When You Give a Creative Writing Class a Deadline

By
Students of La Quinta High School
Westminster, California

When You Give a Creative Writing Class a Deadline

Copyright © 2016 by Garden Grove Unified School District

ISBN: 978-0-6926339-8-4

ALL RIGHTS RESERVED

Edited and Compiled by: Amanda LaPera
Copy Editors: Jennifer Chau, Monica Van
Section Editors: Sadie Adams, Zachary King, Dawn Pham, Alexandra Quang
Design Editors: Kari Nguyen, Richard Trejo
Cover Designed by: Kari Nguyen

Published by La Quinta High School Creative Writing Class

CONTENTS

INTRODUCTION

This book is a collection of stories, plays, and poems written by the first generation of creative writers at La Quinta High School. Despite the title's implication, each piece of writing is a solid product of hard work and dedication.
We hope you enjoy the finished compilation.

We would like to acknowledge Preston Aldous and Jenny Pham for assisting us with the design process for the cover and the La Quinta High School student body for supporting us.

FICTION

ASCENT
Dan Tran

I STARED INTO THE mirror. Eyes, a gold not my own, stared back at me. How was this happening? I blinked, and my eyes were brown again. I shook my head, dismissing it as a trick of the light. I needed to get ready for school.

I bit into the poached egg sandwich and tilted my head back as the yolk ran over my tongue. Delicious. Some of the egg's remains ran over my hands. The rich color reminded me of what I had seen in the mirror this morning. Perhaps something odd was going on. Whatever it was, I couldn't let it make me late for school.

I brushed my hair and dressed quickly, putting on my school uniform and grabbing my purse before heading out of the house. Clouds colored the sky a mottled grey, and cars passed me by as colorful blurs.

"Teachers, please release any ninth grade students for the annual magic check," Ms. Veria said over the intercom.

Did they really think someone would awaken this late?

I followed the rest of my class to the gym and ran into Matt on the way there. "What do you think the results will be today?" I matched my steps to his.

"Surprising. You know, Ellen, the Emissaries only check high schools when they know there's a Sleeper," Matt said. "Who do you think it could be, though? Late Wakers usually end up pretty powerful."

Gold eyes flashed in my head. "I don't know. Kat, maybe? It'd certainly explain all her energy."

"Well, whoever it is, I hope it's not me. I don't have time to defend the city from the forces of darkness." We laughed, knowing that our crazy marching band schedule would subside after Thanksgiving break.

"Congratulations, Miss Zhi." Nurse Alyssa smiled at me. "You're our late Waker. Now, please fill out this form so that the U. E. L. will know what schedule conflicts you may have and can craft you the appropriate Talisman."

"Wait. What? No. I. No. I can't be. You're absolutely sure it's me?" My hands shook as I took the paperwork from her.

"Yes, and what a marvelous Waker you are. The machines almost didn't give a reading for your energy. It was so potent." She indicated the parts of the form I needed to fill out and left me to it.

My hands shook even harder as I wrote out my schedule, school and band, and filled in the personal details at the bottom, ending with my signature. "Miss, I've finished," I said.

A fairy entered, and my heart dropped. This was it. I was consigned to the United Emissaries of Light as a "civilian volunteer" to fight the forces of darkness.

"You will be excused from school this week to participate in the crafting of your Talisman. Your guardian will be notified of your status, and we will assign you a patrol schedule that does not interfere with the schedule you have submitted to us," the fairy said. Her wings fluttered like a hummingbird's and reminded me that I was no longer a free person.

"How often will I have to patrol?" My voice shook, and I blushed.

"Not more than once a week, I'm sure." Her smile offered little reassurance. I would risk life and limb, and for what? The people of the city? No. My friends and family.

"Could you keep this a secret, or at least confidential? I'd rather not have the whole school treating me like Garry Hopper." I looked her in the eye, and she nodded.

"Of course, of course. Your administrators will probably have to know, and your guardian of course, but otherwise, only you will be able to disclose your Waking Persona." The fairy's smile widened, and I smiled back.

"Thank you, ma'am. If that's all?" My words felt hollow but were all I could muster.

"Yes, of course. Please return to class. Another Emissary will pick you up after school."

"Hey, kiddo. Get in the back. We'll drop off your stuff at home and then Mr. Carr will induct you at the local Emissaries' office." Mom smiled at me.

I closed my eyes and my chest tightened. Did she want this? Was she also worried?

"Okay, Mom." I climbed into the car. He was already in there. Mr. Carr's slight figure shifted in the corner of my eye.

"How ya feelin', kid?" he asked.

"Not bad." I shrugged and closed the door.

"Oh, this is all so exciting," Mom said, pulling out of the parking lot. "You're going to be an amazing Waker, I just know it, Ellen. She used to brag that she'd save the world, Mr. Carr."

I glared at her through the rear view mirror.

"Oh, lighten up, Ellen. Ya don't mind if I call ya Ellen, do ya?" Mr. Carr asked.

"Not if you give me your first name." The smile I gave him was all teeth and he laughed.

"Horace." Our eyes met and he laughed again. "I'm sure this'll be a great workin' relationship."

We passed the rest of the trip home with light chatter and more sniping. When I got home, I left my school garb for more casual clothes, a light blouse and dark skirt, before Horace drove me to the Emissaries' office.

My chest throbbed as we passed under a crystalline gate. I stared at Horace. "And what was that?"

"Just a lil' security. We can't let just anyone join the Emissaries, ya know?" He smiled at me with a gleam in his eye and turned his attention back to the road. "The dark ain't above usin' children, after all."

I scrunched my eyebrows. "Wait, the dark used a kid to infiltrate the Emissaries?"

"Yeah, Halloween '05, they almost blew Puerto Rico off the map. We were pretty lucky to have Saint Marth on hand, else we would have lost Lucia, too." He sighed.

"Lucia? Are you talking about Lost Light Lucia? Wait." I stared at him. "Were you her inductor, too?"

"Yeah, I induct all the late Wakers. Y'all are so rare and talented that I get stuck with the job." Horace's lips quirked. "Means I get less work, but the work I do get is a lot harder."

"How long do most Talismans take to craft, really?"

"No more than a day."

"Why am I getting the week off for my Talisman?"

"You're a late Waker."

"And that's so important because...?"

"Your power's so much more potent but so much harder to work with. Smith's gonna need to put in a lot of work for ya."

Silence carried the rest of the drive.

"Amazing. Absolutely astonishing. I've never worked with such...physical Dream, before," Mr. Smith said. They had used some magical machinery to extract a sample of my Dream to see which kinds of Talismans might be viable for me.

"Well, late Wakers always produce extraordinary results, eh?" Horace stared at the machine, eyes half-lidded and half-smiling.

"What does that mean?" I frowned, not entirely pleased with being extraordinary. After all, the less normal I was, the bigger a target I was.

"Oh, not much, not much at all, it's just rather interesting." Mr. Smith adjusted some knobs on the machine and the Dream began morphing, its shape flowing into a hammer, a knife, a pistol, before settling into a domino mask, simple and unassuming. "Hm, it's almost settled already. I usually need to adjust the focus at least three times."

"Is that good or bad?" I stared at the mask, resigned. Perhaps it'd help hide my identity?

"Unusual. Very unusual. I suppose we could try to divine your affinities now, though, before we finalize your Talisman." Mr. Smith frowned at the machine, inputting a few numbers this time.

"Hold on a moment, Smith, are ya sure about that?" Horace looked at him, stunned. "Even for early Wakers, you never try that until the end of the day."

"Yes, yes, the Talisman is nearly stable already, and I'm sure Miss Zhi would rather us spare her the suspense." The machinist looked to me. "Wouldn't you?"

"Ah, yes, sir. If you would." I smiled, maybe this wouldn't be so bad.

"Right, right then, we'll have to check in to use the Moonlight Mirror, but it shouldn't be too hard." He stopped fiddling with the machine and looked to Horace. "Be a dear and tell them we'll be coming along shortly, would you?"

"Alright, Smith, I can tell when I'm not wanted." Horace smirked. "Ellen, listen to what he says, and don't be stupid."

"I'm a high schooler, not an idiot." I scowled. "Just because I have the chance to do something stupid doesn't mean I'll take it."

"Yeah, yeah, you'll do one stupid thing around here by the time we're done. I guarantee it." He strode off, smirk still etched on his face.

"Mr. Smith, is there anything else you need from me?" I asked.

"Yes, yes, just one thing. Answer me this." Mr. Smith adjusted the machine again, "Why would your Dream reflect a forge and the stars?"

I blinked, not sure what to make of the statement. "A forge and the stars?"

"Yes, yes, a forge and the stars." He looked at me. "More specifically, the constellation Scorpio."

"I mean. . . I've always been interested in weapons, and my birthday's November twelfth."

"No, no, I suppose I should be more specific. Why would your very essence consist of balance and equalization?"

"I'm not sure I follow, sir."

He sighed. "I suppose you wouldn't. Very few do. Perhaps, in time, you might. Well, well, we must get on with this. Let's head to the Mirror and see exactly what your Dream is made of."

I greeted the translucent, perfect sphere in the Moonlight Mirror's chamber with a raised eyebrow and a flat stare. After being told that it was an epic artifact made to test the will of new Wakers, seeing something that only rated a five out of ten for the wrong reasons was disappointing. Still, I needed to see what dark secrets I lied to myself about before I could find out what made up my Dream.

"Is there anyone in here? Anything?" The walls reflected my words back at me and I returned my gaze to the Mirror. "How do you work?"

"Just like any other mirror," my warped reflection, gold eyes and curled hair set on my fine face, said. "You gaze upon my surface, and I show you all your faults."

"How. . . cliché. Is this some kind of reflection or meditation that shows me the deep, dark secrets I keep from myself and need to rid myself of before I can come into my own?" I smiled, more than a little disappointed but still relieved. This, I could deal with.

"Well, usually. Your case, though, is different." The reflection frowned, delicate eyebrows coming together. "Here, I'm supposed to give you a positive talk about accepting yourself and saying that it's okay to never find that one thing you're meant to do in life. But we both know it would fall flat. I'm just your reflection, after all."

"And I was never so great at pep talks, right." We shared a laugh.

"So, that leaves me the third route: vigorous debate." She smiled and nodded, a sinister gleam in her eyes, and I shifted slightly. "We will confront the ugly truths of the world. The first topic: religions are shams, except for the ones the Emissaries declared null almost a decade ago."

"Well, yeah, but people need to put their faith somewhere. Their fragile minds can't handle not being significant," I said.

"So they can't, so they can't. Well, why do you still bother with those useless rituals and sayings?" The reflection frowned.

"It makes Mom happy."

"Is that reason enough to keep yourself unhappy, though?"

"Probably not, but it's reason enough for me. Mom deserves better than what my biological father did to her, so I might as well try to be the best for her." I shrugged.

"Point to you. Next topic: why don't you just put in the work at school? You know Mother would be happier for it."

"I'm willing to sacrifice some of my happiness, but I do have limits."

"And of course those limits are schoolwork." She sighed. "So, now that we've confirmed that you probably won't self-destruct or fall into a suicidal pit of despair and throw yourself into increasingly dangerous missions hoping to die --"

"Wait, what?" I made a face, and she raised an eyebrow. "How did you get that out of my answers?"

"You're willing to sacrifice some of your happiness for the better of those close to you, but you're not just going to give up everything for them. So, you have an attachment to life and you're not going to get suicidal to fulfill her every happiness."

"Ah, that makes sense." I nodded.

"Now we can get into the really revealing topics." She looked me in the eye. "Yutada or Kaskada?"

"Why would you make me choose between them?" I glared at her. "You can't compare them, they're both amazing."

"Fine. Queendom Souls or Ring World?"

"Magic beats guns nine times out of ten, and other Wakers proved it. Queendom Souls."

"Sasuke's hot."

I stared at the Mirror, wide eyed and eyebrows nearing my hairline. "Okay, exactly who are you again?"

She smirked. "The reflection of you that bares every shame you hide."

"Does that mean you bear all of my horrible elementary school crushes?" I frowned. "Oh my god, that's horrible. How does it feel to have all those feelings and know that every one of them hated you?"

Tears gathered in her gold eyes and her cheeks flushed. "Why did you have to bring it up? I'd been holding it close for so long now, and you had to bring it up? Really?"

"Sorry. I was just curious."

"How did you even manage this? You come into my chamber, break the rules interacting with me, and make me feel like a horrible person who will never be wanted. Why would you do that?" Her lip quivered, and she half turned to the side. "Leave. I don't want to deal with you."

"Wait." I reached out my hand. "At least tell me what Mr. Smith meant when he said my Dream reflects a forge and the stars."

"Put that hand down. I'm just an image." She pouted. "Besides, how the hell should I know? I just reflect what you're ashamed of."

"Right, right, sorry. Well, would my shame know what my Dream is made of?"

"Forgery, of course. Why, you were so ashamed of your ability to mimic others that you shunted it off almost completely to me." She puffed out her chest and grinned.

"Ah, I see now. Thank you, Mirror. You've been a great help today. I hope someday I'll be able to repay you." I bowed and walked outside, the image of a domino mask and an elaborate battle dress etched in my mind.

Golden motes coalesced above my raised hand, a simple, sturdy longsword forming from the ethereal Dream. The giant invaded San Francisco only a scant few hours ago, and already maps would need to be rewritten. The city would never fully recover from this nightmare.

Ghouls wandered the streets, the dead claimed by the giant reanimated to spread further mayhem and discord. I brought the sword down to remove a ghoul's head and jumped to the side to avoid another strike. Am I really cut out for this?

"Watch out!" Serena sent a wave of fire at the ground behind me, frying the ghouls and giving me time to cut my way out of the undead throng.

"Thanks!" I formed another weapon, this time an unornamented throwing knife, and flung it, catching a ghoul's hand an inch away from her ear and pinning it to the wall.

I jumped up to the rooftops. The swarming dead couldn't reach us up here without coordination, and the giant had more important things to worry about than its minions in the streets.

Lost Light Lucia's voice rang across the bay, the smooth contralto a rallying call for all of us Wakers still fighting in the streets:

"The giant has been labeled 'Tartarus' by the U. E. L." Her radiant figure stood out against the overcast, grey sky, and her arm pointed toward the giant. "It's paused over the bay, and we're assuming it's charging for some sort of massive attack. We need to take this chance to hit it with everything we've got."

She's right. Clouds descended upon Tartarus, covering its hands like the gauntlets of an angry god. Its eyes glowed, a piercing crimson that calls to mind blood and demons and hell. A sword fixed itself in my mind, a black stone blade, half my height, etched with amethyst eldritch runes with a handle wrapped in gold thread, and my Dream came together to form it in my raised hands.

"Everybody, get out of here!" My mouth moved on its own, my voice hoarse for the volume I had never used.

Lucia took one look at the sword in my hand and cursed. "Everybody, we need to evacuate, now."

Wakers and ghouls alike fled from me, all trying to escape the unassuming horror I could barely contain. The runes gleamed with an unholy light, and I strained my arms to keep the blade still.

Lucia appeared before me in a flash. "Hold it. Please, hold it until I leave." Her blue eyes, wide with near panic, stared into my own. I gritted my teeth and nodded.

The ghouls were flinging themselves into the sea, now, and the only Waker aside from me still in the field was Lucia. "Good. Thank you for this," she said, "and for what it's worth, I'm sorry."

She disappeared in another flash, this time so bright the sun couldn't compare, and I screamed as the sword fell.

ONCE UPON A MERMAID DREAM
Aislinn Stolze

Chapter 1

"SOME'NE GIT THE CAP'N," roared a big, burly man to the rest of the crew. He was the first mate aboard the Queen Lady, and no one dared to question him.

The rest of the crew stood around, mouths agape at the sight before them. The pirate ship had been engaging in some illegal fish netting when the net grew heavy. Once it was hauled aboard, a single, pearly white fin poked out of the writhing mass of mackerel.

"What seems to be the problem, boys?" Captain Artemis asked as he made his way to the front. His heavy boots thudded against the damp wood of the deck and various pieces of jewelry jingled together as he strutted forward. He looked like a stereotypical pirate captain with his wide, plumed hat and scuffed black boots.

"There's somthin' in the nets, Cap'n," said Squeaker in his mousey voice. He had a red and white striped bandana tied around his head as if trying to prevent the wind from blowing away the rest of his sparse hair.

The Captain sighed and closed his eyes. "Isn't that the point of having a net, or are you flea-bitten idiots too stupid to realize that?"

"No, Cap'n. It's somethin' that ain't supposed t' be in the net!" Squeaker exclaimed.

"Christov, did we catch more driftwood again?" the Captain asked his first mate. "How many times do I have to tell you to just throw it overboard?"

"It's not driftwood, Cap'n," the burly man replied. "That's why ye were called up 'ere. We ain't never seen nothin' like this b'fore."

The Captain smirked. "Let me see it."

Queen Lady's crew parted, making way for their Captain. He walked past them to the pile of fish, which was growing still. He stared at it with an arched eyebrow.

"What is that, Christov?"

"We ain't got the foggiest bit of a clue. That's why we went an' got ya, Cap'n. We was hoping ye could tell us." The first mate shifted on his feet nervously.

"Well, first things first, we need to get this pile of fish off...whatever it is," the Captain murmured. "Jameie!"

"Yes, sah?" A middle aged man stepped toward and quickly saluted.

"Get some of the men to help you put the fish in storage. They have to stay fresh until we get to Wend or no one in their right minds will buy the lot."

"A'right, Cap'n!" The man shouted orders to the men standing around watching.

"Would ya like t' go back t' yer quarters, Cap'n," Christov asked. "We can have someone git ya when it's all done."

"No, I think I'd prefer to stay, if that's alright with you, Christov."

"Cert'nly, Cap'n."

"Uncle Artemis." A young boy of no more than twelve came running across the deck toward the pirate Captain. "Uncle Artemis! Squeaker said something brilliant was happening. Can I stay and watch? Please can I?"

The captain looked down fondly at his nephew who lost his parents at a young age. Without a second thought, the pirate Captain took him in. Everyone on the crew adored him. Artemis would catch his nephew getting into trouble with the rest of the rowdy crewmates. Where there was trouble, his nephew was never too far away.

"I don't know, Peter. I'd hate for anything to happen," the Captain said thoughtfully.

"Please? I never get to do anything fun around here. You have to let me watch."

"Alright." Artemis sighed. "Just don't touch anything. Try not to get in the way."

With an excited shout, the boy ran off to join in the commotion. Men walked this way and that while hauling fish below deck. There was still quite a ways to go before the mysterious object could be uncovered.

"Do you think I spoil him?" Artemis asked his first mate.

"Without a doubt, Cap'n," he answered. "The whole crew does. That boy 'as 'em all wrapped 'round 'is lit'le fin'er better than the ropes 'round the bloody mast."

"God help us when he starts asking us to fight." The Captain shuddered. "He'd be running off with every knife, cutlass, and revolver we've got!"

"It's goin' t' take more than God to stop that boy."

The Captain and the first mate continued to watch the crew hustle and bustle about. Most of the men were the usual pirate type; big, dirty, foul mouthed, and armed to the teeth. They grumbled and grunted as they carried the mackerel away. The few that stood apart from the motley crew were Jameie and Squeaker. They worked as hard as the others, but there was something about them that made the others doubt whether they could kill a man if they needed to.

"Cap'n! Cap'n! Come quick! It's a gurl!"

"What in bloody blazes...?" Artemis stepped forward to see for himself what all the commotion was about.

He pushed his way through his crew, who were too stunned to move out of his way once again. The men were gaping at someone lying on the deck with a few remaining fish flopping around her. She looked normal in every way, except for the shining tail that replaced her feet.

"What in the name of all that's wet an' slip'ry is that?" Christov asked.

"Is she a fish or a gurl?" Squeaker asked no one in particular.

A wide grin spread across Artemis's face. "Looks like we caught ourselves a mermaid, boys."

Chapter 2

I OPENED MY EYES and tried to pull my mind into consciousness. When my vision adjusted to the light, I looked around and realized my surroundings were completely foreign, and definitely not the ocean. I sat up a little straighter, which caused the water around me to slosh a bit. I was in a bathtub.

I wasn't sure if it was more concerning to wake up in an unknown place or to wake up in a tub. It was one of those white porcelain tubs that had water up to my waist. Whoever put me here must have been very considerate, because I probably would've died had they not filled the tub with water.

Nearby, something made a soft thud, and someone cursed softly under their breath. A small, blonde head poked up over the edge of the tub, and two of the widest cerulean eyes I had ever seen watched me carefully.

"Are you really a mermaid?" the boy asked me.

"What do you think, little one?"

"I-I'm not sure. I haven't seen your tail yet..." He trailed off, but his eyes quickly flickered down to the water.

"You mean this?" I slowly lifted my metallic blue-green tail out of the water for him to see. It shimmered in the dim light, and I couldn't help but be a little proud of it.

"Wow!" His eyes become wider than I previously thought possible. "You really are a mermaid!"

"Of course I am," I said.

"Everything got really crazy when Uncle Artemis said you were a mermaid, so I didn't get to see you before."

"I see." An idea came to my mind, and I decided it was better to act now rather than later. "What is your name, little one?"

"I'm Pe-"

The door slammed open, interrupting the child. Two men entered the room and observed the scene before them carefully. One of the men was tall and thick, but dressed very plainly. The other had on an oversized red hat, a bright navy jacket, form fitting pants, rings, earrings, and thick heeled boots that thudded with every step he took. His whole appearance shouted, "pirate."

"Peter, what are you doing down here? The group going ashore already left without you," the pirate said.

"S-sorry Uncle Artemis. I just wanted to see the mermaid."

The pirate sighed and shook his head.

"Christov, take Peter outside. I would like to speak with our guest alone."

The other man nodded and followed the boy out of the room. I watched as the door closed with a soft click. The pirate moved closer to my tub and I took the opportunity to size him up. I doubted I could beat him physically, but I knew I could beat him mentally. He was human after all, and humans are easily tricked.

"So, I take it you're the leader here," I said.

A smirk appeared on the pirate's face as he sat down on a stool next to my tub. "They don't call me Captain for nothing, love."

"That means I'm on a pirate ship then."

"That's correct. You're aboard the Queen Lady, one of the most feared pirate ships on the high seas," he replied with more than a healthy dose of pride in his voice.

"And that boy is your nephew? Seems odd to have such a young child aboard a pirate ship."

The Captain took a moment to respond. "He's not technically my nephew, but he still calls me uncle."

"But you are related."

"How can you tell?" He seemed curious to hear my logic.

"You both have bright cerulean eyes that resemble the beautiful sea," I said as I pointed to the Captain's eyes.

The smirk instantly disappeared from his face, and he turned a bright red color. Without warning, I was staring down at a sharp cutlass blade being pressed against my throat.

"You're a guest aboard my ship, see, and it wouldn't be very courteous to start any trouble. Do you understand?"

I carefully nodded. Eyes were apparently not to be brought up, ever. He pulled the blade away from my throat and put it back in its sheath.

"So, why am I onboard your ship, pirate?" I asked, regaining my composure.

"That's Captain to you," he said with narrowed eyes. "We were doing some...business further out in the Sea of Hess when we happened upon you. We didn't think it would be right to throw you back in your condition, so we put you here."

"Throw me back? What were you doing?"

"It's not nice to interrupt someone when they're talking, love." He paused thoughtfully then continued "Now, where was I? Oh yes. We kept you here, and now we're docked in Wend unloading some cargo. As soon as we're done we'll be setting sail to drop off one last bit of cargo."

"What would that be?" I was afraid I already knew the answer.

"Well, that would be you, love." The Captain's smirk grew as he continued, "It's not every day we come across a mermaid, and I know someone in Gaal that would pay a handsome price for you."

"That's disgusting." I swore to myself that I would make him pay.

"Is it, love?" He leaned in close and ran his fingers across my jawline. "A pirate has to do what a pirate has to do."

"Then let me go," I gasped. Having him so close made me short of breath, and I began to blush. As disgusting as he was, he was also very handsome.

"Where's the fun in that? You don't earn the reputation as one of the most feared pirate captains on the seas by letting people go you know." He tilted my chin up with his fingers, bringing my face closer to his. My heartbeat quickened.

It was difficult trying to keep my head clear when every part of me was screaming to grab him and pull him into the tub with me. All I had to do was lean in, just a little further, and he would be mine. "Well, I've never heard of you."

"What?" He pulled back in outrage. "You've never heard of me? I'm THE Artemis Lock, Captain of the Queen Lady!"

I could barely hide my triumphant grin. I had caught him hook, line, and sinker. "I'm sorry, but I've never heard of you. My kind do not really keep up with petty human affairs."

That really seemed to tick him off. He was practically steaming from the ears. "Well, be that as it may, I'm still a pirate, and you're still my cargo. We'll be arriving at Gaal in three days."

"Whatever you say." I crossed my arms and rested them against the edge of the tub so I wasn't looking at the Captain anymore. "I'd like to be left alone now, pirate."

"Fine," he practically spat. He mumbled something along the lines of 'infuriating creature' before opening the door. "And that's Captain to you," he huffed, slamming the door behind him.

"I think you meant Artemis Lock," I said to myself once the door was closed. I could feel the magic coursing through my veins, and I knew that he was mine.

Captain Artemis stood next to the closed door for a moment before turning to leave. He wasn't completely unaware of the strange tension between him and the mermaid, but he knew it would be better to not get involved. She was just cargo, infuriating cargo, but cargo nonetheless.

Just then, an odd shiver went down his spine, and he felt a strange sensation come over him. It was like having a rope tied around his chest that was being tugged. The sensation passed quickly, and he thought nothing more of it.

He walked down the dim hall to the stairs that led to the deck. At least the rest of the cargo was gone now and the gold would be coming in. Having a pile of fish starting to rot aboard his ship was not the Captain's idea of a good time. He climbed the stairs two at a time until he reached the deck and was able to smell the salty sea air. It always made him feel better.

A few members of his crew sat on deck playing cards and taking turns drinking from a cloudy bottle. He approached them and watched for a moment before addressing them.

"How long have the others been gone?"

"Couldn't be more than a few hours," one of the grungy men answered.

"Did Peter go with them?"

"Christov took 'im off the ship, Cap'n," another man replied. "'E was makin' them sad eyes like a 'alf starved pup, and we didn't 'ave the 'eart t' tell 'im no."

"I'll expect them to be back within the hour," the Captain said more to himself than the others. He bent down and picked up the bottle to take a swig. "We'll be setting sail as soon as they get back, boys." He looked out over the sea with longing and urgency in his green eyes. "The sooner, the better."

Chapter 3

THE QUEEN LADY SAILED north on the calm sea waves while her crew scrambled about like a bunch of gulls. A call had been raised, and everyone was preparing for the worst. Another ship was spotted on the horizon and was closing in fast. There was only one kind of ship that would be brave enough to chase a pirate ship, and that was another pirate ship.

"Squeaker! What be the word on that other ship?" Christov yelled up to the crow's nest.

"Still comin', sah!" the mousey man shouted back.

"Can ya make out what it looks like? The Cap'n needs t' know what kind o' brainless, no good bunch o' scallywags been followin' us for Neptune knows 'ow long."

"I-it's hard to tell, sah." Squeaker peered through a beat up telescope. "Pink and purple sails, sah! It's got pink and purple sails! Ain't nevah seen nothin' like this b'fore!" Christov cursed loudly. "That be the Bloody Rose. The Cap'n ain't gonna be 'appy t' 'ear this..."

Several hours later, Captain Artemis stood on the deck of his ship and watched as the other vessel pulled in along the side his own. He hated to admit it, but there was no way he could outrun the Bloody Rose. The Queen Lady may have been sturdy, but that by no means translated into speed, and Artemis knew it.

His mood had been in quite foul for a long time, and he glowered dangerously at anyone that walked too close. Anyone except Peter, who ran around the ship excitedly asking questions to anyone that listened.

"Why does that ship have pink sails?"

"'Cause the cap'n o' that ship 'as got a few screws loose up in the ol' noggin."

"What's the captain like?"

"Cap'n James is the most pompous, silly lookin' pirate ya'd evah meet on the high seas, but 'e somehow keeps 'is men in line."

"Have you ever-"

"Enough, Peter." Captain Artemis gave the boy a warning look. "It would be better if you stayed below deck and stopped bothering everyone."

Peter stared at the ground and sunk his shoulders.. "Awww, but Uncle! I never get to see anything interesting!"

"No. You are to stay below deck, and that's final." The Captain's voice didn't leave any room to argue, so Peter bowed his head and walked toward the stairs leading below deck.

A low murmur rippled through the men gathered on deck as the Bloody Rose coasted to a stop. A long plank was dropped to span the gap between the two ships. Captain Artemis tensed as he caught sight of a familiar face grinning at him as the man crossed the plank.

"Ahoy there, Artemis! It's been far too long!

"What do you want, James?"

The flamboyant pirate captain landed on the Queen Lady's deck with a deep bow.

He flashed a cocky grin at the ship's crew before focusing his attention back on its captain.

"Why can't I just pop in to say hello? Aren't friends allowed to do that?"

"You're not my friend," Artemis growled. "Now I'll ask you again. What do you want?"

James sighed. His ruse had been quickly discovered. "Well, the truth is, rumor has gotten around that you've got your hands on a mermaid, and I just came to see if it was true."

"Where did you hear a thing like that?" Artemis narrowed his eyes.

"I was at a bar in Wend, even though I don't usually like places like that, when I heard someone talking very loudly about their captain catching a mermaid."

Artemis swore to himself that someone was going to be very sorry later that day, but first he had to throw James off his trail.

"I don't know what you heard, James, but I assure you there is no mermaid aboard this ship."

The other captain studied Artemis with his blue eyes before flipping his long blonde hair. "Well, that's quite a disappointment. I was hoping to see a real live mermaid." He leaned in and nudged Artemis with his elbow. "They say a mermaid is so beautiful that men can't help but falling in love with her. I'm glad you haven't seen one then, because they also say mermaids are terrible heartbreakers."

"Then you should have been born a mermaid, James," Arthur replied with contempt. He really couldn't stand the womanizing captain of the Bloody Rose.

James laughed, but he also took note of how Artemis tensed at the thought of falling for a mermaid. He didn't believe Artemis's words one bit. There was a mermaid onboard, and he was determined to find her.

"You've always been a funny one, Artemis, and your sense of style never fails to make me laugh. Ohonhonhon."

"Yes, well, my crew and I still have a long way to go, so if you could excuse us."

"Of course." James smirked, turning to return to his own ship. He stopped before stepping on the plank. "Oh, you wouldn't be going to Gaal, would you Artemis?"

"And if we are?" Artemis questioned suspiciously.

"Ah! What good luck! We should travel together, just like old times!"

Artemis grit his teeth. He cursed his ship's slowness under his breath, knowing there was no way he could outrun the Bloody Rose.

"I suppose so," he grumbled.

"Magnifique! Lead the way, old friend!"

With that, James crossed back to his ship and the plank was withdrawn. Captain Artemis silently fumed for a moment before turning to his crew. They watched him warily. Meeting with James always put him in a bad mood.

"What are you gits waiting for!" the Captain roared. "We've got a long ways to go yet, and it's not going to be pleasant in the least if you don't get moving. Now!" He waited for his crew to spring into action before going to his quarters. All he needed now was a nice bottle of rum.

The door to my room slowly opened a crack and a timid face peeked through at me. It was Peter.

"You can come in, little one," I said.

"I-I'm sorry. I didn't mean to bother you."

"You're not a bother." I waved him into the room, and he closed the door behind him. "Did your uncle send you here?"

"No. There's something going on, and he wouldn't let me stay."

"What's going on?"

"Another pirate ship's been following us for a while and they finally caught up with us," Peter explained.

"What do they want?"

"I don't know." He sighed. "Uncle Artemis never lets me do anything."

I let out a small chuckle. "I know how you feel, little one."

"You do?" His eyes looked up at me curiously.

"Yup. I have an older brother that never lets me do anything. It's always 'You're too small, Illia' or 'maybe next time, Illia'."

"Illia?"

"Dammit," I thought to myself, "I'm so careless."

"Is your name Illia?" he asked again.

"Yes little one, it is."

"Well, I'm Peter." He held his hand out to me, and I looked at it curiously. "You're supposed to shake it."

"How? Like this?" I took hold of his fingertips and shook his hand side to side.

"No, no. Like this." He slipped his palm into mine and shook it up and down a few times.

"I'm sorry. I'm not very accustomed to human manners."

"What's it like to be a mermaid?" he asked with wide, wonder filled eyes.

I laughed softly and motioned for him to sit on the stool beside the tub. "Have a seat, little one, and I'll tell you tales that will make your head spin."

"That's what Uncle Artemis always says too," he said as he sat down.

"Well, I doubt your uncle has ever seen the monstrous Leviathan swimming through the deepest, darkest parts of the ocean, has he?"

It took Captain Artemis several hours to realize Peter hadn't reappeared after sending him below deck. The boy usually sat next to the stairs so he could come right back up as soon as the commotion was over, but he had yet to resurface.

"Christov, have you seen Peter?"

"Not since ya sent the lad away, Cap'n," the first mate answered.

"Squeaker, have you seen him?"

"No, sah. Ain't seen him all mornin'"

"Jameie, please tell me you've seen the boy."

"Me apologies, Cap'n."

Artemis stomped off toward the stairs. They creaked softly as he descended. It was still light enough at the bottom that he could see without much trouble, but the oil lamps would have to be lit soon. The Captain took a few steps before pausing. He didn't really have a clue where to search first.

Someone had left the door to the extra storage room open, so he decided to have a quick peek inside. He found his nephew sitting on a stool with his head rested on his arms, leaning against the edge of the mermaid's tub. She was watching him carefully, not even looking up when the Captain entered the room.

"What have you done to him?" he asked with panic rising in his chest.

"Nothing. He just fell asleep."

Captain Artemis narrowed his eyes. The words James spoke about mermaids making men fall in love were still fresh in his mind. "If you harmed him in any way..."

"I assure you he's fine," the mermaid replied, glaring at the captain. "But he may not enjoy your stories quite so much anymore."

Her smug smile made Artemis feel even more uneasy, so he picked up the boy to put in bed. A strange fondness swept over Artemis as he carried Peter to his bed. A fondness that seemed to stem from his heart, although it didn't make much sense to him since he was always fond of the boy.

"There's been a bit of a delay, but we should be arriving at our destination by tomorrow," the Captain said without looking at the mermaid. "I suggest you keep that in mind the next time you feel like causing trouble."

She was about to protest, but Artemis exited the room without another word.

Chapter 4

EVERYTHING HAPPENED SO FAST that I could hardly tell what was going on. I woke up to the sound of a door creaking open. Three shadowed figures crept into my room. There wasn't a light of any kind, so I couldn't see who the men were. They quickly approached the tub, and before I could make a sound, my mouth was gagged and my hands tied.

Two of the men lifted me out of the water and carried me toward the door. I fought and wiggled in their grasp with all my might, but to no avail. The men were too strong. I finally managed to slap one in the face with my fin, and he cried out in pain. He let go of me, and I landed on the floor with a heavy thud.

"'Ey! Keep it down back there!" the third man whispered urgently. "If ya blunderin' idiots wake anyone up, we'll all be fish bait!"

"Yeah, yeah. Quit yer bellyachin'."

"If yew two mangy dogs weren't carryin' the goods, I'd cut ye open meself!"

I bit down on my gag in frustration.

"C'mon then. Pick 'er back up an' let's get outta 'ere. Ye don't want them t' catch us, do ya?"

The two men picked me back up and hustled for the stairs. They softly crept across the deck as to not alarm whoever was sitting in the crow's nest on guard duty.

I was carried across a plank to another ship and taken below deck. The three men excitedly ran through a maze of halls to a room that was a lot smaller than the one I was being kept on the Queen Lady. They shoved me inside and closed the door without unbinding my wrist or taking my gag out.

It was a long time before the door opened again. I squinted against the sudden harsh light and tried to discern who was standing in the doorway. Whoever it was, was a lot better dressed than the pirates who abducted me.

"So, you're the mermaid our good friend Artemis caught," the man said with a grin. He was dressed similarly to Artemis, but a lot more feminine. "Oh, how rude of me! Let me take that off for you, ma chérie."

The pirate removed my gag with a flourish. He bowed, never taking his eyes off mine.

"Allow me to introduce myself. I am the captain of this ship, the Bloody Rose. Many call me the best pirate captain to sail the seas, but you can call me James."

He winked at me, and I couldn't hold back a shiver of disgust. "What do you want with me?" I spat at him.

"Ohonhonhon! A fine question, ma chérie." He flicked his hair away from his face. "Mermaids are the most beautiful creatures in the sea. When I heard Artemis caught one, I had to have it for myself. A beautiful creature for a beautiful man."

These pirates were all the same. To them, I wasn't a living person. I was an item, a thing to collect or trade. Anger boiled inside of me, and I clenched my fists until my knuckles turned white. The ship jerked violently.

"Let me go, you pig, or you'll be sorry!" I growled through clenched teeth.

"I'm afraid I can't do that." His previously playful eyes hardened dangerously. "You're mine now, you see, and I'll do what I want with you."

"Artemis will come after you." I said, hiding the fear resting in my stomach.

James laughed. "I wouldn't count on it, ma chérie. The Bloody Rose is the fastest ship on the sea. There's no way an ugly thing like the Queen Lady could ever catch up to us."

He continued to laugh as he waltzed out of the room. Darkness swallowed me up at the same time as my panic.

Captain Artemis sat at his desk with a quill balanced precariously between his fingers. He was doing some logistics in his ledger book for the last shipment of fish they had sold in Wend. Artemis wasn't the type to let this kind of paperwork slip through the cracks. He liked to know exactly how much gold he had, and how much he owed. There hadn't been any red ink in the book for years.

"Cap'n, we have a problem," Christov said as he slammed open the door to the Captain's quarters.

Startled, Artemis dropped his quill, leaving a messy ink blot on his ledger. "Oh for the love of...what is it, Christov?"

"We found Jamison dead this mornin' sah."

"Dead?" The Captain looked up from trying to wipe away the ink with a handkerchief.

"Yes, as dead as a fishy outta water."

"Well, does anyone know what happened? Did you ask the people he sleeps by? Not that they would notice since they all snore like walruses..."

"He was on watch last night, Cap'n"

This made Artemis's blood run cold. "The Bloody Rose?"

"Gone. And the mermaid's missin' too."

"What?" The Captain jumped to his feet. "Where is she?"

"We ain't sure. We was hopin' ya might have an idea," the first mate answered as he shifted his weight uncomfortably.

"Oh, I have an idea alright." Captain Artemis pushed past Christov and stomped across the deck. "All hands on deck! Everyone get to their positions and wait for my command!"

Peter's blonde head poked up from between some barrels. "Is something wrong, Uncle?"

"It's none of your concern, Peter." The Captain walked past the boy on his way to the helm.

"But-"

"Why don't you go help Squeaker keep a lookout? I'll need sharp eyes up there."

"Yes sir!" Peter shouted happily. He turned to run, but stopped before taking more than a couple steps. "What exactly am I looking for, Uncle?"

"Pink and purple sails," Artemis growled in reply. He gripped the wheel and steered the ship to the northwest. They found the Bloody Rose docked in an obscure town to the west of Gaal.

"We can't just barge through there like a blind whale an' expect t' make it out in one piece!"

"Then what do you suggest?" Captain Artemis asked in exasperation.

"We should do exactly what them rascals did t' us. Sneak in when it's dark an' git the gurl back without them evah knowin' we were there," Christov answered with a nod. "It's the only logical way, Cap'n."

Artemis looked to the three other men standing around his quarters. "Do you agree three agree?"

"It's always bettah t' make it out wit' yer skin still on," replied a man named Cutter.

The Captain sighed. "I suppose you're right. Christov and Lanham," he said as he looked at each man. "You two will be accompanying me aboard the Bloody Rose."

"Are ya sure, Cap'n?" Christov asked. "Shouldn't one of us stay behind t' watch the ship?"

"I need the best men on this mission. There's a lot of gold riding on this, and unless you don't want to get paid, we can't afford to fail."

The first mate nodded. "Yes, sah."

"Good. Now-"

"Can I come too, Uncle?" Peter came bursting through the door, running up to the Captain's desk. "Please, Uncle! You have to let me help save Illia!"

"Peter, you know I-" Artemis stopped short. "Illia?"

"That's her name," the boy told him.

"She told you her name?"

"Uh huh. She told me lots of things. That's why you have to let me come!"

Artemis struggled over the idea for quite some time. He didn't want to put the boy in danger, but he could be useful in making the mermaid cooperate if necessary.

"Fine, you can come, but only if you promise to do everything that I, or Christov, or Lanham tells you, okay?"

"Alright!" The boy hopped around. Artemis couldn't help but smile a little at his excitement.

The four of them got into a tiny rowboat and rowed to the Bloody Rose. Peter was so excited that he had almost tipped the boat over on a number of occasions. Artemis threatened to leave him in the water and not come back, to which the boy responded with silently turning the leather handle of his dagger around in his hand.

Artemis also looked at the handle of his trusty cutlass. He had another dagger hidden in his boot, a revolver under his jacket, a throwing knife up each sleeve, a second revolver at his waist, and a poisoned needle hidden in one of his rings that he had gotten that on a trip to the East.

"Would ya like t' go up first, Cap'n?" Christov asked as he secured a rope attached to the railing of the large ship.

"Might as well."

Artemis grabbed hold of the rope and began to climb. Peter tensed up as he watched his uncle climb, but calmed himself with a deep breath. He grabbed the rope next, and was followed closely by Christov. Lanham brought up the rear after tying the rope to the rowboat.

The four of them quietly snuck around some crates as soon as they were all on deck. The Captain signaled for them to move toward the back of the ship to find a different way below deck. There were several of Captain James's men sitting around the stairs on deck, stairs which led to where Illia was stored.

Christov lead the way with Artemis bringing the rear. His usually loud boots didn't make a sound as the four reached another set of stairs. They crept below deck as quickly and quietly as they could. Lanham blew out a lamp hanging on the wall. It was hard for them to see in the dark, but it was also hard for them to be seen in the dark.

They continued to wander around for quite some time. None of them really knew where they were going, and the Captain was beginning to grow frustrated. That's when he felt something odd.

"Wait," he whispered to the others. They stopped and watched as he peeked around a dark corner. "This way."

"Wot makes ya so sure, Cap'n?"

"I don't know. Just a hunch. Now are you going to follow me or keep asking questions, Lanham?"

"Sorry, sah. Lead de way."

They barely took two steps down the hall when they heard voices from behind them. Captain Artemis held his lips to his fingers as he pushed Peter against the wall.

"What the Cap'n doin' stoppin' at a place like this?"

"Dunno. They say he's sweet on some gurl 'ere. Prob'ly wanna tell 'er all 'bout that mermaid we got."

"Ya seen 'er?"

"Naw, but Temis said 'e saw 'er."

"Yewd 'ave t' be the dumbest dumbo 'round t' believe a word Temis says. Ain't got one truthful bone in 'is whole body that one. 'Sides, why would the Cap'n let an idiot like Temis see the mermaid?"

"Suppose yer right..."

"O' course ahm right! Ahm always right! Ye don' go forgettin' that now..."

The voices faded away as the two men walked away.. A shaky sigh escaped from Peter's lips as they continued down the hall.

"It sounds like they have Illia here," Peter whispered.

"Don't make so much noise." Artemis whirled around to look at the boy. He had gotten another strange feeling when the boy said the mermaid's name. "Say it again."

"W-what?"

"Say her name again."

"Illia?"

Again. Again he got that strange feeling,. "Keep calling for her Peter, but not too loudly."

"Illia? Illia? Where are you, Illia?" Peter whispered into the dark.

The sensation was growing stronger, and the Captain started to move faster. He hurried the men along as the feeling in his chest grew.

"What's goin' on, Cap'n?"

"I'm not sure, Christov, but I know we're getting close."

Artemis led them around corners through twisting corridors. The only sound on the whole ship, it seemed, was Peter's calls.

Finally, the Captain stopped at a door. He was certain this was the one. He twisted the knob. Locked.

"If ya don' mind, Cap'n," Lanham said as he placed a hand on Artemis's shoulder. He held up a set of picks.

"Go right ahead, but be quick."

The pirate went to work tinkering around inside the lock. He pulled up on the pick and twisted the knob.. Artemis was the first to step in the room, and his expression instantly set into a scowl.

The mermaid was laying on the floor of a tiny room with her hands bound. Her wrists were swollen and bleeding from struggling against the ropes holding them, her tail drained of all moisture. The Captain swore under his breath.

"Illia" Peter rushed over to her and knelt on the floor beside her while he touched her shoulder. "Illia! Illia, wake up!"

The mermaid's eyes fluttered open, focusing on the boy. "Were you the one calling me, little one? I heard you saying my name for such a long time that I thought maybe I was imagining it."

Artemis could barely hear Peter when they were walking through the halls.

"How could she hear him?" he thought to himself. He knelt down and lifted the mermaid with care given her unhealthy state.

"What happened to you?"

"I've been out of the water for too long," she replied weakly.

"James is a bloody idiot," the Captain murmured darkly.

"Takes one...to know one..."

Artemis was about to snicker a reply when he saw her close her eyes. Icy cold fear clawed at his chest. He couldn't stand the idea of her fading away in his arms.

"C'mon, love. Pull yourself together. We're leaving now." He stepped out of the little room with the mermaid still in his arm, hoping he remembered the way out. "Hey, snap out of it."

The mermaid struggled to open her eyes and look at the Captain. He shook her, but she seemed to be slipping fast.

"Just keep your eyes open, Illia." At the sound of her name, her eyes opened wide, and she tightened her grip on his coat sleeve. "Don't do that, love. You're getting blood on the coat." Sure, it was silver instead of red, but he was sure it would stain anyway.

"All...you pirates...care about...is clothes."

"A man's appearance is everything." The Captain ran as fast as he could without being too loud.

"What about...what's in here?" The mermaid moves her hands to point at his chest.

"What? What are you talking about?"

"Your heart..." she breathed as her eyes slipped shut once more.

"Hey, you have to stay awake. Illia? Wake up!"

Her eyes slid open again, and she focused on his face as he focused on finding the exit.

"No sleeping!" he said urgently. "You need to stay awake! Illia!"

"Mhmmm? Sorry..."

Just then, the four of them stumbled upon the stairs and climbed them two at a time. A breath of fresh air sounded so good to Artemis that he didn't hear the click until it was too late. Captain James and a large part of his crew stood next to the stairs waiting for them to emerge. He had the barrel of his revolver pointed right at Artemis's forehead.

"Bonjour, my friends. I believe she belongs to me, non?"

"She belongs to me you bloody git." Artemis said as he walked towards the flamboyant captain. He pushed the barrel of the revolver away from his face.

"Mon ami, leave her here and you can go back to your ship. Fair deal, non?" James said, putting his revolver away in its holster.

Artemis glared at James before speaking. "You believe that's a fair deal?" His cerulean eyes darted between the captain and Illia. She was in rough shape. Her breathing became ragged and shallow. He had to do something quick.

"If she stays with me, I don't dump your corpse into the Atlantic. Fair, non?"

"We all go," Artemis said as he stomped on James' foot and kicked him in the knees. James fell hard, giving Artemis and the others enough time to dart to the side of the ship where they had climbed up. Christov picked up Peter and threw him over his shoulder like a sack of potatoes as he caught up with his captain.

"Sorry, love," Artemis whispered. He swung his arm back, and, with a powerful lunge, threw her back into the sea. She hit the water with a splash and sunk below the surface.

"Come on boys," Artemis shouted. He jumped over the rails and landed in the water with a splash of his own. Just before Artemis resurfaced, he saw a bright white fin swimming away. Christov threw Peter over, then jumped in with Lanham. They all swam to the small boat. Artemis cut the rope that was used to secure the boat in place as his crewmates and nephew climbed aboard.

"Head out," Artemis said as he rowed away from the ship.

"Hey Uncle, Where's Illia?" Peter asked, looking into the water.

"Where she belongs."

THE AFTERMATH
Thana Sithisombath

Chapter 1

FIFTY YEARS AGO, WAR broke out over money, power, and control of both continents. Blood was shed, lives lost, families torn apart. Alliances were formed for protection. On the Werra Continent, three clans--the Technicians, the Archers, and the Wereanthros--drew boundaries, each fighting for control of their territory.

Technicians, the intelligent beings, used electronic gauntlets to shoot powerful beams of light and used ground flower petals, roots, and seeds as their fuel source. Archers, the sneaky fighters, blended into the outer edges of the jungle and used bows to kill their oblivious enemies. Wereanthros, the savages, lived deep in the Werran Jungle amongst the dead bodies of their allies. They used natural jungle magic to transform themselves into animals and blend in along with other wild inhabitants of their jungle.

Thirty-five years later, the tumultuous period of brutality and war was finally over, having left the other continent in ruins and only the Werra Continent habitable. The generals of the three remaining clans signed a peace treaty, but kept the terms of the agreement secret from their citizens.

The war had lasted so long that the pre-war era was forgotten. History had been destroyed. Books had been burned. Memories had been erased.

The three generals who signed the treaty made themselves Headmasters to guide their clan brothers forward into a new era of civilization. However, the treaty did not alleviate the wartime feelings of hatred and distrust each clan held against the others. Tension lingered and affected every interaction the clans had with one another.

The new Headmasters forbade all citizens from wandering beyond the borders of their land. This sparked rebellion in several citizens, who wanted to move outside of their territory.

Fifteen years passed since the passage of the treaty and nothing had changed.

I woke up to the smell of smoke, the remnants of the past. Gaining consciousness, I dragged my hand to the nightstand beside my bed to grab the several vials of blue dust topped with velvet bows, my gauntlet, and my phone. I checked the time.

"It's time for my freedom." I jumped out of bed and leapt towards the door. I tiptoed down the hallway and paused next to every doorway to check for noise. At the end of the hall, I approached a familiar teleporter labeled, "Outside."

When I pulled the lever to transport myself, my phone vibrated. "One new message."

I checked the message. "My dear little Alexa, you are so grown up now. I am glad you enjoyed your sixteenth birthday. During mine, all I got was a pat on my back and extra dust for the upcoming battle later that day. The vials weren't a great present, but the gauntlet is the best weapon a Technician can have on the battlefield. The Great War may be over now, but you still need to practice. However, I have another present for you. It's from your parents."

I stopped reading and looked over both shoulders. No one. I sat down on the teleporter and continued reading.

"They told me to give this to you on your sixteenth birthday. It's an image guide. As you know, Alexa, the gauntlet is also a communication and information system. The image guide was programmed with artificial intelligence. A word of warning, the intelligences used are usually acquired from a once-living person, so experiencing random memories of the person the intelligence is based on is perfectly normal. I've attached the code to this message. Just upload it to your gauntlet. I fully support whatever you'll do as an intelligent, young adult. Just follow what you believe in and remember what your parents always told you about life. - Happy Birthday, Alexa. Love, Dem Stert."

"Thank you, Dem," I replied, "For everything. And their present. You've been a great guardian, but I can't stay here. It's restricting." I activated the teleporter. The lights around me spun and blinked. I began to think about the outside, where I'd be able to do whatever I wanted without the threat of danger looming above my head.

Chapter 2

"I KNEW SOMEONE WOULD leave before maintenance started," said Tane, Headmaster of the Technicians. He sat alone in his dusty room. He spun around his chair, rolled to one of the long tables, grabbed a screwdriver, and rolled back to his work station next to his dusty bed. He tinkered with the gauntlet on his desk. The screwdriver slipped out of his hand and dropped to the floor, disappearing under the bed. His grasp was not what it used to be thirty-five years ago, back when he had negotiated the end of The Great War.

"Damn," Tane said, "I'll get the bypass driver later." He pushed the gauntlet aside and lowered himself to reach the bottom drawer of his desk. With his bandaged hand, he grabbed his own gauntlet from the drawer. A dim blue light glowed from a "T" etched into its wrist.

"Those Archers and Wereanthros are too dangerous to be trusted," Tane said, looking at his gauntlet, "Not after what they did to my beloved." Tane pressed buttons on the gauntlet's interface and brought up a photo of a woman's body bleeding on the jungle floor. A tear came to his eye.

"My beloved… did nothing to those Archers, yet she was killed. She was only wandering the jungle for food for us, alone and unarmed, but they were still able to be part of the treaty," Tane said, flipping through the photos again. He stopped at a photo of a wolf creature staring right at the camera. The headmaster of the Wereanthros.

Tane rubbed the tears away. Their customs are so strange, he thought. When one of them is born, he is given a task to complete before adulthood. Complete the task, and he becomes a Wereanthro. Failure to complete the task in time results in death. Why would they do that? The lives of their clan are the most important thing in the world. Why would they let someone else decide whether or not they are worthy? Their freedom is gone as soon as they are born.

Tane put the gauntlet back on his desk. He replayed the unusual security footage recorded from the night before.

He recognized the girl on the security footage, Alexa, but couldn't understand why she would want to risk leaving the safety of their land. Does Alexa feel the same way as the Wereanthros, restricted and raised to become whatever the clan says she has to be?

Tane knew Dem allowed her to escape in the small timeframe, which was uncharacteristic of Dem, his most trusted advisor.

Tane picked up the gauntlet from the table. He thought, am I really no different from the Wereanthros that kill their own people or the Archers that killed my beloved? Does my existence cause others in my clan to feel restricted rather than safe? Do I have the right to live freely in this world? Might as well be a Wereanthro failing his mission.

Tane stared at his gauntlet and turned it over in his hands. He thought, I cannot live in this world forever. My plans for revival are destined to fail. My beloved would want to see me in the afterlife as soon as she could, after what I did to bring peace to this world.

Tane looked down the gauntlet's barrel and, with a heavy sigh, said, "I will see you soon, my love." He fired the gauntlet.

Tane slid off his chair to the floor. Blood oozed from his head, leaving the skull of his lifeless body.

The Headmaster of the Technicians was dead.

Chapter 3

SCREAMS AND GASPS ECHOED through the dark hallways of the Technician city hall. Dem burst into the headmaster's room and gasped. There on the ground was the lifeless body of Headmaster Tane. Dem looked around the messy room. Another man ran down the hallway towards Tane's room.

"Dem, what happened?" A young man entered the room, bearing the Technician's head of security badge.

Trembling, Dem pointed to the desk.

Garcus moved passed Dem to investigate the scene. He leaned against the doorway, staring back into the room. Neither man said a word. "My father's been murdered," he said, breaking the silence. He slammed his fist against the wall. "We must find who did this."

" Garcus, look. The body's position, the amount of fresh blood, and the gauntlet covered in blood on the floor are pretty obvious hints," Dem said. He approached the corpse and examined Tane's head. "One shot to the head. The mighty tactical general of the Technicians dies to a single shot to the head."

"Sounds suspicious," Garcus said.

"What are you suggesting?" Dem asked.

"My father would not have committed suicide. Someone did this to him."

"Who could have done this? The princess is the only person who has talked to the Headmaster in fifteen years," Dem said.

Garcus walked across the room to the long tables, viewing the various scattered mechanical parts and scraps. "But the murder scene is very interesting."

Dem wandered toward the long table. "How could you say this is interesting? Look on the floor. Is this Tane's gauntlet?" Dem picked up the murder weapon. "The meter shows a bit of dust has been used up. It looks like suicide to me."

"It's not necessarily my father's gauntlet. What if it's the killer's?"

"Garcus, this is Tane's gauntlet. It's even got his 'T' etched into the wrist."

"We can't confirm that it belongs to him. Can you find a bypass driver?"

"Nope, Tane doesn't own one in here," Dem said. "Without it, we can't break the gauntlet's voice recognition."

"What's this?" Garcus picked up a small disc from the scrap metal. He rolled up the left sleeve of his black robe, revealing his own gauntlet. He placed the disc on it, making it bing and light up. Holographic images popped up from the side of the gauntlet, swapping back and forth.

"It's security footage before the maintenance," Dem said. "The girl is Alexa."

"Do you have anything to say about this?"

"I have no idea."

"Why would she be at the teleporters before maintenance?" Garcus asked. "She knew about the maintenance and the activation window the maintenance causes when it starts. Why would she escape?"

"She's probably curious about the outside. Her parents did leave a message for her when they…" Dem dragged his thumb across his neck. "They talked about pursuing life without others stopping her."

Garcus walked around to Dem's side of the table. He rolled up his right sleeve and revealed a long, dark scar on his forearm. "Remember this, Dem? Remember the outside, the war, the Wereanthros? I do. This scar - this memento - from the war reminds me to stay inside the walls of the city. Tane agreed with me. This scar is why we Technicians stay with each other in our territory," Garcus said.

"I know the war was devastating to all of us, but do we really need to restrict the Technicians who want to leave and see the jungle?" Dem asked.

"It does. We, my father and I, do not want more people to die to the Archers or the Wereanthros," Garcus said. "We do not care about the treaty. Those people cannot be trusted. We need to protect our clan even if we are bound by these walls." Garcus walked to the bed, holding out his arms.

"Where are you going?" Dem said.

"I'm going to hunt down that traitor for what she did, killing my father and compromising everyone's safety," Garcus said.

"What are you going to do with her?" Dem said. "She's inconsequential."

"I'm going to bring her back so we can discuss her execution."

"Garcus, think about it. You are saying that Alexa, a regular citizen, killed the headmaster with his own gauntlet, and went through the teleporter to escape punishment before the maintenance starts, which is an hour after curfew. Why would she do that? Just because of freedom? I've known Alexa much longer than you, Garcus. She's too smart. Even if she did murder Tane, she wouldn't leave a trail," Dem said.

"It doesn't matter. She broke the rules, and now she will face punishment," Garcus said, exiting the room. "We cannot risk a confrontation with Archers or Wereanthros. I don't want another war."

Chapter 4

I SPARKED THE KINDLING, igniting an ember. It lit up into a flame. Fire roared up from the ground.

"Can I have my arrowhead back? Couldn't you have used your weapon to light it?" Lucas, my new friend, said, grabbing the flint.

"I could, but this is how I always do it," I responded.

"What is this?" Lucas pointed at the gift I gave him.

"It's a phone. Since you're an archer, you never get to see one. It's a device that allows you to talk to people anytime you want," I said, pulling Lucas to a nearby rock and sitting down. "You just need to press this moon-shaped button and press my name. Go on, do it."

Lucas tapped the button. The screen brought up a list of names, and Lucas pressed Alexa's. Seconds later, my gauntlet beeped. I pushed the call button. Two holographic images came out of the phone and gauntlet, images of me and Lucas.

"Awesome, Lucas," I said, looking up at the tree leaves and the night sky. "I want to go on an adventure today, but I got interrupted again. Do you think it's a sign?"

"I don't know. You can ask your guide."

"I did. His answers are always so straight and literal. I want your opinion."

"Okay, Alexa," Lucas said, standing up walking around the fire. "Did you enjoy leaving your town for the first time in years?"

"Of course I did. I just couldn't live there anymore. I had a great guardian, but I had a terrible headmaster," I said.

Crackling sounds from behind, interrupting our conversation. Lucas grabbed his bow and readied an arrow. Silence filled the clearing. A figure jumped out of the bushes in front of me. Lucas, standing behind me, hit it dead-on. The figure dropped to the ground.

"Is it dead?" I said to Lucas.

"I think it is. It looks like a cat," Lucas said, walking to the bleeding corpse and smelling it.

"Lucas! That's disgusting. Stay away from that," I called.

"This cat is domesticated. It's covered in summoning dust," Lucas said.

"Wait, summoning dust? The only summoner on the continent is Garcus. He was spying on us," I said, turning to the blue light of the city. "What should we do?"

"I don't know, Alexa," Lucas said. "If he was looking for you, why send his cat? Also, summoned cats should not be this easy to kill. It should've taken a lot more arrows."

"Maybe he was just scouting the area for something else. Cover more ground. But now, since the cat is dead, Garcus will know something happened to it and will try to find whatever killed it," I said, looking around the clearing. "I think we need to confront him before he finds us, or worse, reports it to Tane."

"Wait, Alexa. Isn't that a little unnecessary? Can't we just leave the area and set up camp somewhere else? Somewhere closer to the Archer and Wereanthro areas, where

Technicians never travel," Lucas said. "I won't stop you from carrying out your plan. But I want you to think about what'll happen if Garcus captures you and returns you to that city."

"I don't know, Lucas," I said as I walked toward the bright blue city.

"Looks like you've already decided. I will go roam somewhere else then," Lucas said, putting his bow on his back. I took one final look back at Lucas, now a shadow in the vast jungle.

"Wait, Lucas," I shouted, running across the clearing to catch up with him. "I'm not going back."

Lucas stopped and smiled. "Then we start a new era, with Archers and Technicians hand in hand."

Our fingers intertwined.

ALIEN INDEED
Dawn Pham

I WAS FLOATING IN space. There was no light anywhere. The darkness was suffocating. It was too hot. I couldn't breathe. I woke up with a start and clawed at my throat, which greedily gasped in air. I tried to look around, but couldn't see anything. Someone was lying nearby. I could feel their body heat.

"Excuse me?" I whispered, "Excuse me? Please wake up." Hearing no response, I nudged his or her shoulder.

"Mmpf," a male voice groaned with a sleep-roughened voice. "What?"

"Could you please turn on the light? I can't see anything and I don't know where I am," I said. "I don't know who you are. I'm not even sure what my name is. Please turn on the light. I won't be able to figure anything out in this blackness."

The man sat up. I heard a click, but no light accompanied it. He didn't seem bothered. Instead, he turned towards me and grabbed my fragile hands. The silence was tense, but his hands comforted me.

"I think there's a blackout," I muttered. His only response was a vague, sympathetic noise. "I don't think your lights are working, sir," I tried again.

His hands tightened for a brief moment before they let go entirely. He sighed. Realizing I'd disappointed him in some way, I shifted, feeling guilty for reasons I didn't understand myself.

"They warned me this might happen," he whispered to himself. "Listen, you got into an accident last week. You're... blind, darling."

I flinched at the word "blind." A lump grew in my throat, and tears built up. Blind meant I had to learn how to live all over again. Blind meant useless. Blind meant burden. Blind was me.

"What happened?" I asked, my voice cracking between my words. "Why am I not in the hospital? How long have I been asleep? Who are you? Why is my memory gone?" My questions tumbled out faster and faster. My breathing quickened.

I felt the man's arms encircle my shoulders. He made soft humming noises to comfort me, but it didn't work.

"You're okay," he murmured. "You're alive, and you're okay. We are going to

34

make it through this."

"I'm damaged goods. I can't be okay," I thought bitterly. A tear slipped down my face, and like a crumbling dam, the rest followed it. I sat in his arms, crying. When my tears stopped, I slumped down, exhausted.

"If you promise not to freak out again, I'll tell you what happened," he said.

I nodded.

"We are friends and were on the way to *Hiraeth,* but unfortunately, your transport crashed. I rushed you to the hospital as fast as I could, and thankfully, you ended up okay. Your vision, however, was not. We left the hospital to our new home, and you have spent the last couple days recovering. The doctors warned me you might get temporary amnesia."

I slapped my hand to my mouth to muffle disbelieving giggles. I shook with silent laughter. Tears rolled down my cheeks again, but this time, they were tears of amusement. "So you're telling me my spaceship crashed while we were moving to a new planet? What are we, aliens?" My laughing fit grew louder.

"Of course not," he faked offense. "We are perfectly human. We have four arms, two legs, and mind controlling voices... Perfectly human, scout's honor."

"Were you ever even a scout?"

"Well... no, but it's the thought that counts," he said in a solemn manner before dropping his act and chuckling.

"I guess I'll have to believe you then, Mr. Boy Scout." I motioned a salute.

"Enough serious stuff!" he declared loudly, jumping up. "We have so many places to explore! There are green elephants, purple trees, and candy mountains! I'll describe it all to you!"

He grabbed my hand and pulled me up, dragging me to the door and swinging it open. Even though I was blind, I felt the sunlight shine on my face. The birds were chirping. The flowers were fragrant. There was laughter everywhere. The air was full of life and happiness.

"By the way, my name is *αλλοδαπός.* It means Alien," he announced before dashing into the fray of people and chaos, pulling me alongside with him.

For the first time since I woke up, I felt at peace. It didn't matter that I was blind, I would be alright. It didn't matter that he was basically a stranger, I knew he cared for me. I didn't even matter to me that I was on an alien planet. I paused at that thought and smirked. *Alien indeed.*

AWAKENING
Hannah Grove

THE GOAT SKULL RESTED on the stone slab in the enclosed cave, dampened by the occasional drops of condensation that marred the silent echoes. A single candle burned in the lifelessness, illuminating etches on the wall which signaled that it was three in the morning.

A dragging sound broke the silence. Moonlight crept into the cave when the boulder door had been pushed aside. A line of five darkly garbed men, hooded and stone-faced, entered. An individual in white, rough, cotton garments, which glowed under the candlelight, followed them. As they approached the slab, the hooded men circled around the man in white.

"Begin." The man in white closed his eyes and raised his chin. His hands fell at this sides, his palms wide open.

The hooded figure furthest from the door stepped forward, dragging red chalk behind him until the image of a star circumscribed within a circle emerged. Each of the hooded men removed a small candle from their robes. They lit and placed the candles onto the points of the pentagram.

The chant-- a chant unheard since the dark times-- began. The voices reverberated in the depths of the cave's chamber. The candles on the pentagram went out one by one, until only one candle burned. The last candle died. Blackness engulfed the cave, save for the sharp rays of moonlight by the door. The chant ended. Silence. The candles flickered back to life, illuminating the dagger now embedded in the man in white's chest. From the stone slab, the goat skull had disappeared.

"Why did you call me here?"

The five hooded heads turned towards the rich, deep voice coming from the back of the cave.

A young man leaned against a wall of the cave, flipping the goat skull, catching it with his long, tapered fingers. His raven hair, long and fine, was tied at the back of his neck. His angular face, porcelain skin, red eyes watched his summoners. His frock coat, cashmere trousers, formal mannerisms--Victorian.

One hooded figure spoke. "We summoned--"

"I will not speak to the one who takes my brother Gabriel's name." The young man scanned the hooded figures' faces. "I will speak to the one called Seth."

A shiver ran down their spines. He knew their names.

Seth stepped forward. He removed his hood, revealing a stern, aging face. "We want you to start the apocalypse."

"The apocalypse?" The young man rolled his eyes. "You called me here for that? I was having fun in hell. Torture racks are in hell. Earth is boring. Apocalypses are boring. The people just run and scream." He mimicked. "'Oh, no. Help me. Help me.' People are so predictable. No, I don't think I will. Now, if we're quite done, I'll head back to hell."

"I invoke, conjure and command thee," Seth said. "Begin the Apocalypse."

The young man crooked his finger. Five necks snapped.

"Fools. To do that, you need my name." He looked around and walked toward the moonlight and out of the cave, feeling the breeze of the mountain and the chill of the air. "Oh well. Might as well have some fun while I'm here."

He raised his arms. Around him, the world hushed. "To all on Earth, dead or alive, Bebbach has returned." His tone revealed a smirk that was hidden in the darkness. Forgetting the bodies in the cave behind him, he strolled into the night.

The world was different from what he remembered. Louder. Noisier. Actual buildings hundreds of meters tall with structure and support now stood. At least the humans had learned something. He recalled watching the Tower of Bable fall. One could only build so high with dry mud. Humans were so entertaining back then.

The humans have evolved, living up to their name as God's favorite creation. He almost agreed. After all, their species was clever, just like his brethren, except more fragile and mushy. That, and the fact that they had a horrible compulsion to suppress their instincts. Why fight what one could embrace? Oh well. That's characteristic of humans, after all.

He wandered near civilization. The mortals startled him. They were different then he remembered. The females wore pants. Strange. A man who passed him had long, flowing locks, like that of a gentleman in the middle ages. Bebbach scratched his chin. His brows furrowed as he stared at the man's attire, short, glossy trousers and a shirt that mixed a hood with a fur coat.

Then he noticed the man's beard. "Fashion sense, eh. But at least they know how to groom themselves now." He nodded.

That's another thing about mortals now. Much better groomed. Demons have an acute sense of smell, and the hygiene of humans was almost up to demon standards, which gave him hope for humanity. Maybe they wouldn't be boring this trip.

"You need to leave. This place is not for you." A hand fell on his shoulder, and a deep voice slipped into his ear. His body tingled with delight. He turned around, beaming at the entity behind him.

"Ansiel. Interesting that the first one to find me is 'the constrainer.' Here to escort me back to hell? That's rude."

The angel beside him stiffened, and the air stood still for a moment, heightening the tension between the two beings.

"No worries Ansiel, I'll go. But I was wondering…" His voice trailed off, and he placed a hand on top of the one already on his shoulder. "How would the constrainer react to being constrained?"

The ground cracked open, swallowing the two men, leaving only the faint scar of a pentagram and a fading smell of flesh.

BACK HOME
Magaly Plasencia

Chapter 1

ADAM PACED ACROSS THE wooden floor, his footsteps echoing throughout the cabin. Pip observed his brother's excitement while munching on the last piece of thick bread.

Adam shook his head, "Come on, Pop. Where are you? Today is the day." He turned to Pip. "Can you believe it, Pipsqueak? I'm finally going to learn how to hunt."

Pip, who hadn't spoken since the day he was born four years ago, smiled and nodded, offering Adam the last bits of his bread. The happiness on his brother's face lightened his spirit.

Adam covered the bread with his large hand. "No thanks, Pip. The only thing that can satisfy my hunger is jackrabbit, and I'm gonna hunt some when Pop arrives."

The door cracked open and in walked a man holding two dead jackrabbits in one hand and a long gun in the other. His pants dragged in dead grass. He wiped his sweat with his dusty shirt and hung up his gun. "Phew. It's scorching out there."

"Pop." Adam ran up and wrapped his thin arms around their exhausted father.

"Hello there, kiddo." Pop ran his thick, calloused fingers through his dark, messy hair.

"I'm ready," Adam yelled. "Let's go."

Pop set the rabbits in the sink. "What are you talking about?"

Adam frowned, his shoulders slumped. "You promised you were gonna teach me how to hunt."

"Kiddo, I promised to teach you when you get older," Pop said.

"But I am older. I turned ten yesterday."

Pop handed him a rusty pot. "Wash this so we can start our grub."

Adam set it on the table. "Pop, please?"

"Look, kiddo, the heat wore me out. Maybe another time."

"Please. It won't take that long. I swear I'll learn it in a jiff."

"Good tarnation, Adam." Pop gestured at Pip whose stomach was audibly growling. "Look at your poor brother, he's starving."

"I'm sure Pip won't mind waiting just a little, Pop. Please."

Pop stared into Adam's gray eyes then looked over at Pip. "Do you mind waiting at all, Lad?" Pip grinned and shook his head and sighed. "Alright, I'll teach you just a bit, Adam."

"Yes! I'm gonna learn how to hunt. I'm gonna learn how to hunt." Adam sang, jumping around the room.

"Quit your dilly dollying and get outside. I'll be out there in a sec," Pop said, pulling a cigarette from his torn pocket.

Adam grabbed the long gun and ran outside. His father walked over to Pip, placed a sturdy hand on his small shoulder, and stared straight into his hazel eyes. "You're an enduring lad, just like your mother."

Pip plastered a smile on face, while turning his nose away from Pop's smoky breath.

Pop frowned. "I worry about you more than I worry about Adam. He can speak and express himself, but you?" Pop's eyes teared up. "How do I know what you're really feeling?"

Pip felt a drop of his father's tears onto his hand. Wiping them off on his shirt, he pointed at the front door.

Pop gulped and took a deep breath. "I'll hurry so we can eat."

A gentle breeze swept Pip's chestnut hair as he sat on the porch watching Pop teach Adam. He inhaled the fresh air and gazed up at the cerulean sky. He examined the shapes of the clouds and drew them in the dirt: a bunny running, a flying elephant, an upside down snail. Next, he drew a large figure next to a small figure. Pip raised an eyebrow at his last drawing and circled it.

Boom. Adam jumped back. "Whooo! That was amazing. Did you see that, Pip? See me hit that rock?" Adam yelled.

Pip smiled and nodded, giving Adam a thumbs up.

"That'll be it for today, Adam. Let's go inside. I can't stand this heat." Pop brushed the sweat off his forehead.

"Next time, can you teach me how to smoke?" Adam blurted.

Pop rolled his weary eyes.

Pip glanced at his last drawing once more before following them in the house and closing the door.

Chapter 2

EVERYTHING HAPPENED IN A flash. Pip felt Pop's bulky arms wrap around his body. The panting of his father worried him. He saw Adam running to catch up from the corner of his eye.

"Pop, I don't want to go," Adam cried.

"We have no choice, Adam. We have to get away from it!" Pop yelled.

Pip looked back at a black blob spreading through their home. It swallowed everything it touched and expanded like a virus. Up ahead, Pip saw a long box with wheels attached to it. After releasing a loud sound, smoked appeared from its top.

"No! It's leaving without us," Pop said, picking up Adam and sprinting to catch up to the mysterious box.

"Pop, it's moving faster. We're not going to make it," Adam cried.

"Yes, you both will," Pop shouted, lifting the boys and throwing them far onto the top of the moving box. Pop tripped and stopped running, allowing the blob to expand further and swallow him whole. He stuck out his hand and bid his boys a last farewell.

"Pop, no! Don't leave us," Adam screamed. Pip opened his mouth, but nothing came out. "Pip!"

"Pip! You awake, Pip?" Adam punched him in the arm. Pip wrinkled his eyebrows and pushed him back. "Come on," Adam whispered, showing Pip a gun in his hand. "We're gonna get some breakfast for Pop."

Pip thought back to his dream and shook his head. He grabbed Adam by the hand and ran outside.

"Whoa! Pip, what's wrong?" Adam asked.

Pip drew a long rectangle with wheels at the bottom and two small figures on top of it. Then he drew a wobbly rock on top of a large figure.

Adam rolled his eyes, "Oh, Pip, dreams are a bunch of nonsense. Let's get going." Adam ran off.

Pip stared at his drawings for several moments before shrugging his shoulders and running after Adam. The wind brushed through his hair and the morning birds' melodies charmed his ears. Pip stopped and rested on the olive grass. He gazed at the cobalt sky, blending in with the honey sun. The trees towered over him, providing shade.

"Pip, come here!" Adam shouted.

He ran over to Adam, who was crouching behind a bush.

"Look what we've got here," Adam whispered, pointing at a jack rabbit chewing on grass. "This is my shot, so don't you make a single sound."

Pip backed away, stepping on a twig. The jackrabbit froze, dropping grass from its mouth.

"Pip. I told you to stay quiet," Adam said.

The rabbit remained stuck in place. Adam fired his gun, but missed. The rabbit fled.

"Don't let it get away!" Adam shouted, jumping up.

The boys ran, trying to stop the rabbit from getting further into the trees. Pip picked a medium size rock and threw it at the rabbit's head, and Adam fired at its neck.

"Whooo! I just shot my first jack rabbit." Adam picked up the rabbit by its long ears. "Wait 'til I show Pop. He'll be so proud to hear that I caught a rabbit all by myself."

Pip frowned and gave Adam a sideways glance.

"Don't worry, Pipsqueak, you'll learn how to catch a rabbit too someday." He patted Pip on the head.

Pip rolled his eyes and huffed loudly.

Adam's eyes widened. "Whoa. Did you just make that sound, Pip?"

Pip huffed louder. "Aww."

"Golly. Pip, you're not silent after all. You can make sounds."

Pip inhaled air. "Aww."

Adam jumped. "Come on. Let's tell Pop about this."

The boys rushed back to home.

Chapter 3

"HEY, PIP," ADAM SAID, panting, "someday when I get older, I'm gonna be the world's best hunter, and you could be my helper."

Pip beamed, his legs moving faster.

"I'll be so good at hunting that we'll even open up our own grub store. Millions of people will come to eat. We'll be rich."

Pip's heart beat faster. He stretched his arms wide and moved them like the wings of a bird.

"Or I can open a collector's shop," Adam said, "Hundreds of animals will be displayed, and heck, who doesn't want a moose's head on their wall? I sure do--" Adam stopped, causing Pip to crash into him. Adam stood still.

Pip followed Adam's line of sight and saw an army truck parked next to their house.

Adam frowned. "Pip, you don't think we're in trouble, do you? You don't think they're here because they heard a gunshot, right?" Pip looked at Adam and tiptoed to the side of the house. He leaned his ear against the wall to hear the muffled conversation between Pop and the man in green camouflage.

"It's a requirement. Every U.S. household must have at least one male member join."

"Am I a U.S household? My cabin, located in the middle of nowhere, isn't near a city nor a town. I moved out here for a reason."

The guard grunted. "This territory is part of the U.S. Therefore, you *are* a U.S. household."

The guard handed a letter to Pop and stomped out the door. He drove off in his truck, leaving behind a huge cloud of dust.

Pop stared at the letter and covered his face with his big hand.

"What is that?" Adam asked.

Pop shook his head and walked outside and took out a cigarette.

Adam glanced at Pip, who shrugged his shoulders. They walked outside and found Pop sitting on a stump, staring at the floor.

Adam held up the rabbit to Pop's face, "Look, Pop. I did it. I hunted my first game."

Pop didn't look at the rabbit. "Boys, head inside and don't come out. I need to think about some things."

"What kind of things?" Adam asked.

"Things you won't be able to handle. Now go and take the lad with you."

"But, I can handle anything. Why won't you tell me?"

"I said, YOU CAN'T HANDLE IT! Now go inside."

"I'll surprise you, Pop. Who was that man? Why did he come? What did he say that made you so upse--"

Pop slapped Adam in the face. Adam dropped to the ground. Pip rushed over to his brother's side. Pip gasped.

Pop shuddered. "Lad? Did you make that noise?"

Pip stretched his lips to form the sounds. "Ye-...yes!"

With his mouth agape, Pop broke down to tears. He embraced the boys. "What am I going to do?"

The brothers looked at each other, confused.

Chapter 4

SEVERAL WEEKS PASSED. POP had been different since the day he received the letter from that man.

Early one morning, Pip rose from his bed. He rubbed his eyes and saw two suitcases placed near the door. He shook Adam awake.

Adam opened his eyes, "What is it, Pipsqueak?" He yawned.

Pip pointed at two suitcases near the door.

"Suitcases? That's odd. Are we moving?"

The door opened and Pop entered, wearing a long overcoat and a hat. "Boys, put on these jackets." He handed them light brown coats.

"What's going on? Where are we going?" Adam asked, putting on his jacket.

Pop ignored him and yanked the sheets and blankets off their beds and put them in a bag.

The boys walked around the house, only to see the house empty. Everything was gone.

"Where's all our stuff?" Adam asked.

Pop walked outside and motioned for the boys to follow him.

"When will we come back home?" Adam asked.

Pop didn't answer, his eyes teared up. He paused, kneeled down, and placed his hands on both of their shoulders. "Boys, I know this is sudden, but I have to go somewhere. I don't know how long I'll be gone. I'm sending you two to a place you'll be taken care of while I'm away." He looked at Adam. "Take care of your brother. Be more than just an older brother." Pop held up a shiny gold compass. "I'm giving this to you because you're a courageous child, always taking chances."

Adam took the compass. "Promise you'll come back for us."

Pop held up his hand. "I promise." He grabbed Pip and hugged him tightly. "James, never be afraid to speak. Be a good lad to your brother," he said with a calm demeanor.

Pip nodded his head and opened his mouth, "Ay… will…Pop," he said.

"All aboard!" a conductor yelled. The train whistled.

"There's not much time," Pop said, struggling to take something out from his pocket. He handed Adam a crumpled paper. "Get to this place and hand them this. Now go! It's moving."

The boys ran to the train and hopped in. They found seats and looked out the window to find their father in the moving crowd.

"Where is Pop? I don't see him," Adam said, looking anxiously.

Pip fogged up the window with his breath and drew the pictures from his dream on the glass with his fingers.

"Pop, where are you?" Adam abandoned the window and curled up in his seat, gripping the golden compass.

"Pip." Adam's eyes filled with tears. "Do you think we'll ever get back home?"

Pip stared out the window."Y-yyess."

Chapter 5

THE OFFICE DOOR SLAMMED open, startling Mr. Calther, a tall middle-aged man, seated at a desk.

An officer marched in, dragging two boys behind him by the scruff of their necks. One looked like a teenager, and the other looked about ten years old. "Calther, I believe these are yours," the officer said, pushing the boys towards the desk.

Mr. Calther looked at them nd rubbed his fingers against his temple. "Thank you, Ted. I'm sorry if they were causing trouble again."

Ted rolled his eyes and marched towards the door. "I lost count of how many times," he said and slammed the door shut.

Mr. Calther stared sharply at the boys. "Adam, do you want to clean all the rooms again?"

Adam shrugged. "I don't care anymore."

"And James, do you want to another night in the cafeteria?".

Pip lowered his head. " No, sir. We… we just want home."

"Look, the war is over. Let us go home. We won't be in your way anymore," Adam yelled.

Mr. Calther stood up from his desk and walked to the window. "You boys aren't old enough to go out in the real world, especially after the war has ended." Mr Calther placed his long fingers through the shutters to take a peek outside.

"What do you mean?" Adam asked.

"The end of the war is only the beginning of other situations to come." Mr. Calther put his hands behind his back. "Your father wants me to keep you two here until it is safe." He held up a crumpled old note.

"He's gone. He's not the boss of us anymore. We don't have to stay here anymore. These past six years of waiting and hoping has only been a waste." Adam stomped on the ground.

Mr. Calther narrowed his eyes at Pip. "James, what do you have to say about all this?"

Pip stared at the floor, " I-I..I--"

Adam slammed his fist on the desk. "Leave him out of this. He's got no idea how to express his opinions. There's no point in asking him what he thinks!"

Mr. Calther sat down on his chair. "You boys go to your room. No dinner for either of you tonight."

Adam marched out of the door. Pip followed closely behind him. Silence filled in the building. Adam ripped off a paper taped to the wall and crumpled it. He kicked it at Pip.

"You promised he'd return," Adam said.

Pip picked up the crumpled paper. It was a list of the fathers who returned. Their dad was not on the list. Adam opened the door of their small room. Cracks covered the walls and the cold wooden floor. Springs were poking out through their mattress. Pip raised his chin and threw the crumpled paper at Adam, who was making another hole on the wall with a rusty nail.

"I- I promise we be home, not pop be here!"

Adam threw his arms up and gave Pip a look. "Either way!" He threw the paper back at Pip and proceeded to make more marks on the wall.

Chapter 6

THE CLINKING OF GLASSES and silverware and jolly voices echoed from downstairs. Adam tip toed through the halls.He carried a medium sized sack and wore a long overcoat. He walked out and closed the door of the building.

" Me go too," Pip said, holding a small backpack.

"Oh, holy, Pip," Adam whispered, placing his hand on his chest and looking up at the night sky. "You're not coming with me. We've been caught too many times."

"Pop says look after me."

Adam sighed. "Don't get us in trouble this time."

The dark clouds covered most of the night sky, and the wind whistled through the trees. "Pip, try to keep up," Adam yelled, yet he was only a few feet away ahead of Pip.

The boys ended up in front of a long fence.

"Where we go?" Pip panted.

Adam pulled out a rusty wrench from his sack. "We're not taking the usual path."

"You sure?"

Adam pulled out the golden compass and turned his head to Pip. "It's worth a shot. Sometimes in life, you just got to take risks."

Chapter 7

ADAM AND PIP TRAVELED for days. The trees became longer, blocking the sky, and the dead leaves covered the cold ground. The boys' footsteps echoed through the forest.

Adam woke up,feeling goosebumps on his arm.

"Crud, we slept all day. Pip, get up." Adam punched Pip in the arm.

Pip rubbed his eyes and brushed off roots stuck to his back.

"Hurry up, let's go," Adam yelled from a distance.

Pip's legs wobbled and he collapsed to the ground. "Go, me can't no more."

Adam looked at him. Rummaging through his sack, he discovered only a quarter piece of bread. " Here, eat this. It will give you a boost."

Pip pushed the bread away. "No, my..." Pip hugged his stomach and turned away.

"Pip, remember what Pop said?" Adam pulled him up.

"I know, listen to you, but me--"

"No." Adam cut him off. "Pop said you're strong. Even stronger than me." Adam released Pip and crouched down next to him. He pulled out the compass. "You endure more pain than I do, which is why Pop loved you more than me.," Adam dropped the compass.

Pip picked it up and handed it back to Adam. "No, he loved us to-geth-er."

Adam brushed the tear from his cheek and helped Pip up. "Let's keep going."

Chapter 8

ADAM CARRIED PIP MOST of the way back home. Nothing but harsh weather was in their way. Pip observed the ground passing by, his arms waving back and forth. He no longer felt them.

"We made it!" Adam shouted, putting him down.

The house looked exactly like it did six years ago, but the grass no longer had a rich emerald color. Instead, it was a dead brown. The boys heard a strange sound coming from the still house.

"Someone's in there," Adam said. They opened the door, careful to not make a creak.

The growling sounds came from their' bedroom. Adam turned the knob. In the center of the room, a savage looking man paced back and forth. His long, gray hair swung with every step. He held cerulean crystals up to his nose.

" Be on a lookout, be on a lookout, men!" the man muttered.

He sniffed the crystals, and his hands trembled. Grease reflected off his skin.

"Pop," Adam said, running towards him. "You're alive!"

Pop turned and pulled out a sharp knife. "Stay away, you savage beasts. We're still winning."

Adam stepped back "Pop, it's me. I'm Adam, your son. Why didn't you tell us you were back?"

Pop examined Adam, still holding the knife. "Son? Adam? I have no children. I devoted myself to serve this country."

Adam showed Pop the compass. "We are your sons. You sent us to an orphanage and gave me this."

Pop's wild eyes roamed over the compass. He snatched it. "Huh-huh so so I d-d-did, Lewis. I remember you now," Pop said, tasting the compass with a small lick and putting it in his pocket. He wrapped his arms around Adam. "I've missed you so much, Clark."

Adam closed his eyes and leaned against his father's chest. "I've missed you too, Pop."

"Adam," Pip hollered, pushing Adam away.

Pop struck his knife through Pip's shoulder. Pip screamed and fell to the ground.

"Pip!" Adam screamed, pulling him away before Pop could strike him again. "Where do you think you're going?" Adam grabbed Pip and dashed out the house.

Pop marched out behind them, holding a long gun.

"Don't let them escape!" he shouted. He began shooting. Adam managed to get himself and Pip into the forest.

"Pip, let me see your shoulder."

Pip shook his head quickly. "No, we go! Go!"

"No, Pip. It's ok. That crazy old man won--" A huge hand pulled Adam away. "Let me go!" Adam screamed.

Pop threw Adam against a tree. Adam fell to the ground. Pop kicked him, but he didn't respond. Pop set his gun aside and pulled out his stained knife.

"I'll do this the fun way."

A huge rock hit him by the head.

"No!" Pop turned and spotted Pip standing with another rock in his hand.

Pop gritted his teeth and breathed harder. "I haven't finished you yet!"

Pip stumbled away. Pop reached for his neck and laid him flat on the dirt. "America lives on!" he hollered, positioning the knife.

Pip closed his eyes and turned his head.

A bullet blasted through Pop's chest. Pop dropped the knife and fell to the ground.

Adam rushed over to Pip. They both stood over their father's body. Or the body of what used to be their father. He still had the compass clutched in his hand.

Adam squatted down beside his father. The compass shone in the golden sunlight. The compass that symbolized the love and loss of Pop. The Pop who taught him how to hunt, who taught him how to love, even after the loss of their mother, and who taught him how to care for his brother no matter what.. The same Pop that was stolen from them by the war.

" Adam," Pip said wearily. "Can't make it. Leave me here.."

"No, no, no, Pip. We're going to be okay."

"Adam," Pip touched Adam's shaking hand. "You're my home. This why I always follow you."

Adam shook his head, his eyes flooding with tears. "Pip, I should've been the one struck with the knife, not you. This was all my fault. I wanted to come back here."

"Loo-oosing you is losing home," Pip said.

Adam wrapped his arms around Pip and covered his shoulder with Pop's jacket. "We need to get you help, Pip. We have to go back to the city."

Pip smiled and laid his head on Adam's shoulder. Adam held him tightly walked back on the trail. "This will be a long way back, but don't worry, Pip. I'll never leave you." Adam gazed into Pip's eyes. "As long as I'm with you, I'm already home."

BENEATH THE BRIDGE
Monica Van

"DID YOU PREPARE THE dynamite, Theo?"

"Is it really necessary to blow up the bridge?"

"Use your head, Theo. The cops will be on us once we have the 3 million pounds." James hid under the corner of the bridge near the shore, slipping on a black mask with 4 tiny slits.

Theodore worked the wired fuses around the legs of the bridge, his fingers trembling as he gripped the remote that would operate the wires.

England slept in silence, its people snug in their beds, unsuspecting.

"Theo, give me that gun."

"I thought we agreed--"

"Just give it to me," James said. "That scoundrel Foswrotes fired the old guard and hired a sharper one last week. He reacts to the slightest creak. What if the old window o'er the top creaks, huh? You want me to be caught?"

James snatched the gun from Theodore's side and crept onto the shore from his escape boat. The bank loomed over the shore, protected only by the guard prowling close to it. James strapped the pouch he would load with riches onto his shoulder and around his back. He threw the nylon rope and grappler, which caught hold of the window. Right, left. Right, left. James creeped up the wall, clinging to the rope for dear life. James's foot slipped. His hand lost hold of the rope. *Crrreaakk.*

"Hey! You!" A light beam centered on James's face..

Having landed on the ground, James scrambled for his gun. The guard went down with a "*BANG!*" The flashlight dropped onto the concrete, bouncing once before turning its beam, revealing the bloody face. James inched forward to examine the motionless body. The face would have mirrored James's, if it wasn't for the red stain of imminent death.

"John…?" James's mind went blank. "John… Why are you here?" he said, both hands clawing at his temples. "They said you were in London, not here in Manchester. A well-to-do in London. John…"

James removed his mask and wiped the beads of sweat from his face. Lights flashing on from nearby windows snapped James from his wide-eyed musings. He fled towards the bridge, the sounds of police whistles following him. He jumped onto the boat.

"Where's the money, James?" Theodore asked, looking into the empty bag.

"Theodore." James panted. "I just killed John."

"We agreed not to-- Did you just say 'John'?"

"John is dead. I…" James's voice cracked. He stumbled onto the seat of the boat, his hands rubbing his forehead, and his dark--now darker--eyes darting back and forth from his partner's face to the bank. "We need to leave."

"What? It's one thing that we've come to rob that scoundrel of his dirty money, but you just bloody killed your brother. No money, a corpse, and you want to leave?"

"Give me the paddle, Theo."

"Give you the paddle? Look at those hands, James. They're stained with blood. Look at them. James--"

Another gunshot interrupted Theodore's objection.

His hands shaking, and his panting out of control, James threw the new corpse overboard. The whole town was awake now. The footsteps of cops running towards the first crime scene echoed through James's thoughts.

He fetched the paddle out of drowning hand and began to row. The bank shrunk as the boat dragged itself through the water, away from the shore. James mumbled to himself, "You didn't kill John. You didn't kill Theo. No, James. You did nothing wrong. Nothing, nothing, nothing."

BLUE EYES, BLACK SKIES
Alexandra Quang

"YOU CAN GO HOME now, Carl, but take the folder with you. Look it over and bring it in tomorrow morning," Carl's boss said. "The press is going to have a field day with this story. Six dead in our town and not a single suspect, only a grainy photo of the killer's eyes."

Carl merely nodded, too tired to even reply. He just wanted to get home to rest, ask his daughter to put some tea on the stove, and then knock out on the couch.

He got into his car and sighed. He should be paid more; the job was demanding and he was no longer as youthful as he was when he joined the force thirty years ago.

Carl opened the file his boss had given him and read through the reports. Six bodies, four males, two females. Four were murdered in their homes, and the other bodies were found near the town pier. He flipped to the picture of the attacker's eyes and his heart nearly stopped. He knew those eyes. They were the same striking blue as his daughter's. The same abnormal blue that was a result of a genetic blip, as neither he nor his wife had eyes that color.

"Jesus, not my daughter. Not my Jessica. Not her. Not my daughter. Not my Jessica, Can't be her. Not my..." It was a mantra that branded itself into his mind.

Carl turned the key into the ignition and his ancient machine sputtered to life. He pulled out of the parking lot in a daze, his eyes on the road but not really seeing. He no longer trusted what he could see and feared what he could not.

"My little Jesse?" he muttered to himself. "Couldn't be." *But yes it could,* a little voice within him beckoned. *Where has dear little Jesse been coming from all those late nights? The same nights those victims had gone missing?* the voice taunted in a lilting tone. *She says school library, but you, sir, are smarter than that.*

Carl swallowed hard. He did know better. The school library closes two hours after school lets out. She always came home well over that time.

The night was dark, making shapes and obstacles hard to distinguish. He drove along the road aimlessly, unsure of whether or not being home alone with a possibly sociopathic daughter was what he still wanted.

The poor man was so absorbed in his thoughts that he didn't notice a shadowy figure standing directly in the center of the road until the split second before it would've been too late.

"Jesus Christ!" Carl violently swerved off the road into a ditch.

Carl remembered a shadow brushing past his window. The last things he saw before he died were pale hands reaching in to take the folder from the passenger seat and a pair of striking blue eyes against the blackening sky.

BONGO
Zachary King

"UGH. WHERE AM I?" I opened my eyes. I squinted, protecting my eyes from the glare of the street lamps. I surveyed my surroundings. Cars occupied the spaces between the faint white lines and gray concrete parking blocks. My chest felt heavy. A lump choked the back of my throat.

I gazed into the distance. A crowd of small children gathered around the neon yellow entrance of a giant technicolored tent. In front of the crowd, a man wore a cap with a hot dog-shaped propeller on top. He leaned against his hot dog stand and chatted with the child nearest him. Did I know this man? Why did looking at his face make mine grimace?

I walked away from the tent--away from the man--and into the abundance of conifers that bordered the massive parking lot. Further up, along the narrow roadway, I waved one arm, signaling any passing car to allow me to hitch a ride. No one. I kept walking.

When I was halfway down the road, a small, soft voice said, "Hey, Bongo, where are you going?"

I looked back. In denim overalls, a blond boy three heads shorter than I, had the string of a cherry red balloon clutched in his hand. He beamed, a smile too innocent to belong in this dark place.

"Are you talking to me?" I said.

"Of course, Bongo." He giggled. "There isn't another Bongo the Clown!"

Clown? I glanced down at my clothes: a crusty shirt with multi-colored blotches of irregular shapes and sizes, , orange and blue cotton overalls, and bright crimson shoes five sizes bigger than my feet. Part of my shirt was crusty and stained brown, although it was hardly noticeable with the rest of the colored splotches.

I smiled at the boy. "That's right kid. I'm Bongo the Clown. There is no other."

He frowned. "That's not your catchphrase, Bongo."

I remembered what he was talking about. "Bongo, Bongo, Bongo. I don't wanna leave the Congo." I cheered.

"Yay!" The boy clapped.. "Why are you out here, Bongo? Shouldn't you be in the circus tent? The lions need you."

"Right. The tent. The lions." The lions? "Hey, kid. Bongo's just gonna get some more… clown fuel. I'll be right back."

"Okay, Bongo. But you're gonna come back, right?"

"Of course, kid." A sense of guilt whirled in my brain.

The boy waved his arms in the air, his balloon bouncing along with his glee. . "See ya later, Bongo." He sprinted towards the tent.

I glanced at the tent and back at the road. Should I disappoint this child? Or should I risk the potential suffering within the tent?

I trudged back to the tent, each step weighing heavier and heavier.

I squeezed through the crowd of children towards the bright yellow entrance. Someone gripped my shoulder, stopping me. I turned around. The hot dog man.

"James," he said. "What the hell are you doing out here?"

"A-a-are you talking to me?" I asked.

"Of course, you moron." He glared at me. "Why aren't you getting ready for the next performance, you idiot?"

"Oh, um, uh." I kept trying to remember who this man was, although it became really clear to see why I had such negative feelings towards him.

"Get going!" He stomped his foot on the ground and pointed to the tent with one hand on his hip.

My eye twitched. I walked to the back of the tent. Men dressed in leotards and overalls like mine gathered near the back entrance.

Entering from the back, I noticed a paper stapled to a post that read: CLOWNS - RIGHT, ACROBATS - LEFT, ANIMAL TAMERS - WAIT OUTSIDE. I turned to my right.

A clown in red and green striped overalls and a frizzy choker greeted me, his mouth outlined with red lipstick. "Excuse me, old chap," he said in a posh accent, "I've been trying to acquire some knowledge of who and where I am. And I don't mean that in the metaphysical sense. Oh no, dear boy. Most certainly not. I seem to have suffered some great amount of physical trauma and can no longer remember anything from before I awoke in yonder parking lot. Do you have any information relevant to this?"

"Actually, I'm in the same boat, pal," I said. "I--"

"Wait. You lost your memory, too?" Another clown asked.

I nodded. "Apparently, we both did."

"Me too." Another clown raised his hand.

Then another. "Memory loss? Same here."

"Can't remember a thing."

All of the clowns beside me nodded their heads. Like a ridiculous noir film, our discussion began to stir, rumors started spreading. Some tried to feign knowledge, but most asked, "Why?"

A voice screamed at us, "Quiet, you clowns. The show's about to start." The clamor in the back of the tent weakened to a whisper then to nothing. A rolling snare drum from further inside the tent broke the silence. A woman dressed in a yellow tuxedo and top hat pulled aside the maroon velvet curtain to make her grand entrance. She strutted onto the stage.

The audience, mostly baby-faced children, cheered. The calliope then the trumpets then the French horns began to play, followed by the rest of the band. In the back of the tent, the performers, myself included, lined up behind curtain.

Two burly men approached the area where we clowns were gathered. One of the men, who had a curled moustache, read a list from a clipboard. The mustached man glanced up and observed the swell of multicolor, confused clowns who stood before him.

"Which one 'a youz is Bozo?" He scanned the crowd.

The clowns looked and mouthed to one another, "Who?"

"Bozo," the mustached man repeated. "Bozo the clown. Iz dere a Bozo 'ere or naht?"

"You moron." The other man, whose face was moustache-free, smacked the back of his partner's head. "Dat says 'Bongo.' Bongo da clown? Iz dere a Bongo da clown 'ere?"

I approached the two men. "I'm Bongo. Or I think I am."

"You're next," the mustached man said.

"What am I supposed to do exactly?" I asked, as they led me to the curtain.

"Juss' do what tha' ringmasta' tells ya'. Ya don' even haf' ta say anythin'. Think ya can handle it?"

I opened my mouth to answer, but the men shoved through the curtain. The spotlights glared into my eyes. Hundreds of people chanted my name.

"And now, ladies and gentlemen," the woman from earlier shouted into her megaphone, "Bongo is going to show you his magnificent pets! Bring out the lions, boys!"

A family of cats made their way towards me, each with fluffy, orange manes surrounding their necks. They cuddled at my feet, playfully pawed at the air around me and jumped at me, purring

"Don't just stand there," the woman whispered at me. "Do something!"

I picked up one of the cats. The audience giggled. I examined it, rotating it about in my hands, making ridiculous faces. The audience laughed some more. I ran around the stage, chasing the cats, letting them chase me, making them climb on top of me and bite and scratch me up a bit. I found some hoops lying around the stage, and let the cats jump through. The audience roared with laughter.

"Alright, Bongo," said the woman, "It's time for these lions to go back to the savannah!"

A wave of disappointment swept through the audience.

"It's alright. You'll be back, won't you Bongo?" a child in the crowd asked.

My shoulders sunk. I put on the biggest frown I could stretch my muscles to. "Bongo, Bongo, Bongo. I don't wanna leave the Congo," I said with a cartoonish, disheartened tone. The audience roared with amusement at that.

Another child said, "It's okay, Bongo. You'll be back next time, won't you?"

I plastered a large smile onto my face and nodded my head. I turned around and made my way through the curtain to rejoin the amusing amnesiacs.

The clowns in the back had all formed a circle with a large gap, but I couldn't push through to see what the commotion was about.

"They just took him. Carried him off like some sort of big game prize," shrieked one woman whose attention I managed to capture. I could practically feel the hysteria radiating off of her. "He was saying something about Jason… Jason… Oh, I wish I could remember. They just took him, but no one wants to go and find him because they told us if we did we'd be dead."

"Who took him?" I asked.

"Those two burly men. They just covered his mouth and dragged him by the arms outside the tent. No one dared to follow them."

I thanked her and headed out the tent. Many people lined up at the curtain tried to stop me, telling me how good I was on stage and congratulating me on my performance. I brushed by them, finding my way back outside.

A large spatter of blood stained one flap of the tent. A blood trail led into the parking lot. I followed it, ducking behind the parked cars.

"You are such an idiot," the smooth-faced man from earlier said, although now there was no trace of an accent. "How did you forget the injection?"

"I'm sorry, man," the other said. "I've had a lot on my mind recently, okay?"

They walked past me, arguing the whole way back. I reached the end of the trail. An unconscious clown laid there, blood oozing from his mouth. I slapped and shook him, trying to get him to regain consciousness.

"Yellow forgets… green remembers…" he muttered.

"What do you mean?"

"Yellow forgets… green remembers… yellow forgets… green remembers," he continued chanting. His voice faded and he fell into unconsciousness once more. I heard the two burly men arguing, their voices inching closer. I scurried to a nearby jeep and hid underneath it.

"I still don't get why we gotta bring the whole box," one of them said.

"It's so I know you'll remember it this time, you moron."

They reached into the box and pulled something out. One of them bent down, gripping a syringe in his hand filled with a yellow liquid. He thrust the needle into the chest of the bleeding man, who jolted awake and screamed out in pain. The other man jumped back, dropping the box and spilling the syringes, scattering them across the little perimeter of his surroundings.

"How many times have we done this? They always scream, you moron!"

Two of them rolled toward my jeep, one with the same yellow liquid as before and one with a green liquid. The two men cursed and argued, and started swinging fists. I snuck off in the opposite direction, ducking behind cars as I went, until I was as far away from the little crime scene as I could get. The man's words echoed in my head, "Yellow forgets, green remembers."

I injected the green syringe into my chest. A million thoughts blazed through my head all at once. As though some light had been suddenly switched on in my head, I remembered.

I remembered Jason Morgan, the charismatic hot dog vendor at the circus I had taken my son to, the circus where I had worked as a clown. I remembered my son, my little boy with his gleaming face and blond hair and overalls, and how I told him to pretend I wasn't his daddy when I was in costume.

I remembered the incredibly huge and strong dynamic duo, Mike and Charlie, Jason's ever-obedient lapdogs.

I remembered how I accidentally got scratched too deeply by one of my cats, how the blood had seeped through my cobalt overalls. I remembered how the two bozos started injecting everyone, even the audience with that yellow serum, making them forget it had ever happened, then dragging me off into the parking lot and leaving me to my fate. I clenched my fist.

I made my way to the front of the tent. Jason shouted at Mike and Charlie.

"You idiots. Do you know how expensive this serum is? I have to import it all the way from Czechoslovakia! Do you really think a circus makes enough money so you can just drop all of it?"

"It was only two, boss-"

"Only two? Only two? That's practically two year's pay for you! Go back and find them! And dump the old man into the lion's pen. The real lion's pen, not the cats' like you did last time. Do you hear me?"

The two men nodded and made their way back to the bleeding man, kicking the ground as they walked. Once they were out of sight, I approached Jason.

"Bongo," he said. "What are you doing out here again? Get back in there and prepare for the finale you insufferable buffoon."

But I didn't listen. I closed in on Jason.

He backed up. "Bongo, what in God's name are you doing? If you're trying to scare me, you should remember that you are in face paint and a multicolored shirt."

I walked faster.

"Now, now, Bongo Whatever it is you're upset about, we can talk about it."

I pulled the syringe from my pocket.

"How did you- where did you- Oh, please no.." He turned around and ran.

I charged at him. I pulled on his collar and wrestled him to the ground. We got into a scuffle, each trying to keep the pointy end of the syringe pointed towards the other. After I wrestled him to the ground, I jabbed the needle into his chest and pumped the serum into him. He screamed like a banshee as every last one of his memories were stripped from him. I stood up, sweaty and panting.

Jason's two goons rushed to their boss's aid. "What did you do to the boss? Did you just inject him?" They tried to shake Jason awake.

"Guys," I said. "let's be rational, here."

"You just wiped the boss's memory."

"Yeah, but is he really worth it, guys? He's verbally abusive, controls people by making them forget who they are, and just in general isn't that good of a person."

They remained silent for a good deal of time.

"Look, man, he's all we got." Mike said, looking at the ground..

"Yeah, we can't remember anything either," Charlie admitted. "He took us in, gave us a job, feeds us, and lets us beat people up without telling the cops."

"Don't you feel guilty about wiping people's memories?" I asked.

"Yeah, but if it's what Jason tells us to do, then we gotta."

"I don't suppose Jason ever told you about the green serum then, did he?"

"No, but Jason told us to use it on him if he ever wiped his memory," they said.

"Do you still have the box?" I asked.

"Yeah, it's backstage."

"Okay, maybe it's time someone showed you what that green stuff actually does," I said.

We made our way backstage. The two led me to a secret cabinet that was hidden amongst the animal care products.

"Here's where we keep the green ones," they told me.

Inside the cabinet was a massive amount of syringes filled with green colored liquids, with a few yellow syringes. Taped to one of the doors of the cabinet read a note: "REMEMBER, IDIOTS. YELLOW FORGETS, GREEN REMEMBERS."

I took two out and injected the green liquid into Mike and Charlie's chests, retrieving their memories and breaking the mental chains that bound them to Jason. The two agreed to distribute it amongst the other performers, making sure Jason never got his hands on any.

I found my son, still holding his red balloon, his blond hair glistening like an angel's. I knelt down and injected the serum into his right arm.

He looked up at me, beamed, then hugged me. so tightly I thought his little arms were going to fall off.

"Da-Daddy?" He tugged on my overalls. "Can we go home now? I don't like the circus."

"Of course," I said, "Because this time, I want to leave the Congo."

CASE 66
Stephany Vivar

FRIDAY, NOVEMBER 13, 2007
7:16 A.M.

I entered a dark room. A dim light appeared, cast on a body. Blood covered the boy's pale face and half of his head. His middle fingers were cut off, his ears and part of his foot, torn apart. A tear ran down his bloody face. Something--something warm, thick, wet-- ran down my arms. Blood. I wanted to scream, but my voice was lost. I could only inhale inaudible air. Lights appeared in another room. Darkness covered the face of another boy. He laughed and said to me, "The ear was the best part. It had more of a crunch to it."

I recorded these nightmares in my black five-star notebook. I hoped writing them down would help me recover. I threw away the stale toast that sat in my toaster, and ate only a grapefruit on my way to work. At my desk, my friend, John, invited me to an isolated glass room to discuss a particular case, Case 66. I had already agreed to help John. I couldn't back out now. A boy named Angel had called in yesterday night, saying that his parents had abused him.

1:34 P.M.

At Angel's house, John and I conducted routine procedures, questioning the parents about Angel. They didn't answer. They refused to let us see him, saying that Angel was in school. They told us to come tomorrow, but just as we were leaving, glass from an upper floor fell and shattered at our feet. From the broken window, Angel, a frightened, skinny, pale boy appeared.

5:57 P.M.

We questioned Angel in my office. He didn't say much, so I asked my coworker, Emily, to get him some food. In about 10 minutes, she came back with two dozen doughnuts and a carton of milk. Angel's eyes opened as if he have never seen so many doughnuts. I placed the boxes down on the wooden table between us and said that if he could answer some questions, he could have them all.

8:36 P.M.

I recalled the thrill in Angel's eyes as he ate the doughnuts. He told me he hadn't eaten in two days. Why? Why did he have to endure this abuse? But I kept my mouth shut.

SATURDAY, NOVEMBER 14, 2007
1:22 A.M.

I called foster homes to request a bed for Angel to sleep on overnight, but all were full or wouldn't answer their phones. I allowed Angel to sleep in the office until I had found him proper foster care.

10:46 A.M.

I received a call from the P.D.O.C (Police Department of Ohio Court), saying that Angel had to testify in court on Monday at 8:00 A.M.. I had found Angel a temporary foster home, but he insisted on staying at the office, where he felt safer from his parents. As much as I wanted to, I couldn't take Angel home with me. I took him to the house of Ms. Rosa, a nice old lady who would provide him a bed more comfortable than the office couch and I promised to visit him.

6:27 P.M.

At 11:35 A.M. Ms. Rosa called, screaming, telling me that Angel couldn't stay in foster care. When I arrived at the foster home, Ms. Rosa was waiting on her sidewalk, pressing a white cloth against her ear. She grasped Angel's shoulder, as tears streamed down his soft pink cheeks. Ms. Rosa shoved Angel into the car, warned me never to call again, and shut the car door. Angel attempted to hide his grief, but soft whimpers grew louder, until his emotions erupted.

He said the kids at the foster home bullied him immediately, one of them started to pick a fight. He only tried to defend himself. When Ms. Rosa tried to break apart the fight, he tried to bite the kid's arm but accidentally bit Ms. Rosa. I comforted him, assuring him that it was accident, that he wasn't at fault.

9:19 P.M.

I brought Angel back to my place, since most foster homes had heard about the incident. They refused to accept Angel, saying that he was a little devil. How could they think that about sweet Angel?

MONDAY NOVEMBER 16, 2007
6:52 A.M.

Yesterday I shopped with Angel for a formal outfit for court and regular clothes. He had worn the same clothes since the day I met him: torn jeans, a white shirt that turned yellow from toxic smoke, shoes that revealed his pinkie toe. I tried to relieve his pre-court tensions and assured him that I would support him.

5:56 P.M.

When the judge charged Angel's parents with multiple counts related to the death of their seven children whose corpses had been partially eaten. The judge ordered the parents to be held without bail. An officer cuffed them and led them away. Everyone in the court cheered except Angel. Angel's parents glared at him. I told Angel that he did the right thing. By reporting his parents, he had sent the seven kids his parents had killed off in peace. He smiled, knowing they were in Heaven.

John and I took Angel out to celebrate. I asked if he would like me as his new mother. He hugged me and said he had loved me ever since he had seen me from the broken window of his old home.

THURSDAY NOVEMBER 18, 2007

5:26 A.M.

After a while, the same nightmare returned, but this time, I saw more. I came down the stairs in my own home, seeing the same kid bleed again. I heard the same laugh. In the light, Angel's face appeared. Terror shook me. I asked him, "Why?"

He said, "It's in my genes. Since I was in my mother's womb, she had fed me human."

I woke up, trembling.

6:16 A.M.

My dreams came to life. My dreams weren't dreams. Right from the start, they warned me about Angel.

THE COFFEE SHOP
Tracey Hoang

IT WAS FINALS WEEK. The coffee shop was littered with frantic students trying to study while chugging down bitter coffee to stay awake. All the tables were filled with laptops and random papers. The manager was nice enough to set up extra tables with fancy umbrellas outside the shop and even had the electricity company install additional outlets, so that all the students could charge their electronic devices when they needed. It was the busiest time for both the students and coffee shop employees.

Still, there were hours when the coffee shop was relatively peaceful, and it was possible for only one person to watch over the shop.

It was around eight in the evening, and Joy was about halfway through her shift when she had her first encounter with Collin. He had run into the shop with his book bag flung open and his clothes a mess. Finals week.

Joy had seen many students come in with wrinkled clothing, some even worse than him, so she didn't blink when he sauntered up to the cash register, his dirty shoes leaving a trail of clumped dirt and grass on the clean floor. He flashed her a big smile, one that made it seem like he was up to no good, and she flashed her perfected "I'm pleasant but only because I have to be for my job" smile and uncapped her pen.

"Welcome to Happy Coffee Days. What can I get you?"

He looked over the menu for a few seconds before replying. "I would like a caramel macchiato in your biggest size. Extra caramel please." He looked up from the menu and took a closer look at Joy. "Your number would be a nice bonus, too."

Her eyebrow twitched and she refused the urge to flush. She was relatively new to this job and was not used to being hit on at work. She kept her smile and quickly scribbled his order onto the cup and set it down on the counter. "Is that all?"

"Yes."

"Your total will be $4.25. Can I get a name?"

"Collin, or Handsome person. Both work."

She chuckled softly and shook her head. This boy was quite shameless. He was fishing his wallet out when they heard a loud booming voice.

"He couldn't have gotten that far, you nitwits! Check the coffee shop or something. That bastard left behind a trail of mud."

Collin muttered a few statements filled with profanity before he flung himself over

65

the counter, miraculously not knocking over the cups or Joy herself. She let out a surprised yelp and backed away to the sink.

"What in the world are you doing?" she said.

He placed his index finger to his lips and motioned her to crouch down.

She warily glanced at him and slowly lowered herself.

"I was never here."

"You mean they're actually looking for *you*? What in the world did you do?"

"Trust me, you don't want to get involved with them. Tell them I was never here."

"Why should I? I don't owe you anything."

He rolled his eyes and forced her to stand up before rushing off to hide in the employee break room. Before she could glare at him, one of the goons walked up to the counter.

"Sorry to bother you. Have you seen this rascal?" He shoved a badly drawn portrait of Collin into her face and looked at her expectantly.

She cleared her throat and shook her head. "No, not really. It's been a pretty slow night."

The goon leaned close to her face, trying to see if she was lying. Joy felt uncomfortable, but she kept her face neutral. Years of drama class taught her how to perfect the art of a poker face.

The male looked across the dirty floor and pointed to the foot prints. "He ran across a muddy field. There are muddy footsteps across your floor."

"The school's soccer team came by after practice. The field is still wet from the recent rains." Joy maintained a happy smile on her lips, but was panicking.

"That could be an excuse."

"I also could be telling the truth. It's your choice on whether you want to believe me."

The goon scrutinized her even more.

"Look at the coffee shop; it's empty. The person you're looking for is not here. Check the bathrooms if you must, but I'm telling the truth."

She crossed her arms and raised a single eyebrow, daring him to push the subject further.

He didn't. He simply narrowed his eyes and shrugged. He didn't speak to her again as he left.

Joy waited a good thirty seconds before she quietly called out the boy hiding in the employee break room. "He left. The coast is clear."

Collin stuck his head out first, checking to see if she was telling the truth. When he determined that the goon was in fact not there, he walked out and reached over to ruffle her hair.

"Thanks. I owe you one."

She huffed and patted down her hair; it actually looked nice today, and here he was ruining it. "Mind telling me what that was all about?" She eyed him with caution, running her hands across the bottles they used to make their whipped cream. It wasn't much, but they were made of metal and it would hurt if she hurled one at him.

He shrugged. "I didn't do much. I just foiled their drug dealing scheme--"

"Wait, what?" Her eyes widened. She stepped back until she bumped against the counter. "What do you mean by drug scheme? Are you crazy?"

"They were ruining my gang's business. I had to do something."

"Wait, you're in a gang, too?" she asked, completely horrified. "Oh my gosh. What if the goon finds out I lied to him and comes back for retribution? I don't want them to hunt me. I haven't even finished getting my degree yet. I haven't even dissected a frog yet. They're going to come get me!" she said in one long breath.

Collin actually had the nerve to laugh at her, not a soft subtle chuckle, but the kind where the person throws their head back because the situation is so amusing. "Calm down, would you? If they come back, just call me. I'll protect you. They're not stupid enough to mess with me."

She looked at him in disbelief. She'd dealt with weird customers before, but this was just surreal. She couldn't tell if he was being serious or not. How could he really protect her? Just a few minutes ago, he was hiding from them. Why should she even trust this guy? He seemed like trouble, and she was not into trouble.

He leaned over to read the nametag resting on her apron. "Is your name really Joy? Your personality does not match."

"Yeah... it is," she said coolly. It was a lie, all the employees at the shop had a nickname they went by, and hers ended up being Joy. She wasn't going to reveal information about herself to this man though.

"Cool. Can I have my coffee now?"

Her hands shook against her side as she walked over to the counter to make his drink. She expected him to walk over to the other side of the counter to let her work, but he stayed where he was.

She could feel his eyes as she poured the caramel into his drink. Yes, she remembered to put in extra caramel, though not too much, because she knew this boy did not need any more sugar in his system. She capped it off when the drink was finished and waved him over.

"Your drink is ready."

His face lit up in happiness.

Joy had a hard time believing he was involved in gang related drama, but she told herself not to judge.

"Well, I'll take my leave now," he said, walking out from the employee-only area. "Thanks for covering for me, kid." He messed up her hair and shot her a flirty wink.

Hands clenched onto her apron, she opened her mouth to protest his nickname for her, but he left before she could say anything. Sighing, she leaned back into the counter. It had been a very long and interesting day.

She closed her eyes and took in a few deep breaths to rest. It was only when she felt her body slowly shut off that she remembered.

Her eyes shot open. She glared at the trail of mud on the floor waiting to be cleaned up, the carton of milk she used to make his drink, and the bottle of caramel that needed to be refilled.

"Are you freaking kidding me?" Joy groaned. This was coming out of her paycheck for sure. "That bastard didn't even pay for his drink."

THE FUTURE IS BRIGHTER WITH YOU
Kevin Ho

AT BUSY INTERSECTIONS, AT occupied bus stops, in congested school hallways, I snuck glimpses at Stella Maxwell. A peasant like me could only admire her goddess-like radiance, her fluttering brunette hair, her luminous smile. Just glancing at her was the highlight of my day. I daydreamed about her all the time. On one such occasion, my thoughts were interrupted.

"You're in love with Stella right?" a girl said. "Let me help you out."

At a midpoint between sunset and evening, violet and marigold blended together, painting the sky. The girl in front of me had serene wintry, gray eyes. She stuck her hands in her pockets and leaned against the sidewalk fence with an aura of confidence. Did she know I would walk home using this route? I stood there in awe. Someone like her existed at my school? I've never seen her in any of my classes. Her beauty was almost on the scale of Stella. She wasn't luminous or glistening, but instead there was something different to her. I couldn't quite put my finger on it.

"Who are you?" I asked. "I don't think we've met."

"I guess you could think of me as someone who's just passing through, someone you're going to meet."

She smiled, but I sensed melancholy and regret behind her smile. I had never met this girl, but she knew I liked Stella. Did she plan our meeting? I don't believe in coincidence.

Without a word, she passed near my right shoulder, turned around and whispered into my ear, "If you want Stella to notice you, then you got to trust me on this. By the way, bring an umbrella with you tomorrow. It's going to rain."

The sun set on my way home. I slung my backpack over one shoulder, scratching my chin. I looked up. There wasn't a cloud in the sky. I refreshed the weather app on my phone. 79 degrees tomorrow. Rain was impossible, just like my chances with Stella. Why would the most popular girl in school talk to a guy like me? My report cards were nothing to brag about. I couldn't shoot a basketball or swing a racket. I couldn't run. All I could do was draw pictures.

"I'm just an average-joe type of guy. There's no way that girl can help me."

The moment I got home, I kicked off my sneakers and set them down by the front. My mom, sweeping the tile floor, told me that a package addressed to me had arrived. I didn't remember buying anything. The box was small, no longer than two feet. What could be inside?

Eventually, my curiosity got the better of me, and I ripped open the box, leaving pieces of cardboard scattered on the floor. An umbrella. Its design depicted an intricate picture of many stars under a night sky. A yellow post-it note attached to the umbrella read, "You probably weren't going to listen to me, so I went ahead and bought you an umbrella. See you tomorrow -- Your helper."

"Tomorrow? What does she mean by that? I don't get this girl at all."

How did she even get my address? Why does she keep referring to things in the future tense?

Who is she? I'm sure I would have known her if she attended my school.

I recalled her blonde curls, her skin, smooth as a newborn's. Her beauty almost matched Stella's.

I should have been weirded out that she knew my address, but this was the first time a pretty girl had ever shown interest in me.

Lying in my bed that night, I rolled over to one side and propped my head up, thinking. Turning back to face the ceiling, I ruffled my hair to stop the headache of confusion. Should I trust her? For whatever reason, deep down I felt that she and I had a connection. I turned off my lights, and closed my eyelids, waiting for tomorrow to come, so I could finally unravel the enigma that was simply known as "the helper."

Waking up to the sound of my alarm, I followed my normal morning routine. I brushed my teeth, pulled a plain gray sweater over my head and put on some jeans, then made toast before running to school. The blaring sun greeted me when I stepped outside. Not a single cloud in sight, but I shoved my new umbrella into the third pocket of my backpack anyways.

"79 degrees, another beautiful day. That girl may be pretty, but she's also pretty crazy."

On my way to school, someone punched me on the back. I turned around. There was my buddy, Michael. From the corner of my eye, I saw a group of girls following behind him, wearing the t-shirts of his fan club. He carried a calculus textbook at his side and donned a basketball jersey. Michael, the varsity basketball team captain. My complete opposite.

"Michael, do you enjoy punching me every day?"

"It's what I live for, Nate," he said.

My friend was a real jerk, but without him, I'd guess I'd be nothing. After all, he was the one who got me into art. I owed him for helping me find my passion in life.

He smiled at me. He had news. Good news.

"Nate, I heard that we'd be getting a new student today, a girl. Actually, I saw her in the office yesterday. She looks like your type."

I didn't say anything. I remembered my experience with that girl yesterday and before I knew it, we had reached our school.

We walked up three flight of stairs to get to class. I always liked to get there early, because I could sneak glimpses at Stella before class started.

When I walked into the room, I saw that what Michael said was true. My class was typically quiet, but not today. Excited students whispered amongst their circles. The new girl must be one hell of a girl.

"Dude, she's super pretty," and, "I heard she's the daughter of a model," spread around the class. I ignored the ridiculous rumors and headed towards my seat. Dropping my backpack on the floor beside me, I slumped into my chair. With ease, I stole a glimpse at Stella, who sat three seats diagonally from me. The person who had occupied the seat between us had moved, so no one could catch me in this disgraceful act.

The bell rang and the teacher came in, "Alright class, we have a new student today. Let's all open up to her. You can come on in now, Jessica."

Time froze. The girl from yesterday.

The dots connected in my head. Was this what she meant when she said I would soon meet her? She and I made eye contact. She smiled. Was she doing it on purpose, trying to mess with my mind?

The teacher told Jessica that she could sit in any empty seat. The two empty seats were the ones next to me and Michael. Normal girls would choose Michael over me any day, but this girl wasn't normal. She walked in my direction and sat down next to me. Staring straight ahead, she whispered, "So, do you trust me now?"

"Well, considering everything you've said, you seem like you knew it was going to happen. Let's talk at lunch. I want answers."

Jessica tilted her head, facing me. The corners of her lips quirked upwards, as if she enjoyed toying with me. She faced forward, nodding to the teachers' lectures, jotting down notes. I was going to get down to the mystery of this girl one way or another. When the lunch bell rang, I invited her to the school rooftop. I was friends with the janitor, and he handed me the keys to the rooftop every time I wanted to be alone.

"Alright," I said. "Spill it. How do you know so much about me?"

Jessica smiled. "Well, I guess I can't keep it a secret forever." Reaching into her backpack, she brought out a journal. "This journal holds the events of the future. You may not believe me, but I can see into the future. Well, when I'm sleeping anyways."

Of all the strange things I've heard, this had to take the cake. "Man, you really are crazy."

She shrugged. She must've heard it so many times already. She crossed her arms and said, "Well, that umbrella's going to come in handy later. You'll see."

The sun shined brighter than in the morning. Still no clouds visible.

"Alright, maybe it will, but why am I in your future?" This was probably the biggest mystery of them all. I felt a connection to her, but I never would have guessed that it was a connection in the future.

She looked into my eyes and gave me a bright smile. "Well, in the future, we're best friends."

"What?" I said. "Why would I be friends with a delusional girl like you?"

I had spent a majority of my life in the company of males, strictly males, and I promised myself that the only girl I'd ever talk to had to be either pretty or not crazy. Being shallow wasn't one of my best traits, but I had to do it in order to eliminate all the potentially bad relationships that could happen in my life. The girl in front of me was nothing less than a knockout beauty, but right now, my head was telling me to get the hell out of there.

"Listen. Jessica, I think I'm done with this. Please don't talk to me ever again from here on out."

Putting my hands into my pockets, I strolled back to the classroom. For the remainder of the lunchtime, I heard rumors that there was a girl crying on the rooftop. Jessica never returned to class.

Looking out of my window, the sunny day had turned gloomy. Gray clouds rolled in from every direction.

"I guess she was right after all." I sighed.

By the end of day, it was pouring outside. The roads resembled ponds. People called for their rides. Today, there was a freak storm and no one had expected it, except for her.

"Why am I thinking about her all of a sudden?"

I tried for a few minutes to call my mom, but she didn't pick up her phone. I reached inside my backpack and pulled out the umbrella. I pressed the button on the handle and popped it open. I decided to walk home, but before I could take a step, someone tapped my shoulder. Turning around, I faced Stella. Her hair was soaked, her clothes were completely wet, yet her face was still stunning. Her shimmering eyes gazed into mine. I couldn't muster up words.

"Excuse me," she said. "Can we share an umbrella? My ride can't come pick me up today."

Was I dreaming? The most beautiful girl in school was not only talking to me, but wanted to share my umbrella? I motioned her under it, because I couldn't speak.

"You're in my class right? Nathan, if I'm correct."

This just became one of the best days of my life, Stella not only wanted to share an umbrella with me, but she knew my name. I could hardly contain my excitement, and I'm sure she could tell. My hands trembled as they held the umbrella, and even though it was raining and cold, my palms sweat. Her shoulder, only an inch apart from mine, yet there was nothing except awkward silence.

"Hey, that's a pretty cool design on the umbrella," Stella said. "I think I see the Orion constellation on there."

"What are you, a secret space geek?" I asked.

She chuckled. Her eyes glistened. I paused and stood in awe.

"Well," she said. "I think the universe is fascinating. Like, most people don't even know the difference between a comet and meteor."

"And you do?"

Along the walk, Stella revealed another side of her. Like me, she was a fan of modern art and a closet anime freak.

I didn't even notice that the rain had stopped. I was still holding the umbrella. I always enjoyed looking at her from behind, but I think being able to stand next to her was even better. An epiphany struck me. I understood my affection for her. She was different from the others. Always true to herself, she could admit that she liked anime, when people like me would hide it and judge others.

Before I knew it, we had already reached the bus stop. Stella waved goodbye and joined the line of people boarding the bus. When she neared the front of the line. I put my hands in my pocket and started down the road. She ran back to me, handed me a slip of paper, and winked.

I mean, I was no Einstein, but I was certain that the ten digits written in curly font on the blue post-it was a phone number.

It must have been fate that I was able to talk to her that day, but then, I remembered something. Jessica was the one who told me about the umbrella. Maybe she could see the future.

Reaching into my pocket, I pulled out my phone. One notice. A missed text message from Unknown.

I clicked on the text icon. It read, "Nathan, you told me to never talk to you again, but you never said anything about texting you. Did the umbrella come in handy today? I know you probably heard about me crying, so let's talk later on, okay?"

I texted her, "Where are you right now?"

A second later, my phone vibrated. "Look to your right."

To be honest, I didn't find it creepy anymore. Instead, I felt like it was something I should expecting going forward. The sky settled into a soothing indigo, a perfect scenery for the night after a storm.

I looked to my right. Winter gray eyes stared into mine. Jessica, with a scarf wrapped around her neck, a parka over her cardigan shirt, brown boots and skinny jeans, waved at me, grinning. I glanced down at my own attire. A hoodie, khakis, worn-out sneakers. I grimaced but waved back.

"How you got my number, I don't want to know, but how long have you been stalking me?"

She shrugged and said, "Well, ever since you guys left the school, of course. By the way, I wasn't crying over you earlier. Dust got into my eyes after you left, and I hit head first into the gate."

"Ah, I see. I'm sorry for saying all that stuff earlier. You aren't weird after all."

I held out my hands to give an apology handshake, but I couldn't look at her eyes. They were too captivating, and I was already blushing enough as is.

"What is this? An apology handshake? I remember the first time you did this to me."

If there was anyone in this world I wanted to hit, it'd be her. Everything she did irritated me, but in a warm, tingly way.

"I guess I'll trust you for now. I'll leave the job of winning Stella's heart to you."

She shook my hand and said, "Well, you should've just trusted me from the very beginning."

Out of all the mysteries that surrounded this girl, there was one I wanted to solve.

"Jessica," I said, "tell me why you're using your future-seeing powers to help me."

She pulled me into a hug and said, "It's because we're best friends."

The wind picked up. I shivered but Jessica had kindled warmth in my heart, the fuzzy happiness to know someone cared.

HOW MIRACLES HAPPEN
Jennifer Chau

"MARK. MARK! GET OUT OF THERE. WHAT ARE YOU DOING, MARK!" his mother shouted. She flung open the front door and dashed down the steps. Mark could hear his mother shouting his name, but he couldn't take his eyes off the bright blue ball, bouncing away towards a car coming up the street. Fearing the end of the ball's life, he dashed into the street. The car screeched as his mother shoved him onto the side of the road. An aching scream pierced Mark's ears, followed by the sound of a buzzing alarm.

Chapter 1

MARK OPENED HIS EYES and reached for the "OFF" button on the alarm on his bedside table. It was 9:00 AM, Sunday. He closed his eyes again, and the scene of his dream flooded back into his vision. That flashback didn't show up nearly as much since it first happened that fateful Monday night six years ago, but it would still haunt him in his dreams every now and then. Mark groaned and thought back to his mother. When he was younger, she always comforted him after every nightmare, cooking him chocolate chip pancakes to cheer him up.

His mother was the brightest and happiest person he knew. She never let him feel upset by anything for too long until she managed to cheer him up somehow. He remembered going on countless walks through the park and trips to the ice cream parlor with her every weekend. Whether he aced his quiz or got a few questions wrong, she didn't care. She would take him to the ice cream parlor and say, "You tried your best, and you learned. That's all that matters to me."

Mark got up from bed, brushed through his dark, brown hair with his fingers, and sauntered downstairs to cook himself breakfast. His dad had rushed off to a wedding up in San Francisco the night before, so Mark and his sister had the house to themselves for the day.

"Morning," his sister greeted, looking up at him before she went back to spreading her butter on a piece of toast.

"I had the worst dream last night," Mark said, taking a seat across from her.

"Was it about mom again? That's so weird. And ironic too, actually. I mean, I had a dream about living in a castle," Elicit said. "Here. Toast your own bread." She thrust the loaf of bread into his hand, knocking the blue, porcelain vase standing on the table. It wobbled back and forth.

"Watch out, will you?" Mark shouted, moving the vase further from the edge. It was a big, round vase that spread out like a flower at the top, and was painted with blue flowers and intricate designs. Their mother bought it during vacation in Japan when he was in third grade. Mark remembered how happy she was when she saw it, the last vase of its kind, sitting in a vendor in a Japanese street market. She always said it was destiny that brought her to it.

Chapter 2

NIGHT ARRIVED, AND MARK sat at his desk writing an essay about *The Joy Luck Club*. "Three pages. Write about your analysis of the relationships and sacrifices Amy Tan describes revolving around mother and daughter relationships. Due Monday morning..." he muttered, groaning.

Elicit flung the door open. "Mark!" she said, slamming the door shut behind her.

Mark jumped in his seat. "What do you want, Elicit? You scared me. Calm down a little, will you?"

"Something's moving downstairs. I don't know what it is," she said, "I don't think it's Dad."

"What on earth are you talking about, Elicit? Stop being so scared of everything. I told you not watch *Horror Story* with your friends."

"Mark, I'm serious. Something's moving downstairs," she said, catching her breath. "I heard the back door open."

Mark looked into her eyes, a gaze of genuine fear and worry. In the same moment, they heard a loud bang from downstairs. Pots and pans were flying from the kitchen shelf.

"Do you hear that, Mark?" Elicit shrieked. "Do you believe me now?"

Mark looked at his sister, her eyes already tearing up in fear. "You locked the door, didn't you?" he asked.

"I did, Mark. One hundred percent. All the doors are locked..." Elicit said, "Who do you think it is?"

"There are several possibilities," Mark said, his voice shaking. "Either Dad drove back two hundred miles from the hotel without telling us, or--"

"Or?" Elicit asked, impatient.

"-- or it's someone else," Mark said.

The two siblings stood in Mark's room, completely still. They stared at each other, careful to not make a single sound. A sharp *ping* followed by an object falling to the ground broke the silence.

"Mom's vase..." Elicit said under her breath, her eyes open wide.

Mark shook his head, his eyebrows wrinkling and his forehead starting to sweat. "It's got to be the wind," he said. He didn't even believe what came out of his mouth, and he had every confidence his sister didn't either.

"No way. There is no way the wind could knock down a vase that big," she said.

The crashing and smashing stopped, and was replaced with a soft, feminine voice humming a familiar tune.

"Is that... *Lullaby*?" Mark whispered. "Elicit, do you hear that?"

"Mark, I'm *scared*," Elicit said. "Why is this happening? Mark, please, do something."

Mark sat on his bed, his hands shaking and legs trembling. He couldn't calm down. His mind flashed back to the last time he had been this afraid. It was six years ago, and he was ten years old. Elicit was only three at the time. He remembered his fear, his swelling heart, his shortening breath, and his tears running down his cheeks as he watched his mother lie in the hospital bed for what turned out to be her last few moments alive.

Mark's heart skipped a beat. "Mom, it's Mom!" Mark shouted, jumping up from the bed and bolting out the door.

"Mark! What are you talking about?" Elicit grabbed his shirt from behind. "Tell me what's going on."

"Mother's vase. You said it yourself, wind can't knock it down. Someone had to have done it themselves. I just feel it, Elicit. I'll explain later, but it's Mom, I just know it. She's here to visit us again, Elicit!" he said, dashing down the stairs. He didn't know if he was excited or scared, but he knew it had to be her. Who else could it be?

"Mark, she's not with us anymore, stop! You don't know for sure what it is. It could be dangerous. Mark!" he heard her call, but he didn't stop. How could he? He hadn't seen his mother in so long.

Chapter 3

AS HE APPROACHED THE bottom of the stairs, he heard footsteps in the kitchen. He paused as he got closer. "Mom," he said to himself. A wave of anxiety swept over him. In just twenty seconds, his thoughts flashed through deep, nostalgic memories that he had left untouched for six years. Now he was revisiting them for what felt like the first time. In the past, he'd shut down every horrible memory of fate tearing his mother away from him.

He closed his eyes, and was blinded by the flashing light of a car. His mother shoved him out of the way, and his body went tumbling down the side of the road. He heard screams and shrieks of panic and commotion. Then, everything was silent. He saw his mother lying on a hospital bed, her heart beating slower and slower, lighter and lighter. He felt her hand loosen its grip on his hand as her life drained away, and he knew it was his fault.

He opened his tear-dampened eyes, and saw his mother leaning against the entrance to the kitchen, staring at him with warmth in her eyes, a warmth he hadn't felt in so long. "Mark," she said, taking a step forward.

"Mom?" he said, tears streaming down his face. "Mom!" Mark ran towards her. She embraced him with a long hug. Elicit watched from the middle of the staircase. "You came to visit me. I missed you so much, Mom. I knew it was you." He paused. "But how?"

"After I died, I was able to extend my life and live as a ghost. A spirit, I should say. It's not easy to come back, however, which is why I waited until now. Regardless, you two have grown so much," their mother said with a smile on her face.

Elicit walked down the staircase in silence, grinning from ear to ear. Mark knew she was shy. She didn't remember their mother as much as he did.

"Both of you, I'm so happy to see you again. Elicit, my baby. You know, the last time you saw me, you were just three years old," she said, giving her two children a hug. "I've missed you two so dearly."

"We missed you too, mom," Mark said.

"Daddy talks about you all the time," Elicit said. "He still loves you and misses you."

Their mother smiled. "I'm glad. I'm sorry I couldn't come see your father today as well. I missed all of you so much."

"How long can you stay?" Elicit asked.

"Do you have to go at all?" Mark asked.

"You're both so sweet." She smiled. "but I have to go now, I'm afraid."

"Wait. Mom," Mark said, "you're going already? But I wanted to be able to spend some more time with you."

"I'd love to spend more time with you, too, Mark, but that would defeat the purpose of me being here. I noticed you were going through hard times these past months, so I came back to give you closure. You need to live your life to its fullest extent. It hurts me when I see you still in pain." She brushed her gentle hands across her children's cheeks. Mark and Elicit stared at her in solemn silence. Then, she turned around and walked towards the front door.

"Mom, don't leave me again. Stay with me, Mom. Please!" Mark ran after her, but she was already on the other side of the street. "Mom!" he shouted again, his tears coming back even heavier than before, blurring his vision.

"Mark, come back! Mark! She's gone! Mark!" Elicit shouted, tears streaming down her cheeks as well.

But Mark couldn't hear anything. The entire world was blocked out of his mind. He could only hear the sound of his own shouts, begging for his mother to return to him. He couldn't let her go again. He ran across the street, tears in his eyes, begging. Then, he looked to the right, and was blinded by the light of a fast-approaching car.

The driver slammed his foot against the brakes, but it was too late. Mark felt his body tumbling down the side of the road, his eyes only catching a glimpse of the shock and disbelief stained on his sister's face as she stood in silence, her eyes and mouth drawn wide open. Mark's emotions spun around his head as he laid on the asphalt, dazed. He couldn't even feel the pain. He only knew that he couldn't move.

Chapter 4

MARK SAW RED AND blue lights flashing all around him. A crowd of murmurs and whispers surrounded his ears. When he opened his eyes again, he found himself in a hospital gown, lying in a bed covered with white linen sheets.

"Awake already, honey?" a voice said from the corner. It was his mother.

Mark squinted as he struggled to open his eyes. His entire body ached, and he felt the world spinning around his head. Mark strained to catch a glimpse of his mother, "M-mom?" he asked, his eyes barely opening and his chest too painful to lift his head to see her face.

"It's me, dear," she replied, in a soft, gentle voice.

"Why did you leave me, mom? If you wanted to come and see me now, why didn't you just stay with me earlier?" he asked. "Why don't you make up your mind?"

"I wanted to go away and let you live your life again, freely, without the burden of missing me all the time, but when you ran after me and got hit by that car..." She took a deep breath, "I couldn't just leave you lying there, Mark. Elicit was smart to call an ambulance for you, but..." her voice trailed off.

The room was quiet again. Mark looked into her eyes and finally asked, "Mom, why did you break the vase?"

"The vase," she said "It was beautiful, wasn't it? I saw what happened this morning with Elicit. She almost knocked it over. You know, if I'd been alive, I would've said something. Might've given her a hard time about it too," she said, chuckling. "You wanted to keep it as a memoir of me, but I could see it was becoming more of a burden. It was time that it stopped."

"I see..." Mark said, his breath dying away. "Mom... I can join you when I die... It's fine with me. My life is empty without you, I need you."

"What kind of mother would I be if I let my only son die?" she said with tears in her eyes.

Mark's eyes teared up alongside hers, and with every last effort, he managed to lend her a small smile.

"Do you remember what I told you earlier? My life was extended because I'm a ghost, but this ghost life can be transferred to your human life." She paused. "This is my last gift to you. You don't have to die, Mark. This is how miracles happen."

"Mom... please don't. If you do, I'll never see you again until I die. If you let me die right now, we can live in the afterlife together," Mark said.

"I appreciate that, Mark. I really do. But that wasn't my purpose for coming back. I wanted you to be able to live your life freely, and this will give you your chance. I was foolish to think that me just telling you that would satisfy you. Mark, I'm always going to be with you, and I'll always be watching my family from above. Take this life, Mark, and live it fully. Make me happy."

"Mom... I love you," he said.

"I love you, too, Mark, and your sister, and your father," she said, "tell them that for me, please." She gave him one last kiss and faded away.

Chapter 5

THE DOOR SLAMMED OPEN and Mark saw Elicit and his father run in, breathing heavily, covered with sweat. "Mark, are you okay?" his father asked.

"Dad... I'm feeling better. It's a miracle, really," Mark said, with a faint smile. "Thanks for coming. Did Elicit tell you about mom? I'm sorry you couldn't see her."

His dad took a deep breath and said, "I'm glad you two got to see her again, kids, but really, I don't mind. She was never gone in the first place, always in our hearts. Thank you, Patricia," he said, looking up and paused. "Now, what do you want to eat, eh?"

"Pizza and soda." Mark laughed.

"Alright, pizza and soda it is. Let's go, Elicit."

The door clicked shut, and Mark laid there, staring up at the ceiling. He closed his eyes, smiled, and muttered, "Thank you, Mom."

IRELAND
Dawn Pham

THIS CORNER OF IRELAND is beautiful. The blue, crystal clear water glistens. The fields are full of colorful flowers, divine scents, and quiet melodies of songbirds. It's such a shame, honestly, that this will all be gone in mere hours.

The waters will be filled with carcasses of humans of every age, gender, and ethnicity. The foam from the waves will climb up the rugged surface of the jagged cliffs and paint them red. The floral wildlife will be consumed by hungry flames. The smell of smoke and death will accompany the piercing screams of the damned, begging for mercy.

"Why?" they would cry, helpless and confused.

If they had somehow found out that I was the cause behind their misery and asked me, I probably wouldn't have had a good answer.

"Why not?" I'd reply.

Perhaps I do it because it's fun. After all, the last three towns that I've painted red gave me quite a thrill. Perhaps I do it as revenge for the innocence that was stolen from me a long time ago. Perhaps I do it because I know that, with the world as corrupt and incompetent as it is, I'll never be caught. I suppose it doesn't matter if my answer satisfies them or not. After all, they will soon be dead.

Tick-tock. Tick-tock. Time is running out, little lambs. Tick-tock. Tick-tock. Can you feel it in the air? Tick-tock. Tick-tock. I'm sorry, truly, I am. It's such a shame. It's such a shame that your imminent deaths and narrow minds prevent you from seeing the true beauty of chaos and death.

Oh, well. I'll be leaving now. I hear the next town over is very beautiful this time of year. It has crystal clear waters, colorful flowers, divine scents, and melodies of songbirds. What a perfect time to visit.

JORDAN & JONATHAN
Ashley Rivera

"TEACHERS, CLOSE YOUR DOORS. This is not a drill. Lock your doors and remain silent." The warning blared through the speakers as soon as I walked into my first period classroom. I set down my purse and squatted in the cramped, little corner next to my best friend Katie.

"Jordan, what's going on?" Katie turned to our teacher. "Mr. Cook, do you know?"

"Everyone just stay seated until this all settles down." Mr. Cook honestly looked more scared than anyone else in the classroom. Muffled screams echoed throughout the hallways. My heart pounded.

"God, this is horrible!" a girl said holding her hands to her ears.

I turned around. Katie was quivering with fear.

"It's going to be okay," I whispered and gave her a hug. "I promise."

"Mr.Cook? Tony doesn't look so well," a student said pointing towards Tony who was holding his stomach.

"May I go to the restroom Mr--" Tony said.

"That's not a good idea." Mr. Cook leaned toward Tony. "You don't even know what's outside."

Tony's eyes changed from a bright blue to a pale gray. He snarled and chattered his teeth. He jerked Mr. Cook's arm towards his face and sank his teeth straight into his wrist. Everyone in the room shrieked.

Mr. Cook glanced at his wound with giant eyes, trembling. His skin color changed from a sun-kissed gold to a discolored green. The tears in his eyes dropped to the floor.

The two walking corpses shambled about the room, scanning faces for their next meal. The students remained in our corner, too afraid to twitch a muscle. The zombies stopped when their eyes stared right into Katie's.

"Run!" I yelled. I ran to the door and pulled with all my strength. It wouldn't budge. I looked over my shoulder and saw the entire class, sitting there staring back at me. "Aren't any of you going to help?" I fumbled again with the door and shoved against it with all of my weight.

The door swung open. "Everyone out!" I ordered. I turned around to find Katie, who had now suffered the same fate as our classmate and teacher. Horrified, I couldn't move.

Some guy from the hallway grabbed my arm and yanked me out of the room along with some others. The door slammed shut behind us.

I looked up into the brightest green eyes I had ever seen. It was Johnathan.

"Dude," he said, "we could've gotten killed in there. Let's go."

"I can't," I said. "That was my — "

"No time to explain. Come with me." He grabbed my hand.

I ran with him through the hallways, dodging the frenzy that swarmed against us. We ran for what felt like hours, but we had only made it across campus into the cafeteria.

"We need to stock up on food and water," he said. He looked at me. "Are you okay?"

I shook my head. My eyes teared up.

"Do you want to talk about it?" he continued, "I mean we seem to be in a pretty safe place." He squeezed my hand. "At least for now."

"That girl back in the classroom was my best friend." Tears rolled down my cheeks. I turned away.

"Hey, I'm here for you." He smiled and wrapped an arm around my shoulder for a short reassuring hug. "You're Jordan, right? We don't really know each other. I'm Johnathan."

"Thanks," I said. I took my phone out; ten missed calls from my mom.

He looked at my screen. "Go ahead and call her back."

I dialed the number. "Mom?" I said. My voice quivered.

"Sweetie, get home right now. The street is surrounded by these things and I'm not stepping a foot out this door, bye," and she hung up.

"It's like she doesn't even care if I die trying to go the house." I looked over to Johnathan. "Do you want to call anyone?" I asked, tossing my phone at him.

"No. I don't really have family." He gave me back the phone.

"Well then I guess we're just gonna have to stick together. You did save my life, after all." I stared at him. "What do we do now?"

"Let's try to open that kitchen door."

"It's locked. Can you kick it in?" I said.

The door slammed open with one kick. We walked in and saw nothing of use. Just pots and pans.

"Where's the food?" I asked. There was nothing but scraps on the counter.

"Let's get some of that," he said. "It's gross but we'll need it."

I took it all and stuffed it in a backpack that had been abandoned in the cafeteria.

"Let's leave already," he said.

"Leave? Where would we go? What if there are more of those things outside?"

"Why don't we start out and have a look around?"

I could feel in my gut something wasn't quite right about his plan, but I didn't see a better option. My hands shook. My eyes darted around, making sure those things weren't hunting us.

"We're outside now," he whispered, "so we need to be more careful."

The school had two buildings labeled 200 and 300 with trees and lockers in between. Usually the school was full of loud, annoying kids, but now, it was dead silent.

"It's too quiet."

"I know." Jonathan grabbed my arm and led me to the main school office. "We need medical supplies. I'm pretty sure the nurse has some." He held his finger to his lips as he opened the door.

I held my breath while we tiptoed in, peeking around every corner. The only sounds in the entire room were the ticking clock, our footsteps, and our pounding heartbeats. We hastened our pace, and soon were sprinting in panic, dodging filing cabinets, and pushing chairs out of way. Among our reckless carelessness, we heard a groan and we froze in our tracks.

Pushing Jonathan aside, I stepped closer to the nurse's office door. My hand was just about to touch the doorknob when I saw oozing red liquid seeping out from underneath.

Jonathan was already pulling me away when the door swung open and the zombie latched onto my shirt. "Don't panic, Jordan," I kept saying that to myself. It didn't help. I shoved the zombie back. We both fell to the ground, causing a flurry of papers to fly around us. "Jonathan help me," I cried out to my newest friend.

"Hey, over here!" Jonathan yelled.

The zombie turned its head and fixed its gaze on its new victim.

Picking myself up off the floor, I darted to a nearby computer and yanked all the cords out of the walls. The zombie had Jonathan pinned against a corner. It unhinged its jaw and lunged at Jonathan, and would have bitten his face clean off if Johnathan hadn't ducked so quickly.

I threw the computer at the zombie, knocking him to the ground and saving my new friend's life. I guess we were even now.

"Follow me." I tiptoed back out of the office and into the hallways, leading Jonathan to the school theater. The lights were flickering. My footsteps echoed through the now-empty hallway.

Once again overwhelmed with panic, our pace hastened, and before we even realized it, we were running down the halls at full speed. I threw open the theater door, and was met with a group of gasps. I stopped in place.

"Who are you?" a frantic voice shouted in my ear. I turned to find an axe hovering above my head, held by the shaking arm of a boy.

"I'm Jordan, and this is Jonathan," I said.

The kid lowered the axe.

"We just came from the office. There was one in there, and it nearly ate us both," Jonathan chimed in as we made our way inside.

"My name's Chris," the axe-wielding boy said with a grin. "We were in PE when we heard the announcement on the PA system. I told everyone in the class that this would be the safest place to go, and twenty of them agreed. The whole school was in such a frenzy. People got lost. People got trampled. Maybe some of them even got infected. All I know is, we ended up with only seven by the time we finally got here.

Guess we're nine now."

"We should leave, Chris. We can't stay in here forever," one of the PE students said.

"Yeah, there's no way we can stay in here long-term," said another.

Soon, the whole theater was overrun with voices all discussing our new plan to pack up and leave. Everyone grabbed their backpacks and purses and headed toward the door. It creaked open. We heard footsteps coming down the hall. We jumped back in and slammed the door shut and waited.

"Shh! It's one of those things, I just know it," Chris whispered.

The group fell silent. The footsteps got louder and louder. They stopped right outside the door. The doorknob twisted and shook, and the door was nearly ripped off its hinges from the other side, revealing a police officer pointing a gun right between Jonathan's eyes.

"More survivors?" the officer asked.

"Yes, sir," I replied.

"Good. We're evacuating the entire city. There's a safe zone over near the Super Duper Mart. How many are in here?"

"It's just the nine of us, sir," Chris said.

"Good. I'll take you to the squad cars. When you're there, we'll register your name and find your folks. Follow me."

We didn't run into any trouble on the way out to the parking lot, where a group of SWAT team members and other cops stood pointing their rifles at the school. They hurried us into the squad cars.

Jonathan made sure to stand near me so we could ride together. As we drove out of the school, he grabbed my hand.

"We're safe now, Jordan." He smiled. "We're safe."

LILY'S LEGACY
Nancy Le

ALL I COULD REMEMBER was the hard ground. The gray sky illuminated dark energy as the trees swayed back and forth. For a while, it seemed peaceful until lightning crackled, and thunder echoed across the sky.

"Woah…where am I?" I murmured to myself as I tried to stand. I couldn't. Evergreen trees towered over my frail body, which had fallen down once more. A snap sounded from somewhere behind me. I turned around. A brunette girl stared at me.

"Hi, I'm Lily. I think you must've hit your head hard on that rock over there." She pointed to the large boulder to my left. As she helped me up, I took another chance to take a look at her: petite frame, brown hair flowing down her back, hazel eyes, and freckles lightly dusted across her face.

"Is that your baseball cap?" she said, pointing at the ground.

"Huh? Oh." I dusted off my hat and placed it on my head. "Why are you up here?"

She avoided my stare. "I was making sure no one gets killed by the bloodhounds. It would've been such a shame if they got to you before I did. That's what happened with the last person, a girl who was out here. The only thing left of her was a bloody jacket and a left shoe. It'd be a shame if the same happened to you; you're quite cute."

The wind picked up and shook the trees. The sky darkened.

"Let's go," Lily said. "We need to find shelter."

She helped me out of the thick woods and onto an unfamiliar dirt trail. The trail widened and curved around a few trees to where her gray Audi was parked. We got in and buckled up.

"You should be more careful out there." Lily reached behind her seat and shoved aside a blanket. She pulled out a golden shotgun and placed it into my lap. She reached for a second one hidden under her seat. "You never know when you're about to be prey."

"Are you planning to kill me or something? Why do you have these in here?" I fumbled with my seatbelt and debated whether or not to bolt out of there.

"Calm down, will you?" she said. "It's for all the bloodhounds and Minotaur that run around this side of the woods. Put your seatbelt back on."

She started the car and drove down the winding two-lane road.

Thunder boomed in the night sky. Lily continued to drive for what seemed like hours.

I realized that I had no idea how I ended up in the woods. I couldn't recall anything that had happened. A howl sounded in the far off distance. I tightened my grip on the golden shotgun and looked at Lily for reassurance.

"You know, I never got your name. I probably deserve an introduction because, after all, I was the one that who saved you," she said, never taking her eyes of the winding road.

"My name is Matthew, but you can call me Matt. It seems more natural to me." I slipped once again into deep thought, racking my brain for a reason why I would have been out in the woods. Did I have a family? At least I remembered my name. That's about all I could remember.

"Well, today's my lucky day, isn't it. I save a stranded, likely-to-be-killed boy and he doesn't even have the decency to have a conversation with me," Lily said. "If you see anything come up the side of my car, shoot it. Monsters lurk at this time of day. They can smell your scent lingering because of how long you were in the woods."

"What do you mean shoot?" The thought of monsters made my fingers twitch. "Are you seriously telling me to shoot something?"

She opened her mouth to reply but was interrupted by a loud crash. The impact on the back of the car triggered both fear and memories. I remembered that I was walking towards a giant golden door. It almost made me lose grip of the golden shotgun in my hand. I tried to roll the window down when I heard Lily's voice.

"Shoot! Shoot now. Hurry!" Lily screamed as she floored the gas pedal and swerved to escape the source of the impact.

Whatever it was attacked the side of the car again. We fishtailed to the left. Lily straightened out the car and took evasive measures. Her tires screeched.

"Where do I shoot it?" I tightened my grip on the golden shotgun, fear and adrenaline rushing through my body. I dared to sneak a look out my window and my blood ran cold.

It was the biggest creature I'd ever seen in my life. It stood on hind legs, but it had a body of a bull with what seemed to be pounds of rippling muscle. Horns protruded its grotesque forehead, his black, beady eyes looking directly into my own.

"Shoot it in the eye. Trust me on this one. Hurry up," Lily commanded as she made a sharp turn onto a narrow asphalt road.

The sound of two gunshots and a blood-curdling scream echoed through the air. Blood splattered all over the windshield. The creature hastily retreated back into the dense woods.

"We almost got killed." I pushed my black hair out of my face, and a sticky substance stuck onto my fingertips, leaving a crimson stain. My head throbbed and warm blood dripped down my neck, making it harder and harder to see straight.

"You're lucky that wasn't you, you know that, right?" Lily said. "Wait a minute. What's wrong with your head? Are you bleeding? Hold on, I have something for that. Just stay still and don't move."

Lily reached over to the glove department once and pulled out what looked like an ordinary blue fine point fountain pen. The only difference was that the gold writing on the top read, "AD54."

I needed a bandage, not a pen. I was about to voice that thought when I felt a sharp pain in my lower abdomen.

She had shoved the fountain pen deep inside of me and continued to apply pressure. The new wound hurt and bled more than the one on my head. The pen sank into me. All the physical evidence of the injury disappeared.

"So you are trying to kill me." I held onto my side, wincing.

Lily merely smiled at me and turned back to the wheel.

My head pounded, but the blood on my fingertips and neck had dried and faded. I stared out the window again.

Silence consumed the car. Lily did not say another word to me, only glancing occasionally in my direction to see how I was doing.

"It was to stop the bleeding," she said, "and to keep the poison streaming through your blood from making it to your heart. When you fight a minotaur, don't let it touch you, no matter what. They have a special poison located in their fingertips. One scratch can result in death." Lily slowed down the car in front of a gray stone path leading up to a mansion built of glass.

She turned off the ignition and opened her door.

I saw points at the top of her ears which I hadn't noticed before. My stomach cramped.

"Let's go," Lily said.

Did I just see a fork in her tongue? I stumbled out of the car. Another sharp pang shot through my body like an electric shock. Out of the corner of my eye, I could've sworn I saw a tail poke through Lily's jeans. My vision blurred. There was a sign alongside the path. I squinted to see it: *Science Research Center*.

"We're here" was the last thing I heard her say before everything went black.

LOVE IS
Emily Chau

Chapter 1

I SETTLED DOWN ONTO the bar stool near the counter and asked my best
friend, "Hey, Mia? I'm not interrupting your night with Dean, right?"

Mia prepared two bowls of ice cream and topped them with whipped cream. Then
she walked to the counter and passed the two bowls to me. "Ophelia, nonsense. It's a
date night, but also a party—a party you're invited to." She gestured to Dean, who
perused through the fridge in search of food. "See? He understands the situation,"
Mia said. "Babe?"

"Got it," Dean said. He walked into the adjoining room with a bag of chips and
sandwich in hand.

Mia closed the door after he left. With Dean out of earshot, she placed spoons into our bowls of mint ice cream. "Now, tell me what happened with Dave Sterner:
contestant sixteen," she jested, taking a seat next to me. "How far is he in the running
for Ophelia's heart?"

I gripped one of the bowls of thawing ice cream, jabbing at the chocolate chips
with my spoon. "He didn't call me back."

Mia widened her eyes. "What do you mean he didn't call you back? It was going so
well."

"I thought so too." I sighed, swirling the spoon.

"You just haven't tried all the dating sites yet. What about E-mate?" Mia took a
bite of her ice cream.

"Mia, believe me. I've tried them all," I replied. "Maybe I'm not destined for love.
Maybe I'm destined to live with seventeen cats and call them my children. Maybe I'll
end up like my namesake in Hamlet, all crazy and confused. Either way, I'm done.
Not everyone can have the relationship you and Dean have."

Out of all the ways to meet a perfect lover, Mia and Dean met through an online
dating website. Their relationship just clicked, which led to ongoing communication
that lasted for several years. They decided to meet up, and have been absolutely smit-
ten with each other ever since.

Used to my dramatic spiels, Mia couldn't reign in her snickers. "To this day, I still don't understand why your mom would name you after such a tragic character." She paused, slipping the melting ice cream into her mouth. "Fee, you're not going to end up single for the rest of your life, and while I *do* agree Dean and I make an amazing couple, no romance or love story is the same nor perfect."

"Yours is, Cinderella," I said. "C'mon, how many people do you know have tried these websites in hopes of finding a connection that will actually follow through, but have their hopes destroyed in the end?"

Mia gave me a look. "Even though we were talking on data-mate for several years, Dean and I didn't make our relationship official until we were both ready. I do recall that that took a long time."

"Hah. Two months," I countered. "Dean is a good guy."

"Well, you'll get yours someday," she assured me, nudging me, "You know why?"

"Why?"

"Remember Walter? If you survived Walter, you can survive anythin--".

"Don't remind me."

Mia burst out laughing. "He was something, wasn't he?" Her smile widened. "I remember you would always tell me he had a delicious six pack and bulging biceps that could bake perfect brownies; he was that hot, right, Fee?"

Back when I met Walter on Perfectmatch, another dating site, I liked his amazing physique. It was the only thing I focused on when it came to him. Was I ashamed? Of course. It was partly because when I recounted everything about the date to Mia, she found him so ridiculous and hilarious that she brings him up every chance she gets. Mia obtained some ammo against me, and I learned a lesson: looks aren't the only important thing. Never again.

"Mia?"

"Yes?"

"Shut up and finish the ice cream."

After finishing off her portion of dessert, Mia dropped the spoon in the bowl and moved it aside. "You know, since Data-Mate didn't work, I have one more thing for you to try before you completely decide to swear off love," she said, crossing her arms.

I tried to play along because this was Mia--known not only for her optimism and confidence, but also for her creativity and spontaneity.

"What? Is this another one of your crazy ideas?" I teased, "You're not going to have me kiss fifty guys in two weeks, are you?"

"Of course not." A few seconds later, she giggled, her eyes gleaming, "Well..."

Chapter 2

TWO DAYS LATER, I learned exactly what Mia wanted.

After getting into a mess with my coworkers and humiliating myself in front of my boss at work, I drove home and slumped down on my couch. I poured some wine in a glass, turned on the television, and turned to the first soap opera I could find. Mia slammed my front door open, almost breaking its hinges.

"Mia! What the heck? Easy on the strength, Hulk." I gave her a hug. "I don't own this place, remember? Mrs. Winchell would kill me if anything gets broken or out of place."

In her little black dress and stilettos, she towered over me. She hugged me back, and a familiar gleam appeared in her eyes. "My dear, we're going downtown for a surprise." She glided across the room, landing on the worn out couch. She lifted her head to address me. "Fee.."

I gave her a blank stare. We surveyed each other up and down for a few moments.

"You're changing--"

"--I am not changing."

I sighed. "Look, I just wanted one day to relax, to wallow in misery after Dave decided not to call. Please?"

"Nuh uh, sweetie. This is why we're not wallowing in misery. You always do this whenever someone leaves you hanging." Mia gestured to the wine and television set. "All you do is watch soap operas for weeks and drink your wine like there's no tomorrow." She straightened her posture. "We're doing something new. It's mating season."

"Mating season?" I questioned, exasperated with her. "And not always."

"Well, that's the whole point, isn't it? I thought you wanted my help."

"I do, just not--"

"--No negativity or buts. You'll thank me later," she said. "Get your butt up there and get dressed." She pushed me up the stairs. "It's divine intervention, babe."

"What's so divine about this?" I asked, trying to distract her. We reached my room.

"I'm divine. This is my intervention. It's me," Mia quipped, and with a final push, she closed the door behind us. "Now, shush and get dressed."

"You won't even tell me where we're going?"

Mia raised her eyebrows. "Well, if I did, it wouldn't be a surprise anymore, would it? Now shush."

"Pushy and secretive," I muttered. "I wonder how Dean tolerates your wackiness."

"Well, if he didn't, you would have no choice but to sacrifice yourself for the job. Face it, you love me."

The establishment in the dingy neighborhood Mia brought me to was a far cry from what I had expected from her. With blinking lights and flies buzzing around it, the creaking sign in front of me had a tacky cupid logo with the words: "The Love Doctor's Dating Service: Distributing love cures since 1986."

Speed dating.

I repeat: *Speed dating.*

I groaned. "Dear God. No. No way." I turned around to face a smirking Mia. "This is your surprise? Please tell me you're kidding." I really wanted to punch her. She may have been my best friend, but sometimes I just wanted to break her nose for all her silly antics. Heck, we always made obnoxious jokes about people who went on speed dates. She had to be teasing me, but the light in her hazel eyes and that amused smirk--the one full of mischief--adorned her face in full force.

Nope, definitely wasn't kidding.

"Mia, I love you, I do, but right now?" I told her, "Not so much."

"I'm one hundred percent serious." With that smirk on her face and her arms crossed, she persisted, "C'mon, give it a chance. My Aunt Winnie-"

"Aunt Winnie? Wasn't she the one who went on a speed date with a guy who stole all her money?"

"Okay, fair point, but I doubt it would happen to you. You're different." She shrugged. "You've got nothing to lose. You might even get something out of this... experience."

Like losing my dignity and personal belongings?

"What do I have?"

"Well, for starters, you're young," she replied in a casual manner. "Hey, hey I'm kidding."

"Mia…" I backed away. It wasn't that I had an issue with speed dating as a whole. Five minutes, in my opinion, never determined love or a genuine connection. But I'm sure you can meet a great amount of creeps within five minutes.

Mia placed her arm around me. "Even after that disaster, Aunt Winnie didn't stop trying." She patted my back. "She found a good guy eventually, which goes back to that dating service."

"But it wasn't *through* a dating service, which is a completely different situation."

"Details, schmetails, who needs them?" She nudged her elbow into my side. "Look, just a few dates, Ophelia. Experience a bit. If anything, you can make some new friends and create a lonely hearts club. You won't wallow alone."

"Fine. Four speed dates." It was better to just go along with Mia. She's one relentless nut job.

"Nope, seven dates, and I'll give you ten bucks if you do it," Mia said, "and I do mean seven dates. None of that running away business that you're so fond of."

"*Seven?*" my voice squeaked. I shook my head. "Mia, by speed date number seven, you'll find my name on a headline announcing my disappearance. Five dates only."

"I'll throw in ten more bucks for that bet I forgot to pay you for."

"The poker one?" I asked. She gave me a thumbs up. I gave her an incredulous look. "That was two years ago, and if I do remember, you were in denial about my winnings and refused to pay me back. You owed me twenty."

"I wasn't denying anything, and well, I'm paying you now, plus the extra ten, which equals thirty," she said.

"Fine."

Mia whooped for victory.

"I'll try, but no promises."

I laughed a little. She's something. I placed my arm on her shoulder. "Let's go inside, you booger."

After a few minutes, Mia whipped away before I could grab her arm. "Yup, don't forget to tell me everything when you get back. Toodles!" she chirped, wiggling her finger at me.

With that, Mia skipped to the car and drove off.

Chapter 3

THE TIMER BUZZED, SIGNALING the first speed date. We had five minutes.

I watched the man in front of me. He seemed normal enough. Back and forth, he switched from looking straight at me and onto my 'general info' sheet, a card the "Love Doctor" had asked participants to complete. The man looked like an average guy you'd see on the street. Dressed in a suit too big for him, his arms dangled at his sides, but he was pretty cute. He reminded me of a coworker I had once been interested in.

I looked down to his info sheet.

Tyler Johnson. Twenty-five years old.

Yep, definitely normal.

Dragging his chair towards my side of the table, he angled his body towards me and leaned closer, invading my personal space. "Your face is so smooth and symmetrical. It'd be perfect for our future kids- if we have any." Pausing for a moment, his eyes widened in excitement. "How many kids do *you* want? My mom wants eight. She's crazy, so I'm offering you one. Two is the max. That's because I don't have that much... stamina, if you know what I mean," he whispered, winking at me.

I take it back. He's not normal.

Horrified, I blinked at him, trying to make sense of what he said.

"Um, alright buddy." Nervous laughter. "Tyler, could you back up a bit? You're invading my air bubble." I placed both my hands on each of his shoulders and pushed him back into his seat. "And to answer your question..."

I slammed the timer, leaving four minutes left on the clock.

My next date shuffled in his seat, but didn't say anything.

Trying to help him, I initiated the conversation. "So, what are your interests?"

Silence. He continued to stare.

"Okay, well, I love watching soap operas, drinking alcohol, and eating salt-water taffy," I rambled in sake of filling the silence. "My occupation is-- "

"--Listen. You sound like a lovely young woman."

"Oh, I'm sorry. If it's the alcohol, I only drink if I'm unhappy... I didn't mean--"

He raised his hand to stop me. "No, no. It's just... I'd hate to disappoint you, but I'm not interested in this... speed dating thing," he said, "nor did I come here on my own accord."

Well, we were both in the same boat; at least I could make a new friend.

"Oh, well that's fine," I said, resorting to small talk. "Let me guess, some friends with good intentions decided that you needed to put yourself out there and find someone?"

He sighed. "Yup, but they don't know."

"Don't know what?"

He dug into his pocket and pulled out his wallet. He opened it and placed it in front of me.

I leaned over the table to see that it was a picture of him and another man in a loving embrace, locked in a kiss.

Oh…I get it.

"If it helps, we could still be… " I paused. "This isn't gonna work out, huh?"

The man nodded. "Sorry." Shrugging, his hand reached towards the timer.

With my cell phone pressed against my ear, I stood outside the building watching light rain drizzle over the city, waiting for Mia to pick up her phone. Okay, I'll admit it. I broke my promise to her. Having three dates was already pushing it. After the third one, I ran out of there as fast I could.

That night was just a disaster and definitely not one of Mia's best ideas. Date number three turned out to be the creepiest one. After exchanging simple pleasant-ries, he climbed onto the table with his arm extended over his head like an antenna, rotating in a half-round circle as if he was calling for aliens.

Yeah.

The dial continued to ring in my ear, "C'mon, Mia. Pick up, pick up," I muttered.

One, two more dial tones.

Then, I heard her familiar voice. "Hey, it's Mia."

"Mia, hey. Can you--"

"--I'm not here right now, duh," she giggled into the phone. "Well, physically here here. That's why your phone won't go through. Anyway, leave a message or some-thing. Toodles."

Voicemail. Dang it.

I pressed the end call button, rolling my eyes. "Of course." Out of all the times she could have not picked up her phone, this would be it. I decided to walk home. I took off my heels and held them in my hand.

Now… did we make a left or a right?

Chapter 4

TWO HOURS OF MINDLESS walking brought me to an unknown neighborhood. My hope of finding my way out of there shrank and my anger at Mia grew. If she had just picked up her phone, I wouldn't have been in this situation. I'd have been snuggled in bed after a nice round of good ol' soap operas. Out of breath, I realized that no sign of life existed in this part of town. The relentless rain pattered against the uneven streets and soaked my clothing. That was when I saw a small park with a swing set, a seesaw, and... *a bench.*

I needed that bench.

My body drooped in exhaustion onto the weathered stone bench. I groaned. As cold as it was, I felt happy that my sore legs were able to relax. The rain wasn't so bad; it was peaceful and quiet - sort of. I closed my eyes and drifted off to sleep.

Hours later, an intruding bright light forced me to open my eyes. "Hey, you're not supposed to be sleeping here."

I looked up to see a man standing in front of me. A tall and lean figure dressed in a security uniform towered over my sleepy body, his callused hand holding a flashlight that reflected off of his blue eyes. He had a scar running down his arm to his wrist. With a gruff voice, he said, "The park is closed. No loiterers, lady. Find some other place to sleep. This park isn't for you."

I bristled at his statement. Granted, I looked bad with my dried up tear stains, but it wasn't my intention to doze off on a park bench.

"Sir, I apologize if I caused any trouble," I said, "but I didn't mean to fall asleep on the bench." He seemed unimpressed. "In fact, I was trying to find my way home and got lost."

"Miss, I've heard that excuse a hundred times before. You need to leave. Like I said earlier, the park is closed."

"I know. I don't need you to repeat, sir. However, I do need--"

A phone broke through my sentence.

"Let me get that," the guard said, digging into his pocket and grabbing his phone. "It's the twentieth call." He muttered, running his fingers through his blonde hair. "Hello? I know. I'll wire the money tomorrow morning. Stop calling me, I'm on the job." He hung up and sat down on the bench next to me.

"Bad night?" It seemed that I wasn't the only one having a terrible time. Despite his attitude a minute ago, he seemed defeated in a way.

"You could say that," he said, as if he had forgotten he had just told me to leave. He rubbed his eyes and turned to face me. "Look, I want to apologize. I'm just trying to do my job and--"

I raised my hand to stop him. "I get it. I had a bad night too. If anything, we'll just let this blow over." A moment of silence followed. "I'm Ophelia, by the way."

"Ophelia," he said, "as in the Hamlet-Ophelia?"

I rolled my eyes. "Yeah, I know. My mom is an English teacher," I brought my hand up to shake his. "What's yours?"

"My name is Hamlet," he replied, his face turning serious. "To be, or not to--"

I raised a fist.

"Okay, I'm teasing." He raised his arm in defense, laughing. "It's Theodore, Theo preferred."

"That's a cute name, did your mom name you after the chipmunk?" I mocked.

His mouth quirked up in amusement. "Nope, not really."

After the introductions, a conversation followed. Thinking that we wouldn't be seeing each other again, sitting on the bench divulging into the details of our terrible days and having nonsensical conversations about life brought a positive side to our rough start. We bonded in a way.

"So, how does a girl dressed for a night out end up sleeping on a park bench?" He asked.

"Best friend decided dragging me on a series of spontaneous speed dates after an online date ditched me," I said. "What is it with online dating? It never delivers."

"Most of time, trusting online dates isn't the way to go," Theo said. "Not even speed dates for that matter. If you want a true connection--"

"--It's difficult, you know…"

After ignoring her for a week, I relented and returned Mia's calls. She and Dean had decided to throw another party, and she wouldn't relent until I agreed to come.

"The conversation I had with him…I felt like he understood," I told Mia. "However, I do regret not getting his number to keep in touch."

"You didn't keep his number?" Mia asked. "Can you at least describe him?"

"He's a security guard… with blue eyes. He ruffled his hair a lot, and he had this huge scar--"

Mia's eyes widened. She pointed her finger at me. "A nasty scar that ran from his left mid-arm to his wrist? And he has a mom that named him Theodore, but he prefers Theo?"

I looked at her, bewildered. How did she know?

"Yeah, exactly that," I told her.

She screamed, "Fee! I know him."

"You know him?"

Mia explained that Theo and Dean were once childhood friends. "And guess what? He's coming tonight!" Her eyes twinkled with cheer. "He's single. Divorced, which means he's ready to mingle."

I scoffed a little, "Mia, no more of your match-making. I still haven't forgiven you for ditching me."

"But you met Theo," she quipped.

"Through my own way."

"Well, missy--" Before Mia could finish her sentence, the sound of a doorbell had cut her off. She continued as she walked toward the front door, "That should be him."

"Very funny, Mi-Mi." I replied, following her.

Mia reached the door and opened it.

"Oh, hey, Theo." She turned back at me, giving me a look that said: *would you look at that?*

Theo laughed and reached out to give Mia a hug. "Hey, how have you been? Wedding bells lately?" He was so wrapped in the hug until he opened his eyes and noticed me behind her.

"Ophelia?" he asked. "You're here."

I laughed, feeling nervous. "Yeah. Small world right?"

"We need to talk, I'd reckon."

Mia cut in before she raced off. "Well, I'll just leave you guys to chat."

Theo and I walked out to the porch and sat in silence.

"So," he started.

"Yeah," my voice overlapped.

Theo sighed. "Ophelia, about our talk the other night. I won't deny that we had something, but there's still a lot to take care of in my life right now, and--" He paused, his forehead wrinkled. "I still want to get to know you more as a friend before jumping into something that's probably based off of hormones..."

He made sense. That night, Theo taught me that there was more to what romance is, a true relationship. I'll be honest, I found myself more than willing to take it slow, especially with him.

I turned to him and grabbed his callused hands. "Let's start off as friends."

THE LOVE THAT FOLLOWS
Richard Trejo

BEFORE THE CLOSE OF my first year of college, I first caught the glimpse of a female shadow tailing me on the way to class. Out of curiosity, I decided to strike up a conversation with her.

"Hello there, I'm--"

"The one," she said. "Sorry, I've been following you for a long time. It's just, you make me feel good inside," she said, blushing.

She flattered me, so I, against my intuition, continued the conversation.

"I'm sorry, but what's your name?" I asked.

Her face reddened even more. "Sherry. But my friends usually call me Stardust. Don't ask why."

"I'm--"

"Richard. I know. Or do you prefer Dick? I also want to know what you're doing with someone else behind my back."

"Excuse me, behind your back? I never even knew you existed."

"Your heart belongs to me. You just don't know it. But you will soon," she said and walked away.

After the strange interaction with Sherry, I met up with my girlfriend after her psychology class. She lagged behind everybody else. I knew she wanted to change her major, but her parents didn't permit it.

"Hey Lola. So, what's the problem today?" I joked.

"Oh shut up, Dick. You and I both know how much I hate these classes. Besides, I've got another lab due in a week. Silver lining, I need a subject for it, so it's your lucky day."

"What is it this time?"

"I just need to show you some images and measure your heart rate to see if your heart and mind are connected. The images may be a bit graphic."

The only graphic picture depicted a surgical disaster. According to her *accurate* studies, my heart rate only increased after I had seen certain images of women and on the graphic one out of fear. After the project, the night sped by uneventfully until one in the morning, when there was a knock on the door. I opened the door to find nothing but a box in lavender wrapping paper with a note attached. Inside was a framed picture of me taken before the *beginning of the second semester*. I skimmed the note but my eyes lingered on the signature line: Sherry. *How did she get that picture of me?*

"What is it, Dick?" Lola asked, coming out into the living room.

"Nothing." I hid the photo in my shirt. "It's nothing important."

Days after that incident, I looked for Sherry. I found her playing with her hair in front of one of the lecture halls. As soon as she saw me, she blocked me from entering.

"I see that you've finally found me," she said, "or I've found you."

"Two things: One, this is my lecture hall and two, if you wanted to see me you should've come to me instead of hiding."

"It's more romantic to have the boy find the girl. Wouldn't you agree, Dick?"

"Listen, I have a girlfriend. I'm sure you already know that. Stay away from me and Lola." I forced her aside and entered the hall.

After the lecture ended, I stayed behind to help the professor, so I was the last to leave class. When I had stepped outside, Sherry jumped me, pushing me down. I tried to get up, but she knocked me down again.

"So you want me to leave you alone now?" She stepped on my chest. "I don't *roll that way*. Oh no, if someone I love turns me down, they pay. In fact, something like this has happened before with another boy. It didn't go well for him."

"If you're going to come after me, then I'll just hide from you."

"Every shift you make, each pace you take, I'll be watching you."

Fear grew even as she left me alone for the day. But what she said still bugged me. Days passed as my fear of what she'd say or do next grew, but my life remained mostly normal. Lola and I kept a steady relationship until she brought up the picture I hid from her long ago.

"That night I used you for my psych lab, what was at the front door?" Lola asked.

"Nothing, like I said."

"I've been honest with you for the longest time, so I want you to do the same."

"It's nothing. Just leave it at that," I said, panic setting in my voice. "Please, just leave it at that."

She never did leave it be. Days after, she continued to ask me the same question, soon escalating to the point where she tried to pilfer it from my room.

"What are you doing?" I asked her, as she looked through my drawers.

"Uhhh, nothing."

"Don't lie to me."

"What did you get the day you helped me with my lab?"

"Nothing important."

"So you admit that there was something you picked up?"

"Why do you want to know so much?"

"You and I are in a relationship, so we shouldn't hide anything from each other."

"I don't want to creep you out though."

"How would it creep me out? It's not like it's a photo of you or anything."

"Actually... it is. The day I helped you, this present was left outside my door. In it, was this picture of me and my dog during the break after first semester." I felt horrible for not telling her. After I told her, she sat herself in a nearby chair. Her eyes were wide open and her breathing was slower.

The next day began like any other, but entering the lecture hall without seeing Sherry worried me.

As the lecture ended, a text on my phone appeared from an unfamiliar number. My heart rate quickened as I read it: "Love is a battlefield." I shut my phone off and proceeded to exit the building. From the corner of my eye, a figure dashed across the door, so I used the other exit. Chills crept up my spine as I entered an empty hallway to the exit. I reached for the handle, until I heard footsteps coming in my direction. The handle didn't budge and I heard chains from the other exit.

"Can you hear me, my beloved?" a voice asked. "You and I are together in the school now. There's no way out of here. We belong together. Forever."

"Leave me alone. I don't need you, I don't want you, and I don't love you. You're insane," I yelled back.

"You remind me of my first beloved. He said the same thing to me."

There was no response after that but I still couldn't find an exit. The windows were too small to get out. The doors were locked. The only way out was through the connected women's studies building. I thought back to when Sherry had insanely left me an earlier text of her schedule. Her decided major was women's studies.

Walking towards the hallway, I heard footsteps nearing my direction. I opened the door and tiptoed out. I hightailed it to the adjacent building. Locked. No matter how much force I exerted, it wouldn't budge. Behind me, the door opened. The janitor-- thank God--had also been cleaning up the building, so he let me out once I lied about helping a professor.

I arrived at my apartment late to find all my belongings littered across the ground. Even with my bedroom wrecked, I still noticed the items that had been stolen: a small black book with my contacts, my phone charger, and a picture of my girlfriend.

There was a small note attached to a ripped picture of my girlfriend, which originally also had me in it. It read, "Let it go. She doesn't love you at all, but I do. I know that you secretly think about me, but you don't have to think anymore. I'm coming after you, but only after the middle figure is gone. Love, Stardust."

She's after Lola.

Descending into the garage, I noticed a hooded figure but ignored it. I drove off towards Lola's dorm.

I raced around to the front of the dorm, dashing right through the lobby. I rushed up the stairs and ran to Lola's door, which was already open. The room was pitch black, but I could make out the traces of destruction: the mattress was flipped over, closet doors torn from the railings, computer monitor on the ground. Her phone sat on a perfectly clean cabinet.

A message had been left on the screen: "The interloper is no more. Now it's just you and me. No matter what you say, I'll keep on loving you."

I screamed, flipping the table and smashing everything within reach. Upon turning around, I felt a sharp pain on the back of my neck, and I slowly sunk into a fuzzy unconsciousness.

"Good morning, Starshine. The Earth says hello," a calm, feminine voice said.

Dazed and confused, I struggled to move my wrists, then realized they had been bound to a chair. I looked up. Sherry.

"Where am I?" I muttered.

"Our house, in the middle of the street."

"Where is Lola?"

"Not dead. In another room."

"Don't do this Sherry. I'm begging you."

"So now you beg. Well, guess what? It doesn't matter. She'll die, and then it'll be just you and me."

I struggled to get out of chair, but it was bolted to the floor. Sherry had noticed, stood up, and stepped on my left foot with the spike of her heel.

"The only way to stop me is to catch me," she said, closing the door on her way out. Even though the door was closed, I could hear her humming happily.

Teetering left and right, I tried to bring the chair down with me. After about two minutes, the chair fell, one of its arms collapsing onto the ground. I began working on the ties when the door opened. Sherry stood there in awe.

"I knew I should've used desk chairs instead of wood." She walked over to me and kicked me in the forehead with her heel. It felt like being stabbed by a knife, and caused me to cough out blood. She kicked me again. Was she planning to kill me?

The light swung wildly after she slammed the door and walked out. With one arm still free, I tried again to undo the tie but I couldn't tell what I was touching, or if I was touching anything at all. Colors blurred, forming a spectral white. Blood trickled down my hand, and I felt like I was going to die. There was no way she'd let me die; she loved me. Fear ran through my body at the thought of her love disappearing, which may serve as my only salvation.

Trepidation tried to triumph my thoughts, as my mind plunged itself into madness. Red continued to fall from my mouth and forehead, until my eyes closed against my will. Carpet rubbed against my clothes. My hair stretched to the threshold of pain; I couldn't move or speak. Even the air against my skin stung like salt on open wounds. Something whisked me away, placing me on a plush surface, almost like a bed. I opened my eyes to see Sherry sitting in a chair. She looked at me, smiling as she twiddled a knife between her fingers. I looked behind me, seeing a mirror with the phrase, "Whatever we deny or embrace, for worse or for better, we belong," in blood.

"You taught me the ways of desire, but now, it's taking its toll," she said, with a malicious grin. "You're the right kind of sinner to release my inner fantasy."

"Whose blood is that?" I asked. "Tell me."

"I believe we both know the answer to that one," she said, walking over to a closet door. As it opened, I saw the most horrific thing, something I never wanted to see again.

"Lola? God, no. LOLA."

Sherry got up, but I shoved my head into her chest. Still bound, I hopped over to the door only to fall down. She stepped over me and kicked me aside as she walked out the door. After she had exited, I loosened the rope around my legs and tried to cut the rope on the window sill. That didn't work. I almost gave up until I remembered something I saw on a fictional television show. Using my bound hands, I punched out the standing mirror and grabbed a shard of glass. Blood continued to pour out of my hands, but I continued to cut the rope. One layer came loose, then another, and another, until finally the glass shattered in my hand.

Sucking in the pain and glass shards in my palms, I stretched my arms. The rope slid off. My phone had been sitting on the desk next to the mirror. Grabbing it, I checked the screen: no new messages, battery at fifty percent. I turned on my phone to dial the police, when the room turned pitch black.

I walked outside of the room. Candles flickered in the hall. Staying near the railway, I slowly crawled my way through the halls, holding my breath in intervals. My phone light was off, but if any text were to come through it would immediately turn on and reveal my location.

I tried not to open any doors but when I came across a slightly open one, I couldn't help myself. My interest was piqued, so I slowly moved towards it and nudged it with caution. I looked inside every cabinet and drawer that was open, each one filled with pens, paper, baseball cards, cigarette packs, even trash. One cabinet stood alone in the room, its door wooden and locked. Looking around for a key, I found one on a desk. I walked towards the cabinet to see what the skeleton in Sherry's closet was. Unlocking it, I realized it wasn't so much of a skeleton as it was a rotting body, as some of the flesh was still on it. The body of a man stood inside with a puncture near the heart. I lost my footing and fell on my back, looking at this suspended corpse. There was no ID but I feared I was looking at my own fate. Negotiating with her would be impossible without some kind of weapon.

Sneaking into the dark halls again, I wandered around, almost passing out. I propped myself up against a door when it opened, causing me to fall backward. The room was almost like a study, books lining every shelf except for one which was labeled fantasy. An globe sat next to a desk that had a single lamp on it. A book laid open on the desk, flipped to a page near the end.

"Love Under the Stars? What a stupid title." I started to read the passage and soon became immersed in the book itself. Apparently it was a love story about a girl from the stars and a young king. The girl tried to get the king to marry her, but for the first few chapters, she kept failing. She had followed him to study his routine, she retaliated when he angered her, she tried to lock him in with her, and she even went to the point of threatening a loved one's life. It was so familiar.

I kept reading into the end. In the final chapter, the girl killed the loved one, trapped and followed him inside his own castle, but eventually did get him to love her. Through all the pain and agony, the king didn't want to be alone so he forced himself to marry her because he knew she wouldn't give up. The girl died a year after the marriage and where she died was where I understood its title: "Underneath the stars, the queen and her king had one last moment together before she would disappear. She wanted to make the most out of it, but she could not. She had to return to the stars for she had been on the Earth for too long. Her body started to turn to dust and was blown by the wind into the night. She had exited the Earth the same way she entered: as stardust."

Everything became clearer now; she wanted to recreate the events of the book. She was obsessed and thought that I was going to willingly accept her. She's completely insane. Whoever the guy in the wardrobe was, I became sure it was the first love she warned me about, the one "that didn't go so well." There was nothing in the room that could help me subdue her. The lamp would give me away and books weren't exactly the best weapon, so I resorted back to my hide-and-seek tactic.

Searching every possible room on the top floor, I thought about heading down the stairs. If I did that, it'd be easier for her to find me, but more rooms for me to hide in. No sounds emanated from the hall behind me so I thought the coast was clear. Standing up, I slowly walked towards the stairs. I continued to look all around me in fear that the stairs' noises would give me away.

As I approached the final step, I heard a loud *BOOM* from outside. The thunderstorm had finally started, just as I thought I was safe. The rain could be heard as if it was a monsoon outside and the wind chimes were being blown constantly. Everything this storm did made the house even more unpredictable. Walking towards a door to what I thought was a kitchen, my phone went off: a text from the maniac stalking me.

"Here comes the rain again, falling on my head like a new emotion. Is it raining on you?"

I ignored it as I was focused on getting out. Past the door wasn't the kitchen, but instead was a dining room. The windows were locked, and looking out I saw a steep hill with a path leading to an outdoor shed. I entered the adjacent room, which turned out to be the kitchen. Finally. Something useful has got to be in here.

Searching through every cabinet, even pulling out some of the drawers, I couldn't find a single object. The pantries were empty, the drawers were empty, and the knife holder had nothing in it. No usable weapon could be salvaged and no food either. *There has to be something, anything in here that can help me*, I thought to myself. This girl, there is no easy way to stop her because she is unpredictable.

"If you're lost, you can look and you will find me," echoed through the hall. She was getting close. I assumed the noise I made ransacking attracted her. Another door was in the kitchen so I sprinted through, as it had no locking mechanism, I found myself in some room that served only to connect to the back porch. Reaching for the door, I felt a cold wind blow down my neck followed by a blow to the back of my head, knocking me down onto the floor.

Waking up, I saw I was put in front of a body sitting in a chair. Like him, my wrists were bound to the arm rests. There was a note attached to his chest that I could barely make out: "Don't you mess around, no, no, no. Just tell me that you want me."

She's never going to let go of me. I had to accept this. On closer inspection of the body, another piece of paper was attached to his right thigh. "Daddy, this is what happens when you patronize me."

"She killed her own father." I said to myself. My head spun. My phone was put on my lap, blood on its screen. Most likely it was my own. I rotated my hand to try and find the end of the cord and undo it, but the arm rest scratched against my skin. I was able to get some space between the cord and rest though, so the pain was worth it.

The chair I was in wasn't like the one in that basement; this one had wheels so I could move. I rolled closer to the body and tried to grab the knife pinning the note. Leaning forward, I started to roll backwards but my head was close enough to knock the knife out his chest. It fell onto his lap, but I was unable to move my legs to kick the knife off. I twisted my body and angled my bound hands towards the knife.

Success, I thought to myself as I clenched the knife. In order to cut the rope, my hand needed to be at an angle. Rotating gently, I moved the knife to a position where I could cut the ropes but I needed to be careful in the movement of it.

Cutting slowly, the ropes started come off and I was free in a matter of minutes. I broke my right arm free and diverted attention to my left arm. Blood dripped slowly from my right arm; the wound was pretty deep, but time wasn't something that could be wasted. My left arm was free and in turn, my legs.

"She has to die," I told myself, clenching the knife even harder. *Can I do it? Can I bring myself to harm another human, even one as crazy as her? Of course I can, but would I be sacrificing my humanity? Debating now is just wasting time, time I could be spending getting out of here. I'll decide when the time comes.*

With not much of a resolution, I walked out of the room into more darkness. The storm outside was getting even worse than before. Thunder was nonstop, rain and wind collided, whipping against the outer walls. Lightning came down almost every ten seconds, and the flashes got brighter and brighter. It was as if God had come down to this very house to judge us. Sweat fell from my forehead, seeping into my wounds and blood came slowly oozed out of my arm and legs. "I guess I need to work on my knife skills."

I felt sorry for what happened to her dad and that guy I found in her wardrobe, but I had to worry about myself at the moment. Thinking about their past would only cloud my judgment even further. Walking aimlessly, I found myself in the foyer, alone in the dark and multiple entrances available for a surprise attack. Turning around constantly as thunder boomed louder and louder, I heard someone call out to me from above.

"This day was going to be perfect, the kind of day I dreamed since I was small."

It was Sherry, standing on the baluster above. She was toying with me, like she has been doing this entire evening. This is it, the time to end it all. The time to kill her is now; walking toward her, tears came out of my eyes. What was going on? Was I feeling sorry for her? Am I actually the villain here, or am I not fully understanding her intentions for bringing me here?

"What have you done to me?" I questioned her, stopping on the staircase. "Why do I pity you instead of feeling anger and hatred?"

"If you're lost, you can look and you will find me. Time after time."

"Stop this, now. Do you honestly think this a joke?"

She chuckled under her breath. I continued to ascend the staircase, but slower than before. Caution was flying through my mind, blocking all my hatred. Here is the woman who killed someone who rejected her, killed someone who didn't understand her, and killed someone who I loved. Why can I not just run to her and plunge this knife right into her heart?

"Why did you do this? Why did you do this to your first love? Why kill your father? Why kidnap me? Do you honestly think that I'd develop some sort of love for you?"

"Bookmarking, she's getting closer," she said to herself, I assumed.

The storm outside was getting even heavier than before. The windows behind her shattered. The chandelier above the foyer rocked back and forth, the curtains flew from their post, and rain poured into the house.

"Just say that you love me." Tears dripped down her neck. She was actually crying, genuinely crying. I didn't think she could harbor an emotion like that. Here I was, the love of her life, the person she obsessed about, trying to kill her. No, I'm not the bad guy.

"Say something that makes sense. Don't hide behind fading song lyrics. Give me an answer," I told her, standing straight with the knife still in hand. Clenching it brought out more blood, but I didn't care. If I was going to die, I might as well take her with me. All the kicking and beating she put me through, and yet I'm almost complaining about how my arm hurts. My forehead wound opened up again. Blood dropped between my eyes, my arm continuing to bleed; I was almost sweating out my own blood.

"Talk to me, like lovers do," she said.

"I won't walk with you; I won't let you harm anybody else. I can't let you harm anybody else."

"If you don't love me now, you'll never love me again."

"I never loved you. Why would I love somebody who tried to kill me?"

That was it, her snapping point. When she heard that, it was like her universe fell apart. She walked slowly to the edge of the baluster. Either she was going to jump, or she was planning something else. Moving closer to me, she lunged forward at me in a last ditch attempt to kill me. I wasn't fast enough; she stabbed into my chest but I wasn't going to let that stop me. Taking hold of her, I held her up against the railing and we continued to fight. Tossing and turning the other, I was finally able to stand up to her. In a flash, I shoved her over the railing and onto the floor of the lobby. She wasn't dead. Sherry just got back up and walked over to the stairs.

"How are you not dead?" I was tired. All of my wounds were open and my chest was bleeding profusely. Limping towards the stairs, I saw she too was limping. Both of us being injured, the real question going through my head was "Who was going to pass out first?" I got down the staircase and she stopped in center of the lobby, waiting for me. Both of us were armed with only a knife, and were ready for a battle.

"Revved up like a deuce?" She asked me.

"I'm not some runner of the night," I replied. The thunder outside cracked its loudest that moment. A couple of alarms were activated. This weather is one of destruction, the alarms continued into the night but a distant siren could also be heard. Whether it was coming here or not, I knew that this battle with her had to end fast. Running forward, she attempted to swing at me but I kept moving backwards until I bumped into the wall. I ducked underneath one of her swings and head-butted her to the ground. She tripped me and my head hit the ground. Hard.

My pain was intensifying, but that didn't matter. Looking down, Sherry had stabbed her knife into me but that was actually helpful. I still had my knife and her this close meant she couldn't dodge fast enough. Hoping to hit her, she pushed me away and was unscathed; or so she thought. Around her neck, droplets of blood fell out onto the floor. She dropped to her knees, her eyes widening on me and her smile changed into an open mouth.

"Freeze!" An officer kicked down the door, his gun aimed at her.

She turned around, only to fall on her knees.

"We need medical attention, stat," he said into his radio. "I've got two people down here who are bleeding, medical evacuation is necessary."

My vision started to fade, and the last thing I saw were four medical personnel running into the building. Although I couldn't see, my hearing wasn't affected. The voices swam through my head and formed into broken phrases.

"The two of them … make it… alive. Let's hope… they are strong… survive."

I woke up in the hospital to find out I'd been unconscious for a week. During that time, I had four IV's in me to keep me alive as well as stitches in my chest. Morphine bags were in the trash beside my bedding and a doctor walked in only to drop his clipboard. He stood there in awe for a good five minutes until he decided to walk towards me.

"How are you up already? With the wounds you came in with, you should have woken up next week."

"I remember what one doctor said."

"What was that?"

I looked into his eyes. "Survive."

"Well, the woman you were with also survived. She's in critical condition and if she too wakes up, she won't be the same."

"Fine by me, I don't know her that well."

The doctor had me stay for the whole day just to make sure my body was recovering well. Based off of the medications given to me, my blood was leveling out to normal levels. I was escorted out of my room, and saw Sherry being escorted by the police. She also recovered from the attack and the stitches around her neck were visible. We were walked out to the front of the hospital, left to go our separate paths.

I walked to the left and she was escorted to the right. Looking back, I saw her eyes stare into mine. Not a single sign of happiness was in them, only a burning flame.

A year passed and there was no investigation in the death of Lola, mainly because they never found a body. They searched high and low in that house and turned up nothing. The owner of the house was Sherry's father, but he had been dead for ten years. I was able to get my uncle, who was a psychiatrist, to evaluate Sherry's past based off of the house she grew up in and the books in the study. Any documents turned up were seized by the police, but I recovered some that were hidden in corners of the rooms. The final conversation I had with my uncle will be burned in my mind until the day I die.

"What did you turn up?"

He looked at me with a horrified expression. "This girl, she was really screwed up." He pulled out a file with all the information and just threw it on my table. "The journal entries you found are probably worse than the ones the police have. The first entry is about how she killed her neighbor's dog because it barked too much. It goes into detail about everything she did to it: how she trapped it, how she killed it, and how she even buried it. The second entry is when she started to hate her father. He was abusive to her whenever he had alcohol, which was frequent based off of the globe he kept in the study."

I looked at my feet. "What other things did her journal reveal?"

"Some were about her feelings toward a boy named Jonathan. The dates about Jonathan were spread out so it was tough to gather information, but there was one that detailed his capture, torture, and death. She did similar things to him that she did to you. He was kept tied up in her basement, girlfriend killed in front of him, and his death due to blood loss. To paraphrase her words, 'He was weak and unfit. One kick and he was coughing up blood, so she just killed him.' The last two entries were about you."

I looked at him with a stern face. "What did they say?"

"Are you sure you want to know?"

"Tell me," I slammed my fist on the table. "I need to know what she was like so I can understand."

"Fine." He sat down in a chair and cupped his hands together. "She detailed her plans with you. First, she'd lure Lola into some trap and either drown her or hang her; she couldn't decide on which one to do. Then, she'd lure you into a trap, which by the looks of things she succeeded, and keep you tied up in that house. Over time, you'd develop Stockholm syndrome for her and you wouldn't want to leave. If anybody came to the house, she'd kill them."

"What about the second entry?"

He didn't respond. I pushed the folder onto the ground to get him to react. "What did the second entry say?"

He stood up in front of me, hands to his side. "She was getting closer and closer. She figured out your routine." He then pointed directly at me. "She was going to drug you after school and drag you to that mansion if she had to. Lola was weak in her mind, but you were strong enough to survive the pain that Sherry would put you through. Any attempts at resistance and you would have ended up dead. She didn't care if you lived or died; it was all for herself."

"You don't know that."

"You're right, I don't know that. I can only hypothesize based off of this data you collected." He once again raised his finger to me. "Also, why are you defending her actions? She killed your girlfriend and tortured you and yet you act as if she is the victim. You're the one who's delusional."

"She is a victim to herself. Her mind is in the wrong place --"

"And you think you can fix that? I've met people like that. Heck, one of my former coworkers was insane. There was no way of fixing him, no matter how many sessions I gave him. His mind was broken beyond repair."

"Stardust and your friend are different people, she --"

"They are in the same situation." He grabbed me by my collar. "If you won't listen to my studies, then listen to your uncle. They can't be fixed. If you try to make her normal, you will fail. She is too far gone."

I didn't talk with my uncle for a while after that. I deleted his number from my contacts, but kept it on a note in some drawer; in case of emergency. I returned to Stardust to see how she was doing and she had left a note for me on the table. Searching her room, I couldn't find any of her possessions in it. No bags, no clothes, not even dust was in her room. Deciding to read the note, I dropped it shortly after reading it.

"That's everything." I said, bringing my head up. "Everything up to this point has been normal. I haven't heard anything from her but I've kept in touch with my uncle."

A detective walked in the room and sat across from me. "Actually, that's not everything. We didn't find this note you spoke of."

"I burned it, alongside my photos of me and Lola. I don't want to relive this ever again."

"Well, I hate to tell you this but there is a chance that she'll come back."

"What do you mean detective?"

He pulled out two bags of evidence. One of the bags had a knife while the other had a note. "These were found at a crime scene in some big house that was secluded in the woods. The body we found had the note pinned to it while the knife was still stabbed into the victim." He showed me a picture of a body with a heart scarred into the chest and the throat slit. "This is the body that was left. The DNA from the knife and the note happens to match that of Sherry --"

"Stardust."

"What did you say?"

"Her name is Stardust."

"Are you insane?" He stood up and slammed his fists onto the table. "We know of the past events with you and her. That woman, Sherry, she is completely insane. We went to three other psychologists from around the globe. They all agree that she is mentally unstable. There is no saving her."

"There is a way. You just don't know it."

"I don't know it, but the man from Oxford, he knows it. The man from Stanford knows that there is no saving her. The woman who leads the psychology program and graduated from Yale with a doctorate in psychology insists that the only way to save her is to put her six feet under. Sherry's plan was to get you to love her, and it looks like it's working."

I stood up and almost attacked the detective. "I don't love her. She killed my girlfriend; there is no way that a man could love her. Not unless he was from an asylum, that girl can't be loved. She can be saved though."

He grabbed me by the collar and put my head against the folder. The pictures inside were easily visible now and I saw that the body found in the closet was in a worse condition than I originally thought. On his back, the word love was cut into it. His face had cuts and lashes and the chest puncture was only one of seven.

"You're being played Gray, and you don't even know it."

"I'd like to have my lawyer present."

The detectives let me go since I wasn't being charged with anything. However, I couldn't help but think about what that detective told me. Does the road for salvation lie behind death? How dangerous is she? I pondered the question as I began to enter my apartment, only to stop at the door. A letter rested on the ground addressed to me. Inside my apartment, I sat on my couch and ripped open the envelope. The first thing I take out is a picture of Sherry holding a sign that reads "I remember." The next of its contents causes a lump in my throat.

Dear Lover,

Time is of the essence so I'll keep this as short as possible. I'm leaving your company. This town is one that only brings back terrible memories. It was fun getting to know you on a deeper level, Dick. I've already passed the boundary of the town, don't ask how. I know the police will be looking for me, and I know they'll be led by Detectives Gash and Amity.

Everything was supposed to be perfect, the life I wished since I was small. I dream at night, I can only see your face. We belong together, but I'm trapped by your love and I'm chained to your side. Your love has set my soul on fire, burning out of control. I can hear you saying that you'll never break the chain. If you're lost you can look and you will find me, time after time. I don't wanna sleep, I just want to keep on loving you. Talk to me, like lovers do.

Goodbye to You,

Sherry "Starlight"

THE MATCHMAKER

Amy Tran

THE TWINKLING STARS ILLUMINATED the night sky as Chriselle stood from her balcony, peering through her telescope. Orion's constellation came into view. She scoped further to find Saturn's rings when multiple spheres of bright light shot through the sky. *Shooting stars?* The spheres zoomed in on Chriselle. *Those are not shooting stars.* She rushed towards her room for cover, but tripped. She felt a monstrous jolt. Dust fell off her ceiling and objects fell to the ground. The spheres had hit her room.

Silence. Having barely escaped death, she opened her eyes. A foreign breath tickled her cheek. She turned her head to find a handsome face that was framed with brown locks only inches away from her own. She covered her mouth to keep herself from screaming. The man was laying on top of her. *Is he asleep? What do I do? Do I push him off?* Glancing to her right, she saw two conventionally attractive gentlemen in unfamiliar school uniforms.

"Hey, Taurus, how long are you going to be on top of that lady?" the blue-haired one asked, smirking.

The blue man rummaged through Chriselle's belongings, ignoring her incredulous stares. The blond one grabbed the back of the the blue man's collar, glaring at him.

"Did you forget? We're on a mission, Aquarius." His voice was firm.

Mission? Who the heck are these guys? Kidnappers? With renewed panic, she attempted to free herself from the man dubbed Taurus's grip. The second she touched his shoulders, Taurus's eyes shot wide open.

"H-hey," she whimpered.

Taurus picked her up and stood there, carrying Chriselle as if she were a bride.

"She's quite heavy," Taurus joked.

She blushed, hiding her face in his neck. Peering over his shoulder, she noticed a sadness in Aquarius' blue eyes and paused. *Taurus? Aquarius? What in the world?* Still holding her, Taurus hopped onto the rails of the balcony. Chriselle shot a look downward and flinched. She on the second floor.

"W-wait," she begged.

"Miss, if you don't stay quiet, you'll wake your neighbors," Aquarius warned, joining Taurus on the balcony rails.

The blond man followed their lead and climbed onto the rails as well. Chriselle's empty stomach churned, but she kept her mouth shut.

"It's a go," Aquarius cheered.

The three gentlemen, Taurus, Aquarius, and the unknown blond, jumped off the rails. They shot through the sky like meteorites, as if an invisible gravitational force had vacuumed them up. Chriselle lost all consciousness.

"How long is she going to stay asleep?"

"I have no idea. When it's time, she'll find the light and awaken on her own."

Distant sounds of droplets echoed. A flow of energy surrounded Chriselle and filled her with warmth. Her eyelids fluttered open and she gaped at the sight before her. Before her was a mini galaxy of stars, all connected to become a web of light. She stood up, feeling lightheaded and unconnected to her body. Covering her eyes, she treaded towards the center of the blinding light. She reached out to touch it and woke up, in the real world this time. *What was that? It felt so real? It felt like I had been there, even though I wasn't fully in control. Astral Projection?*

"Ah, you're awake?" a feminine monotone voice asked.

A young girl with fiery red pupils leapt through the window of the room that Chriselle rested in and landed on her feet like a ninja.

"Nice to meet you, Miss Chriselle. You can call me Gemini," she said.

Gemini's voice and aura were so soothing that Chriselle had to pinch her arm to reassure herself that this was reality rather than a dream again. Gemini's long, dark locks and pale skin reminded Chriselle of a porcelain doll. Gemini batted her lashes and stared at Chriselle's face. Chriselle couldn't tell whether it was because her own face looked amusing or if Gemini was trying to remember something.

"The headmistress is waiting for you in the office," Gemini said, strolling towards the window and leaping out again. *This place is filled with freaks.* Chriselle got up from the bed and saw an outfit that had been laid out for her. It resembled the dress her childhood doll wore, only it was more gothic than her doll's royal garments.

After she made herself look presentable, she looked to the window. The girl had not returned. *Well, there's no way I'm leaping out. I'll find another way.* She exited the room via the door and wandered around the empty hallways. Constellation patterns decorated the walls. The carpet, a flawless blood red, contrasted with her dress' pastel blue. *This place is huge. How do I find the office?* A strong breeze blew past Chriselle and a large door appeared at the end of the hallway. On the wall to the right of the door was a nameplate with the words "Headmistress Blake" engraved on it. *I guess I found it.*

"Come in," an unfamiliar voice said. Chriselle entered. The ceiling was a sky engulfed with stars. There were floor to ceiling bookshelves lining the wall, as if she were in the library. At the center, she saw a tall, slender woman clothed in a simple monochrome suit. Her hair was tied back into a low ponytail. After flipping through some pages of a book, the woman slammed it down on the table, closing it.

"You are Chriselle?" she asked, eyeing her from head to toe.

"Y-yes," Chriselle stuttered.

"The Lost Souls that brought you here, to this academy, what do you think of them?" the headmistress asked.

"Excuse me?" Chriselle asked. *Lost souls?*

"Oh, Miss Chriselle, stop acting so oblivious. I mean, you have already met Gemini, Aquarius, Taurus, and Capricorn," she said, scoffing.

Capricorn? I guess that's the name of that blond man.

The smirk that had been on the headmistress' face disappeared in a matter of seconds. "Well, Miss Chriselle, I guess you can go now,." She signaled for her to leave.

Chriselle bowed her head and followed the order.

Once the door was securely closed, the headmistress chuckled to herself. "Oh dear, I wonder what happened to the poor girl. She must have hit her head pretty hard to give me such a confused look." Realization flashed across her face. "Well, I wonder why all this happened? What exactly did you do to the girl, Victoria?"

A bookshelf beside the headmistress' desk swung outwards revealing a spacious room. In it sat a young girl, dressed in an outfit similar to Chriselle's, sipping tea.

"My, I don't know what you mean, dear Blake," the young girl replied, putting her cup of tea down. She wiped her mouth with the handkerchief that had been on her lap. "I only did what was necessary to protect her."

The headmistress sighed and rubbed her temple with the tips of her fingers. "Let's hope it works out like you planned, Victoria. It may seem like a game to you, but one wrong move on her end, and we will all suffer."

Victoria nodded nonchalantly and returned to her tea.

As one, all the Zodiacs turned to face the night sky, each seeking out their own unique constellation. Something big was coming, and Chriselle was going to be right in the middle of it. They could only pray that she was strong enough to face it.

A ball of darkness in the middle of the web of starlight widened.

Chriselle wandered the corridors of the building. Her mind raced through the information she had been given. *Lost souls? Gemini? Taurus?* Chriselle shook her head in denial. *It's okay, Chriselle. Everything will soon return back to normal in a blink of an eye. Everything will--*

"Ah, it's her! It's her!" a loud and childish voice called from behind.

Chriselle turned around to see a young girl struggling to get down from a tall teenaged boy's shoulders. The boy had a calm demeanor and gave her a warm smile, which seemed to reflect kindness.

"Sorry, about that," the boy apologized. "This one is quite wild." He walked over to the bench nearby and placed the child down onto the seat. "My name is Virgo, by the way. The small girl here is Aries." He stretched his arms out, massaging away the tension that had built up on his shoulders due to Aries sitting on them.

Virgo, huh? At least this one seemed a bit sane. Chriselle extended her hand. "Nice to meet you. I'm --"

"Chriselle!"

Chriselle was again interrupted by Aries who was buzzing with energy. Suspicious, Chriselle stepped back. "Wait, how do you know--"

"Your name? Aries is sad," the girl said. "Aries is sad that Chriselle doesn't remember a single thing of her real past," she whined, on the verge of tears.

Aries ran up to Chriselle hugging her tightly, burrowing her face into Chriselle's torso.

Chriselle squirmed with discomfort.

Virgo prevented it from going on any longer by picking Aries up and allowing her to cry onto his shoulders instead.

"Sorry. I know this must be a lot to take in," Virgo said, backing off. "Are you okay? If you don't feel like talking anymore, it's okay."

"No, no!" Aries struggled to escape from Virgo's arms, tears dried up now. "Let me go! Chriselle needs to know. She needs to know."

Virgo covered Aries' mouth with his hand and forcefully carried her away.

Chriselle looked on in confusion but shrugged off the commotion as something insignificant. Her head throbbed. She headed back to the room from which she awoke.

Aries's declaration bothered her. She kept turning the words over in her head, unable to fall asleep. Not until the sun peaked out from beyond the horizon did sleep overcome her.

Unlike before, Chriselle didn't find herself in front of the light web. Instead, she found herself facing an ordinary oak door. The door creaked open and she peeked through the crack. Behind the door was a child who resembled her at the age of seven or eight. The child was playing around with other children in front of a mansion that Chriselle didn't recognize.

"Oh? So, you've decided to face your past, Chriselle?"

Chriselle turned around to find a young girl wearing a dress similar to what Chriselle had been given and was now wearing.

The strange girl twirled the handle of a lace umbrella in her hands. She took a step toward Chriselle. A grin spread across her face. "Well, what are you waiting for? Why don't you go in?" She gave Chriselle a push.

"Poor child. She doesn't know the truth about her parents," the caretaker murmured.

"Well, it can't be helped. The two of them were matched as star-crossed. It was inevitable that they would become magnets of misfortune," the soothsayer pointed out, watching over the children as they played.

The younger Chriselle continued to play, oblivious of the gossiping happening behind her. She wouldn't have cared anyways. Chriselle had been raised to believe that she was an orphan. Unlike other orphans, she had no interest in finding out who her parents were. The only things she cared about were her twelve best friends, who consisted of six boys and six girls. Little did she know, her friends weren't ordinary.

The Chriselle of the present walked towards the lively group of children, mesmerized by the scene she was witnessing. The children, the ghosts of her past, ran right through her as they played their game. One of the children fell, scraping her knee. All of the others circled around the fallen girl, pulling up her pants leg to take a closer look. In doing so, they revealed the pisces symbol on the girl's ankle. Startled, Chriselle took a closer look at the other children. Now that they were still, she could see that they each had a horoscope symbol on their bodies.

"You finally noticed?" The strange girl in matching dress reappeared next to Chriselle.

"Who are you?" Chriselle questioned, unsure if she was a friend or foe.

"Pardon my rudeness. I haven't introduced myself yet, have I? You can call me Vic. It's short for Victoria. Now, the reason I am here is to be your guide. As a guide, I will be able to reveal the truths of your past. Your memories had been blocked for your safety and mental stability, but now I feel like you can handle it."

Victoria walked passed the transparent memory as if it wasn't there and disappeared through the door that Chriselle had entered. Chriselle hesitated, debating on whether she should follow the girl or wait for herself to naturally awaken. However, questions piled up and she couldn't resist the urge to find the answers.

Chriselle ran to catch up with Victoria. Right as she reached her, Victoria twirled her umbrella and a gust of wind came out of nowhere. When the air settled, Chriselle found herself in the galaxy of starlight yet again.

"Now then," Victoria said, "shall we get your answers?"

"Yes," Chriselle answered firmly.

Chriselle opened her eyes. Sunlight filtered through the thin curtains, hitting her face. Everything felt too bright, too intense.

Her childhood friends, six of whom she had remet recently, were not human. When they were born, they were bound to a constellation, more specifically the Zodiacs. Their powers depended on their starlight. They were star agents and the Lost Souls assigned the job of keeping the universe stable. They fought every day to keep the darkness from consuming all life. Chriselle was meant to join them, but the others cared too much about her to let that happen. They had begged Victoria to bind her memories in order to let her live out her life normally.

However, a new force had emerged, and with it came an overwhelming darkness. The darkness threatened to consume the starlight and the star agents were losing their power source. The universe's balance was no longer stable. According to the soothsayer, Chriselle was destined to bring back that balance. As a result, despite the Zodiac's protests, Victoria gave her back her memories.

Chriselle had been living her entire life never knowing that her most precious people had been watching over her, protecting her. This brought tears to her eyes. They had protected her and the universe despite their waning powers. Now it was time for her to do the same.

She would defeat the darkness and bring back the starlight. She would do anything in her power to protect them, to save the lives of the Lost Souls, her long-lost friends.

MIRROR
Yen Tran

"GO TO SLEEP, AZUSA, or else the boogeyman will get you," Chester told me, patting my head.

"Okay, okay," I said. "One last room before I can save."

"Honestly little sis, you're in front of your computer all day, every day. It's really unhealthy, not to mention bad for your complexion." With that parting remark, he left, shutting my bedroom door.

I rushed to the full length mirror next to my computer desk. *I don't look that bad, do I?*

A notification lit up on my computer screen, shaking me from my vain thoughts. I returned to my desk, determined to finish the next level.

Lightning flashed and thunder rumbled outside the safety of my house, but that wouldn't deter my focus. *I must get out of the doll room before I lose my sanity.*

Thock. Thock. Thock. Gnarled branches knocked at my window. *Did that come from* inside *my room?* It sounded like it was coming from the reflection of the window in my mirror rather than from the window itself. I shivered. The thought gave my goose-bumps.

I saved my game and went to bed.

Bits and pieces of cotton were strewn across the dollhouse room. With my mouse, I grabbed another doll. The ringing of a distant clock grew more ominous with each passing second. Panicked, I glanced at the blank screen in the dollhouse game. A blue hand reached out, ready to capture and consume me.

"Key, key, key, key," I muttered.

The ringing grew deeper, the whispering insistent.

Dong...Dong...Wide, saucer-like eyes stared back at my own. Dong...

"Ahhaahahahahah." The blue doll cackled, its claws drawing close to my neck. "We could be together forever...together forever!"

"Gahhhh."

I jolted myself out of sleep.

"Oh my gawd. Still alive." My eyes adjusted to the dimly lit room.

"What...It's not even morning yet?" I reached around for my blanket. Nothing. I scrambled onto my feet and glanced around, spotting an aged sign that hung on ivy-covered walls. It read: "You have one hour. Don't touch the walls."

"Ooh-kay." I breathed out. "Once I get out of this, I'm never going to touch that computer game again."

I trudged down the warped hallway. My muffled footsteps echoed. Ivy curled against the wall, with its tendrils trailing onto the floor. I watched the vines hoping there would not be any dark, ghostly hands reaching out to drag me down into abysmal darkness.

Clunk. I bumped into an antiquated chair that adorned the hallway, pushing it against the wall. Sighing, the ivy curtain wrapped its vines around the chair and pulled it deep into its leafy depths.

I looked ahead. A pool of luminous blue light glowed in the distance. Around the pool stood thirteen marble statues. A figure of a young boy rested at the pool's center, ink streaming down his unblinking eyes.

"Miss, help me find my friend. I don't know...I don't..." a ghostly voice whispered.

I traced the path of ink that trickled from his pearl stone eyes. The ink spattered on a board at his feet, almost obscuring the words underneath: "Find the child's friend. You have 55 minutes left."

I've been playing too many of these games, I thought.

Avoiding the puddles of murky water, I entered the next room. Along the side wall was an image of a woman. One arm splayed at her side, the woman sat, tears streaming down her face, clutching her heart. Underneath the painting was the caption detailing me to end her misery by destroying the cause of her grief.

"Another riddle...how lovely." I sighed.

Upon further observation, I found that the painting's background included mermaids, the ocean, and a palace. *How do I end her misery?* My fingers trailed across the picture frame's golden surface, stroking the intricate shape of a knife carved into it. The knife jiggled a little. I raised my eyebrows and felt around the edges. I pushed my finger against its outline. A hollow clunk. It seemed there was a small space in between the knife and the back of the frame. Bending down, I inserted my fingernails into the cramped crevices and pried the knife from its frame of gold. It may have been a trick of the lighting, but the scales adorning the knife's hilt played the fluid pattern of the ocean waves.

"A knife and a woman with mermaids in mourning in the ocean," I recited, listing a tongue-twister of what I assumed were clues. "Now, there's a palace, so there must be a royal...perhaps a prince or princess will do?"

The mermaids in the painting had directed their gazes at me, staring with blank eyes from the canvas. I shivered and took the change in their position as an agreement with my deductions that the woman needed a prince. Discomfort crawled along my skin, making me glance back every step or two, but the mermaids' gazes didn't leave me until after I exited the room.

In the next room over, shifting and replacing items as I went, I arrived in front of a handsome sculpture so realistic that his chest seemed to rise and fall. All around the room lay various items and exquisite trinkets, and along the walls, painted windows depicted the image of the sea.

Hm...it was a prince after all, I thought, unsheathing the blade in my hands. *Sorry, but I have a request to fulfill, so please excuse me.*

I approached the statue, examining the best spot to stab him. His chest seemed to breathe again. Golden and turquoise hilt met crumbling stone as the silvery blade pierced through the his stone chest. Spurts of black ink spattered my shirt.

Click.

A door had opened somewhere. I scurried back into the mermaid room, trying not to touch the mysterious substance that stuck to my shirt. A staircase leading down into the painting's ocean awaited me back in the mermaid's room. Soft whispers and contented sighs floated out from the entrance. A subtle, salty breeze cleared the stuffy atmosphere. For a moment, I stared into the gaping abyss. A plaque at the top of the staircase read: "Do wander astray, lest you let your soul wander away." *What did that mean?* Before long, I had descended into the darkness.

Pitch black encased my surroundings. My footsteps echoes in the endless darkness. I kept going. A dim glimmer surfaced from the wall of black nothingness and freed me from the oppressing magnitude of my surroundings. Reaching toward that minuscule ray of light, I could barely make out the tip of my fingers: gray and unreal.

An empty warmth surrounded me, muffling the thumps of my heartbeat, and my thoughts became disjointed. One thought here, another thought there.

With those unreal fingers, I pushed toward the dim light, which convulsed and expanded, becoming more blinding with each second. Music tinkled in the background, and the laughter of merry children chilled the air. My vision returned in patches of pink and blue, and eventually, the colors evened out, returning my vision to being whole.

Another sign on my right read: "Great job. You made it out on time, but this is not the end. You still have 30 minutes."

Something about that sign irked me.

Who does it think it is to patronize me like that? I am well aware of my current-- Oh. Everything makes sense now. I am me. If I had spent any more time wandering in that tunnel, I would have lost myself to that emptiness. *To be arguing with a wooden sign. Am I still sane?*

Crunch.

I looked down. Shattered china littered the ground. Around the room, shelves filled with broken trinkets and torn stuffed animals adorned the wall. Music continued to play in the background, but there were no children in sight. I shivered, and goosebumps once again graced my skin.

"There are no such things as ghosts. There are no such things as ghosts," I chanted. "There are no such things as ghosts. No such things as ghosts. No such--eep."

"Mew."

A little black kitty brushed its tail around my leg and proceeded to rub its sleek frame against my leg.

"Oh...aha...ahahahahahah...it's just you. A cat." I reassured myself. "Well, it seems like there's nothing in here."

The cat followed me with its amber eyes, its ears perked up in interest. I was bothered, not because I don't like cats but because I felt that I might have to sacrifice the cat to the little boy statue. *If you look at me like that, it will make it hard for me to hand you over, you know?* I sighed and snuck a glance at it. It cocked its head in response. *Urghh. Darn this little kitty. Darn this stupid maze. This sucks.*

"If you follow me, you might end up dead, you know?"

Those amber cat eyes turned up to acknowledge me before they turned back to the hallway. The shadows were less menacing with the cat beside me, so I let it be. Eerie azure light brightened just enough for me to make out the shadowy outlines.

The shadows turned to face us, and the sight of their unwavering eyes unnerved me, sending trickles of cold down my spine. Warily watching the shadows dance along the stone bodies, we proceeded through the onslaught of icy, lifeless expressions. From the corner of my eye, I spied the cat looking up at me, but I looked ahead, determined not to meet with its gaze.

Sorry, kitty, but I guess it's bye-bye. Time for you to go with statue boy.

"Hey kitty," I said. "come here."

The cat just peered at my outstretched hand. Then, convulsions racked its slender body.

I observed in horror as it retched a damp mass of fur onto the palm of my hand. "What the heck? Gross!" It trailed a path of saliva across my hand.

"Aaahhh. Elizabeth!" Statue boy exclaimed. Ghastly cracks ran along his fingers and carved rivers down to his stone base. "Elizabeth." From those dark depths, the yellowing dome of a skull smashed through the stone, followed by twiggy arms with bits and pieces of foul matter clinging to it. Its jaws clacked open and shut as one milky eye lolled about in its wide socket. "Elizabeth. I sense you. I sense you!" it screamed.

It staggered toward me, its wicked odor burned the air between us. Groping the air blindly, but accurately, the statue boy approached me.

My limbs stiffened. My heart thrashed within my chest, and all my reason escaped the clutches of understanding. *There's a zombie before me, and I'm stuck. How lovely.*

Hiss. The kitty flashed out of sight. My limbs loosened. I followed pursuit, flinging the furball at the zombie boy.

"Ah?" The clacking sounds faded away to slower, more controlled beats. "Elizabeth? It's been a while…"

Hah? Did it catch the cat? I risked a glance back. My hands covered mouth. My eyes watered under the waft of malicious smells.

"Oh. It's been so long. I'm so glad. So glad…" Zombie boy's voice trembled above the hard clacking of teeth, and from the furball emerged a few tiny bones, glowing inside the shape of a transparent mouse. "Elizabeth," he whispered to the mouse. It scampered up his arms, and its squeals echoed across the chamber. They both withered away into sand and dust, along with all the other statues in the room.

In the piles of sand, silver key glinted. A note was attached to it: "Achievement unlocked."

Somewhere, a sharp but distant click broke the silence, notifying me that I was given permission to pass through an unlocked door.

"If that was the door...then this key is for something else?"

"Meow."

My eyes jerked up to meet the cat's steady gaze. It twirled and walked off to the left.

"Wait." Pocketing the key, I raced off after the cat. "Wait for me!"

The cat twitched its tail in front of a large oaken door. Its eyes seemed to glow brighter in the light dark, and above it hung a sign: "You have reached the end. Pass through the door to escape."

Yanking open the door, I rushed into the darkness with the sleek shadow of a cat by my side. My breathing grew ragged, and only the nudging of the cat could encourage my heavy legs to stumble forward. Darkness parted to reveal a dirt path under my feet. The nudging became more insistent as a crossroad crept closer under the fading fog.

Another sign. "You now have 5 minutes remaining. Go left, and you can escape. Go right, and you will be free."

To escape or to be free. Don't they imply the same thing?

"Meow." The cat circled around my legs, still energized even after such a long run. "Meow." Steadily, I was turned toward the right, away from the passage promising escape. It mewed even louder, as if it was trying to dispel my hesitation.

Tick. Tock. Tick. Tock.

Time counted down. I had two minutes left. Considering that it had helped me, what did I have to lose by trusting the cat?

"Okay." I swept up the cat and bolted.

Wistful lavender mist curled up from the path, and patches of dark green grass sprouted out in scattered patches. The mist blurred my vision, but I could make out flashes of trees and flowers. In my arms, the cat grew heavier and heavier as it squirmed out of my embrace and lept from my arms.

It landed somewhere behind me, but I needed to keep going forward, before time could run out. My legs gave out from under me.

The sky above was filled with towering trunks and shadowy evergreen leaves.

Strange laughter echoed off the trunks of the strange forest as light footfalls approached me, and the stranger swept me up onto my feet. *Urghhh.* Nausea lapped at my consciousness, and the whole world turned.

"Ahaha, a little unsteady are you?" He sounded oddly amused, but my ragged breathing prevented me from retorting. "It feels so good to be out here again." He pushed me away from him and chuckled. "Couldn't have escaped with my own power, so as my thanks to you, I shall give you passage home."

"Huh?"

The ground left me, and I felt myself falling back. A pair of glowing amber eyes and shiny teeth was all I could make of my converser, and curls of violet fog closed in on me. From below, light reflected onto the purple veil. It was only for a split second, but I sensed a membranous layer break away underneath me before I was sucked into a gelatinous body of water. It was almost blinding as I sunk deeper and deeper into the jelly.

"Wha--"

My back was suddenly attacked by the sensation of cold air. Next were my ears and the rest of my body after. In front of me was the reflection of my room, distorting and wavering until the ripples upon the mirror's surface had calmed down and stilled.

"Whu...What the heck..." For a moment it looked so malleable, but now my bedroom mirror was as firm as it had always been. Remembering the pocketed key, I pulled it out. *If I insert this into the mirror...*

"Azusa. Are you coming down for breakfast or what?" Chester called to me, impatience tinting his cheerful voice, "It's getting cold, you know?"

"Coming, brother."

With one last fleeting look at the mirror, I left to join my brother at the the dining table. A shadowed being watched me from behind the silver glass. Its hands reached out to touch the surface, which rippled like water before fogging up. It traced out a message, backwards so that it was readable from the real world, which said:

"Thank you for helping me, Azusa. I may not be able to join you in your world, but you hold the key to play in mine anytime you wish."

ON HIS COLORED FACE
Jennifer Chau

THINGS WERE SIMPLE AND easy in my early life. I had no care in the world for the things that happened around me. I didn't care which presidential candidate was campaigning, nor did I care about his values. Why would I have? I couldn't vote. I didn't care about the radical abolitionists striking raids in the North, but my father and my husband cared a whole lot. Both of our families were rich and owned slaves for as long as I could remember.

I was a woman named Alice Miller, born and raised on a plantation in Georgia since December 8, 1788. I cleaned the house, cooked three meals, and washed the men's clothes every day. Sometimes my husband would come home happy, and we'd embrace lovingly for the rest of the day. On other days, he scolded me and told me that I could never understand his business. I didn't expect things to change, but my life took a turn after I met a slave who changed my life.

I looked out from the porch of my home at a vast, green meadow. Songbirds chirped gaily, and a little apple tree grew in the corner of the yard. The grass extended outwards forever until it met the edge of town. On the other side of the house, the scorching sun whipped the swollen backs of slaves, who labored in the plantation until the sun set. Thousands of crops stood in line, waiting to be picked by a colored man's weary hands.

When my husband was away, Father often came over and sat in his chair, holding a leather whip and grimacing at the new slaves working in the fields. One in particular was a black man named Thomas. I knew him because whenever I got bored, I would sit out on the back porch where he would sometimes talk to me.

Before Thomas, I had never conversed with slaves. They always kept to themselves. I didn't mind Thomas's company though. He helped time pass on days where my husband went off for business. Thomas would stop in his work for a small break, lean his body against his shovel, and say something like, "Hot day, ain't it, Ma'am? Been out here all day picking this cotton. What've you been doing, eh?" Then I'd say, "Well, I've been cooking and washing the men's clothes."

Thomas saw me sitting by the porch, greeted me his usual way, and began telling me some stories. "Got a beautiful wife and newborn baby back home," he said, "and those darn white rascals took me away from them. It was only two days after she was born."

"How's your wife?" I asked, but in truth, I thought his stories were trivial and un-important. I figured, slaves are slaves, incapable of compassion or love, until he an-swered, "My wife would've been the most beautiful lady you'd ever seen, Ma'am. I remember our wedding as clear as yesterday," he said, closing his eyes. "We promised to be together forever." Thomas teared up, and his voice choked between his words. I knew he loved his wife and missed her.

"I got cuts and blisters from picking so much cotton. The master presses me to work harder than I can every day. I just want to be free," he said, looking off into the direction of town. "What's it like to matter, Ma'am? What's it like to do whatever you want?" he asked, turning to look at me again.

I looked at him with a mournful smile and said, "Doing whatever I want is... Well, I never thought about that, really, but now that I am... I don't think I know, Thomas." I looked at him. It was true. I never realized it, but he and I were more sim-ilar than we thought. "Being a woman in this kind of society," I told him, "I don't get much, either. I can't do anything without asking my husband first, but the truth is he often doesn't let me anyways. Nor does he let me say what I want to say."

"Well, what do you want to say?" Thomas asked.

"My opinions. There's a lot I have to say and a lot I want to advocate. Ideas build up when they've been bottled in for so long. Nonetheless, I do love my husband; don't you misunderstand me, now. I guess it's just the way things are that he doesn't want to listen to me."

Thomas looked at me and said, "I won't misunderstand you. There's a lot of things wrong in this world."

"Why don't you take a seat here on this bench with me, Thomas?" I asked, feel-ing empathy that I hadn't ever felt to him before.

"Thank you, Ma'am, but I can't," he said. "I'd be whipped if the master caught me."

"Nonsense! Neither my father nor my husband would do such a thing," I said.

After a few moments of hesitation, he sat down next to me.

We continued for half an hour talking about his wife back home. "She didn't want me to leave," he said, "so I promised I would return to her and our daughter someday. Someday, when I'm free."

He began to tear up again, and eventually had his entire head down to his lap, his hands covering his face. I stared at him, speechless. I didn't know what to say or do. I knew my family kept our slaves for decades. The chances of him becoming free were slim, and we both knew it.

When I looked up, I saw my father standing on the steps of the porch, hands on his hips with a cold, firm look on his face. "What do you think you're doing?" my father shouted. "Get away from my daughter, you damn negro!" He ran up the porch steps and pulled Thomas off the bench, shoving him to the ground.

"Father, what are you doing? He did nothing to me! Stop!" I shouted.

"You don't have to feel obligated to protect him, Alice. I won't let him hurt you again."

"He wasn't hurting me. He didn't do anything, stop!" I begged, but my father didn't listen to me. He never did.

With a hard foot, he stomped on Thomas and kicked his head against the dirt pathway of our home. I saw him kick Thomas so hard that clouds of dirt became the only thing I saw. For the first time ever, I ran out to my father and pushed him away. He only pushed me back harder. I fell backwards and landed on our porch steps.

"What are you doing, Alice?" He shouted, "Get out! This isn't your business!"

I laid there on the steps, watching him continually thrust Thomas around in the dirt, and I knew that was all I could do.

Tears, blood, dirt, and agony smeared on Thomas's colored face. His eyes met mine. He didn't say anything, but I saw him tell me something with his eyes. He was lost, confused, and so was I. We were wondering the same thing: Why did things have to be this way? What besides the color of his skin made him so hated by society?

"Don't worry, Alice," my father said, "He'll never come close to you again." Father smiled at me as if he were my savior. To him, however, it wasn't quite enough. He proceeded to take out his thin, leather whip.

I sat there, watching him strip away the life of this man, a man whose heart filled with love and compassion for his family. As I watched him, I thought back to them: his wife, his newborn daughter, and his promise to return to them, a promise I knew would be unfulfilled.

Since that day, I knew I wouldn't allow the cruel and evil nature of slavery to exist any longer. Thomas was never able to speak to me again, but I always kept the conversations we had in my head. I was a woman, but I didn't let that stop me. I knew that both my husband and my father would disapprove and scold me terribly if I let on about my vow to free all the slaves. So, I never told them.

Over the months, I stole chunks of money from my husband and hid them in my mattress. I was ashamed to have been reduced to a petty thief, but this was the only way I could get enough money to escape. That's exactly what I did, too. Once I had enough money, I snuck out in the middle of the night. For the first time in my entire life, I was free.

Thomas, who was outside nursing his wounds of the day, saw me. I offered to take him with me and he jumped at the chance. We got on the train headed North, posing as lady and slave. Going north wouldn't reunite him with his family immediately, but there were more advocates for women's rights and the abolishment of slavery up there.

With the help of Thomas, I fought for the lives of the victimized African American slaves. My voice would not be ignored, not like it was in the southern plantations.

On December 6, 1865, two days before my 77th birthday, slavery was abolished. Thomas had left my side a few years earlier to rejoin his family and I worried for him. However, now I could finally rest easy knowing that he would never be recaptured again.

The abolitionist movement had worked. Our voices had been heard. My vow had finally been accomplished. Knowing that I had spent my life had been spent on such a worthy cause, I could die in peace.

PICKING UP THE PIECES
Christina Nguyen

THE MOMENT SHE AWAKENS, the young girl finds two pairs of eyes staring straight at her.

"Look, she's awake!" a teenage boy pipes up, a smile on his lips as he reaches out to touch her.

She flinches away.

"Hey, don't scare her." A girl scolds, knocking the back of his head. Her lips are pulled back, eyebrows furrowed and voice hushed.

"Who are you?" the girl who just woke up asks, fingers clutching her sheets as her eyes scan each person. She doesn't know these people, or perhaps it was that she didn't remember them. She can't recall any aspects of her life, or any information about herself. She can't even remember her name or her appearance.

The two people who were previously arguing turn to look at her, a grins across their faces.

"I'm Estella," the female says and turns to her male companion. "And he's Clyne."

They don't seem shocked that she doesn't know them. In fact, they're exuding happiness at the fact that she seems to be interested enough to ask for their names. Dread pools in her stomach and she hesitantly asks the next question on her mind. "Then, who am I?"

"Well, that," Clyne says, a sheepish smile playing on his lips. His eyes dart towards Estella, who is urging him to speak. He looks at the girl on the bed. "We don't know who you are. We found you passed out on a flower bed. You didn't seem like you were injured, but you wouldn't wake up for days."

Estella adds, "Yes, we had to lift you up in order to feed you."

This doesn't brighten up the mood. The girl's lips tightened shut as she stares at the two in front of her. If they didn't know who she was, what was she supposed to do? How would she be able to recall her identity?

"Hey," Clyne says, breaking her from her thoughts, "until you find out who you are, why don't you join us? We can give you a name for now, if you really can't remember."

The girl contemplates the idea, eyeing them warily before averting her eyes towards her hands. She doesn't know anything about them. For all she knows, they may be cold-blooded killers out for their next prey. However, they would be able to provide her shelter and food. The girl figures there isn't any harm in accepting their proposal. She would rather die in their hands than die of starvation. "Okay," she says, answer curt. It's enough to bring the smile back onto their lips.

"Great!" Estella exclaims, clapping her hands together. "What do you want to be called?"

"We can help you pick out a name if you can't think of anything," Clyne adds, leaning forward in his chair placed next to her bed.

The girls mulls over the possible names in her mind. Minutes pass before she finally comes up with a name she likes. "Yuy, call me Yuy."

She hears a deep grumble of, "Of course she picks a hard name," before Estella elbows Clyne in the side. He jumps out of his seat with a loud squeal. Estella watches in amusement as he falls down before facing her. "Yuy, is it? Welcome to our guild, Neo Moon."

"Wait." It takes her seconds to process the information before she protests. "I didn't agree to join any guild. I thought I would only be staying here."

"It's not that simple," Clyne piques up, reaching out for his seat. He pulls himself up, plopping down on the chair once again, though more cautious towards the girl sitting beside him. "Once you walk in, you're immediately a part of the guild."

Yuy's eyebrows furrow in confusion. "I didn't even walk in here by myself, I was dragged here by you two. I wasn't even allowed to make my own decision!" she wails.

"Too late," Clyne sings. "You're part of the guild now." He bounces on his chair, edging closer until his knees knock against the side of the bed.

"Can I quit?" Yuy asks, tone wary. Having just woken up, she knows absolutely nothing. How is she supposed to handle a guild?

"The only way you can leave is by death. Guilds are important in this world, basically a family. If you leave, you die," Estella hums, voice grave.

Yuy sighs, resigning to her fate and allowing them to tug her out of the bed in order to meet the rest of the guild members. The guide is warm and welcoming. Many walk by, ruffling her hair and patting her back to welcome her. Laughter resounds throughout the building. They go through the basics of the guild, giving her a guild tattoo, and showing her around the house. Her dirtied white dress is replaced with a black shirt and pants, new sneakers on her feet. By the time she looks in the mirror, Yuy is a completely new person.

After the first week of the guild passes, Yuy begins her training. She's appointed a swordsman. Holding a sword in her hands feel familiar, as if she's been a swordsman her whole life. The movements taught come to her easily. She wants to believe it's because she's a natural, but Yuy knows, somewhere in the back of her mind, that her past is tangled with swordsmanship and fighting.

Suy spends most days holed up in the training room, hacking away at the dummies provided by the guild. The sword is always heavy in her hands, yet it moves easily and precisely with her actions. Sometimes, it sparks disjointed memories from before. Her mind always throbs before she can make sense of the image. It's like her mind purposely represses the memories trying to spill out and uncover the truth. When that happens, she takes a break from training. She either stays in her room and waits for her headache to ease away or spends the time with the other guild members, strengthening their bonds with every second.

Months passes before her tutor tells her she's good enough to go out on quests and train on her own. She wishes she could feel the swell of pride in her chest, but all she feels is her gut sinking, warning her that being here, doing what she's doing, is going to bring nothing but more violence.

She forms a small group with Estella and Clyne, accompanying the two on their journeys. Their bond and teamwork grows stronger with each quest, with each shared victory. Yuy relearns how to love.

She watches fondly as Estella stomps on Clyne in the common room. Clyne begs for her to relent and for his life to be spared. The guild that was unfamiliar has become family and now life without Neo Moon would be unnatural.

"Alright, alright, break it up." Yuy laughs, approaching Estella and Clyne.

Estella is still pouting, but she moves her feet off of Clyne's body.

Clyne cries out with glee as he rolls away from her, shouting in victory as if he himself had escaped from Estella on his own.

"Yuy is my bodyguard. Anything you want to say to me has to go through her." Clyne snickers, sliding behind the said girl for protection.

Yuy snorts, elbowing Clyne who then crouches down in pain. "Don't make me throw you towards Estella again, idiot." However, when she catches his eyes begging for mercy, she relents, patting his head to show that she wasn't going to do that anytime soon.

"He ate my pastry even though it had my name on it. Make him buy me a cheesecake," Estella whines, the usually composed girl breaking down to a childish fit.

"Clyne, go buy her a cheesecake," Yuy orders. Before he can retort, she adds in, "It's your fault for eating it without her permission."

Clyne gives a sigh of defeat and heads out of the guild building. Estella skips behind him with a smile on her face.

Yuy follows them, but stops and leans against the entrance to watch Clyne and Estella bickering as they make their way to the shop. Too engrossed in watching over her companions, she fails to notice a pair of eyes staring directly at her.

A man draped in white robes walks out of the shadows, approaching her with a look of disappointment and anger. The man brushes his blonde bangs aside, revealing a small tattoo on the side of his face. "You'll pay for going against Dragon Dust, Sei."

Yuy recognizes the tattoo. Her mind flashes back. Her stomach tightens. It's him.

The man nods. "Now, you remember." He pulls out a sword, which glimmers in the sunlight. "Now, you will die."

She reaches for her sword and widens her stance. "Not this time."

REMEMBERING
Emily Plasencia

Chapter 1

DEAD SILENCE GREETED ME as I awoke. My head throbbed with pain. Soggy, damp air filled my nose and murkiness blocked my vision. The darkness faded. Tall walls covered with overgrown vines formed a narrow passageway. *Where am I? Who am I?* A harsh gasp escaped my throat, and my hand clutched a long deep cut along my side. *What happened to me?* My long brown hair plastered against my hot forehead. *Come on, think! There must be something I can remember.* An image flashed in my mind. It was of my little brother, his eyes widened in terror and his clothes torn, covered in blood, staring at me. My legs trembled.

Ignoring the mind-numbing agony, I staggered around, using the walls as a guide. My hand brushed upon a flat metal object: a sign. I looked at its old faded text. "Don't touch the walls, you only have an hour." My eyes widened and terror overwhelmed me. I drew back my hands and ran. The walls trapped me within the repetitive passageways. A maze.

I stopped to catch my breath in the middle of a large, open space. The moonlight faded away into darkness, and I heard a distant moan. A chill ran down my spine. The moon shone on the maze again. I was not alone.

I turned around only to be met with a dead, decaying face. His bloodshot eyes sunk deep inside his skull. His pale, white skin and rotten flesh clung to his scalp. I scrambled away as far as I could before I tripped over a vine. I raised my head, only to be met with more rotten corpses chasing me. I scurried away until my back hit the brick wall. Trapped. I covered my eyes. *Please wake up. Wake up. Wake up.*

"Why are you running?" a voice called out.

I trembled as I opened my eyes. The corpse was talking to me. I stared at it, confused.

"My, you look like you saw a human being, honey." He chuckled.

"I told you she would do it again," muttered another voice.

A small figure emerged from the shadows. My brother, Austin. His wide blue eyes stared back at me. His clothes were torn and soaked in dried blood, just like in my flashback.

"Dad, how many times do we have to tell her not to try to go back to the world of the living?" he asked.

Dad? I gasped. *That's right, the maze, my second chance to regain my life.*

"Your older sister is just going through a phase," my dad reassured, interrupting my thoughts. "She had one chance to escape the maze and regain her life, like the rest of us did, but she touched the walls and couldn't make it." he continued.

"Poor thing."

I jumped at the new voice and turned to a woman with long tangled hair. My mother. Her dead eyes bore into me.

"She still believes that she can still make it to the living world, but whenever she tries, she ends up losing her memory and wakes up at the same place over and over again," she continued.

Ignoring my dead family, I limped passed them toward the maze to try again.

"Carla, wait." Austin shouted.

I ignored his cries and broke into a sprint back through the maze.

Chapter 2

LEAVES CRACKLED UNDER MY feet as time passed. My pace slowed, I grew dizzy, and my legs screeched with pain. My eyes were heavy. I trotted aimlessly through the paths. *Come on, Carla… stay awake…* Everything around me turned black. The silence was deafening.

I awoke with a start. The throbbing in my head increased the thundering sounds of my beating heart. I blinked, sitting up. *Who am I?*

No. I closed my eyes tight. *Come on, Come on!* I thought to myself. *I need to remember!* I stood up and observed my surroundings. There was nothing but walls with tangled vines. Anger and frustration arose within. I broke into a run. A sharp pain in my chest made me double over and fall. Gasping for air, I reached up to the wall and glimpsed at the faded sign. My memory returned. I pulled back my hand in disgust and shrugged down in defeat. The moonlight faded to black, and then returned once again. I looked up. My family stood in front of me, dead. They died a long time ago, and yet here they were, standing in front of me.

"Given up yet?" Austin asked.

"No," I replied.

My father stepped in. "Come on Carla, you need to stop. You had one chance. All of us did. You have to face reality. The living is no longer for you."

I shoved my way through them and headed for the maze to try again. *Nothing is going to stop me.* My mother stepped in my way, staring at me with a blank gaze. She was not going to let me go.

"Carla, you can't go on living like this!" she protested.

"You are right, I'm already dead," I retorted.

"Carla. You can't speak to your mother like that," my father scolded.

"Oh, so you are the responsible father now. Where were you when I needed you the most?" I demanded.

My father frowned and turned away without a word. I looked back at my mother. She stood staring at me with her expressionless face, until she sighed and stepped aside to let me pass.

"Thank you," I said.

The maze walls began to shift, metal rubbed against metal. I broke into another run. The maze was beginning to close for the morning. I ran faster, trying to reach the end before it closed. I was inches away. The gap was narrowing. I reached out, but the walls closed shut. I pounded the obstacle with anger.

"I need to go back!" I shouted at the walls. I groaned. The maze wasn't going to open until evening. The moon was replaced by the sun. I closed my eyes and sighed before letting myself slip onto the ground in defeat.

I stood up and walked passed my family. I did not dare to look at them. The maze's center was at least half the size of a football field. I walked until I reached my corner. The vines were torn off the walls and several marks were drawn on the bricks. Collapsing in exhaustion, I fingered the dirt and added the 20th mark on the wall. I huddled against the wall with my back facing my family. Hugging my knees, I drifted off to asleep.

Tomorrow for sure, this time. I'll be able to return. The maze won't hold me forever. I recalled the first time I came into the maze. I was just 16, an orphan living in the world alone. I watched my family die one by one. *How did I die?* That was the question, but I didn't care... my mind turned blank. A soothing wind swept my face, *Cons,* my conscience.

Carla? The faded voice echoed through my ears.

Yeah? I responded.

Are you ready to go? it asked, its melodic whisper sent chills down my spine.

No.

Why?

Because I need to go back.

Go back? Go back for what? Cons persisted.

I still don't know yet. I just need to go back. I answered.

Carla, you need to let go, you are dead.

Don't say that, I still have an hour.

Time has already run out Carla.

Just leave me alone, Cons.

Carla...

What?

Remember?

When I awoke, the birds were still singing. The clear blue sky shone high above me. I sat up, confused. The old apple tree that grew on my house's front yard stood beside me.

"Carla, get up. We're going to be late for school!" shouted Austin, running down the house's porch steps. He no longer wore his blood-stained clothes.

I stared, speechless.

The house changed into an elementary school right before my eyes. Austin ran toward it. Before entering the open doors, he turned around and waved excitedly.

"Bye, Carla. I'll see you at home after school. Mommy and daddy are finally letting me go walking home, all by myself," he boasted.

After going through the doors, Austin and his school disappeared. The strong winds and dark clouds indicated that it was late evening. I stood in the living room. My parents sat on the couch. My mother held the phone with trembling fingers.

"No, he wouldn't run away. He was supposed to come home at 2:30, after school. Today was his fifth day walking home..."

Once again the scenery changed. My living room disappeared. From my bedroom window, I watched a crowd of policemen hoisting a small child-like figure out of the sewers. I heard my mother's wail as the paramedics tried to calm her down. The officers covered the bloodied body with a white bed sheet, shaking their heads.

Austin...

I felt faint. The ground beneath me started to spin. I caught glimpses of a small girl, an axe, a dark figure coming closer and closer. My vision and feet gave away as the world spun faster and faster. Voices echoed against my ear.

Don't do it....
Help me!
ZOE!
A scream escaped my throat, "No!"
Everything turned black.

Chapter 3

I SAT UP SCREAMING, the voices echoed against my eardrums. The familiar scenery of the maze's 10-foot walls welcomed me back to my true home. I heard the maze's door open. For a moment, I looked at it. I turned away as I paced through the center. "Mom? Dad? Austin?" I called. No one. I turned my attention to the maze's opening. "I'm going in."

I entered the dark passageways. As I walked, my memory flooded with what happened on that night when I was alive. Austin was supposed to come home, but he never did. A month passed before they finally found him, dead in the sewers. His eyes were wide and frozen. A lump formed in my throat, the maze began to fade to black. My uneven steps grew slower and slower. Everything turned dark and silent.

Who am I? The question ran through my mind as I stood up. I groaned at the sharp pain from the deep long cut on the side of my chest. Closing my eyes tight, questions ran through my mind. *Where am I? What is this? A garden?* I began to walk, cringing with every step. The walls looked menacing with the overly grown vines. They formed dark passageways with only the moonlight to light the paths. I continued to walk until another pain forced me to brace onto the walls. My head brushed upon a flat metal. Wincing, I looked upon it. It was a sign.

"You have one hour. Do not touch the walls." I read aloud.

The last five words echoed through my ears, *do not touch the walls.*

I gave out a gasp in terror and pulled myself from the walls. A gust of wind brushed my face as my memory returned.

I moaned, "Oh, Come on!"

My feet pounded the ground as I walked in despair, waiting for the same routine: Darkness, moonlight, going back into the maze.

However, this time was different. My legs trembled, my vision grew blurry, and I felt a weight drop on my shoulders, making me crawl on my hands and feet. My breathing slowed as the darkness surrounded me. Silence.

Carla!

I jumped back in surprise.

"What?" I questioned. The walls seemed to have grown taller. The vines fought through the bricks.

Carla... The voice whined.

That voice...

"Wait a minute. Cons is that you?"

Yes...

"But I am awake, Cons why are you speaking to me?"

May I remind you that I am your "Cons"cience?

"I know that, but you only speak to me in my dreams."

How do you know that you are not dreaming now?

I paused for a moment. "Wait, are you telling me that I am dreaming?"

Yes...

133

"But-"

Shhh... Carla, you have to stop fighting me. Cons commanded.

"Fighting?"

Carla, you must remember... he whispered.

"Remember what?" I asked, irritated.

Remember... Your father, your mother, your little brother Austin. When they were alive. You were so happy...

"Stop that," I said.

Cons' faded melodic tone turned to an angry rasp. *No! I tried to get to you all this time after you died.*

"Leave me alone Cons! I don't even know how I died."

Not yet, but first you must remember the others. Your family. He said with sorrow, switching back to his earlier faded tone.

I covered my ears. "No, I don't want to."

Then why do you wish to return?

"Because-"

Because what?

"Just because!" I shouted in anger, yet Cons' voice continued in a melodic rhythm *Carla... you were only 14 when Austin died. Your mother was so devastated. She mourned for him. She claimed that he was still alive...*

"Cons, I said I don't want to remember." I snapped. "Besides, I already know how she died, everyone knows how they died," I paused, thinking. "Everyone ... except me. Cons, just leave me alone. I need to go back into the maze and complete it, I need to go back to the living." I said, closing my eyes. Silence.

"Cons?"

I gasped as the air returned back to me. I sat up. The center.

"Carla?"

"Cons, leave me alone!" I shouted, only to see that the voice came from Austin. He was confused and hurt.

"My name is Austin," he said, playing with his fingers.

I gave out a sigh. I apologized, got up and walked past him toward the maze.

"Why do you have to keep doing that?" he shouted, anger in his voice.

I stopped on my trails. I flashed him an angry look before asking. "Doing what?" He cowered at my stare.

"Going back into the maze, to try again," he said.

"Because I need to go back," I responded.

He looked up, his eyes glistened with curiosity, "But why?"

I gave out a sigh. "I don't know, but I feel that something wants me to go back."

Looking away, I started for the maze again. The dead grass crunched beneath my footsteps.

"I also felt that when I came here," Austin muttered.

I stopped and looked at him. "What?"

Austin looked at the ground, hesitating before giving me an answer. "After I was killed by the man, I went through the maze but I didn't see the sign until my hour was up. After that, I was here all alone with no one… and no matter how hard I tried I couldn't help but feel that I needed to go back and try again… but I never went back into the maze because I was afraid that something bad would happen."

I stood, listening. "Do you still have that feeling?"

"No, not anymore."

His words repeated in my mind. *After I was killed by the man…I went through the maze… I couldn't help but feel that I needed to go back…*

"Wait, Austin, do you remember who killed you?"

"No."

"But you said 'the man'."

"Yes, the man who killed me was a stranger, don't you remember? Mom and Dad let me go walking but I was kidnapped and killed by the man--"

"Yes," I interrupted, "and your body was found in the sewers. Mom was so devastated."

Austin looked up. "How come you guys never told me that?" he asked.

"You didn't know that?"

"No I didn't. All I remember was that I was walking home when a white van pulled up beside me. A man promised me a toy helicopter then he took me into the forest. I cried because I wanted to go back home then he stabbed me and… and… then I was sent to the maze." He paused. "You guys found me in the sewers?" he asked, pain and distraught in his voice.

I couldn't answer his question. Heavy silence overcame us. Loud metal walls rubbed against each other. I gave out a loud gasp, and rushed towards the maze's closing walls.

"Carla, wait! You are never going to make it!" Austin screamed.

I closed my eyes, ignoring his warning. I ran with all my might until the shadow of the maze swallowed me. *Slam!* I breathed hard as I opened my eyes. I made it. Though the sun's ray illuminated the maze, the walls remained dark and the basil-green vines consumed the bricks, long thorns fought and twisted.

In the newly lightened maze, my painful groan echoed against the walls. A splitting headache overtook my body and I dropped to my knees, wincing. With one last breath, I collapsed.

Cons' faded voice echoed through my ears. I plunged into darkness.

Remember…?

Chapter 4

A BOWL OF CEREAL sat on the table in front of me. I forced the soggy breakfast down my throat as my mother paced around. Her tangled hair laid undone and her bathrobe and nightgown clung to her frail body. I looked away and stared at the empty table seat where Austin once sat digging through the cereal box for the prize. A lump formed in my throat. The scene faded away.

I stood watching through my bedroom window. Outside in my front yard, police, paramedics, and crying parents surrounded my mother.

My father tried in vain to defend her. "She didn't do it!"

"We have proof, Mr. Bacia." said one of the policemen. Behind him were three boys around Austin's age. Each one crying and clutching onto their parents.

"She stole my child!" one of the parents screamed.

My mother stood in silence. Her eyes had dark circles around them and her long brown hair laid tangled. She looked dead.

"Your wife kidnapped these boys." The policeman continued.

"Please, I assure you, she is just going through a phase. She is still recovering from our son's death."

"Sir, it has been already a year since that happened. Your wife's condition is serious. She needs to be sent to the hospital."

As he said this, a group of paramedics grabbed my mother's frail skinny arms and forced her into the ambulance. Her eyes grew wide in terror.

"No! I can't go now. I have two children, they need me!" She screamed. "Austin! Austin!" She called. "Come here sweetheart! Show them that you are alive! Show them that you need me!" She screamed as she kicked and waved her hands.

My father tried to get to her, but the police held him back. My mother's piercing scream echoed through my bedroom walls. I watched them shove her into the ambulance. Her eyes wandered to my window.

"Carla! Carla!" She cried before they shut the doors.

Darkness.

Everything lightened up with a dull gray. My father was on the phone. I sat on the living room couch, fingering the detailed stitches from one of our homemade couch pillows. *Sewn with motherly love*, it stated, a red heart surrounding the dainty lettering.

"What do you mean, my wife's case is classified?" my father asked angrily. He slammed the phone down. Without looking at me he stomped through the living room and went outside, slamming the door behind him.

Making sure that he was gone, I pulled out a newspaper from underneath the couch pillow. It's headlines stated in bold, ***Screaming at Mental Hospital finally silenced: Locals relieved but petrified.*** Tears glistened in my eyes, I looked out the window to seek comfort. A dark eerie figure across the street caught my eye. Pain overcame me, I closed my eyes. The world began to spin. Voices rasped and whispered in my eardrums. I opened my eyes and images flashed: the entrance to the forest, the full moon, a small girl crying, and police sirens that flashed but gave no wail. I groaned as I felt myself collapse onto my knees. Voices.

I know who you are. I won't let you kill her.

I gave out a loud painful scream. The world turned black. I sat up screaming and grasping the dead grass beneath me. Walls with tangled vines stood at it's normal height. The sound of my uneven breathing echoed against the lonesome barriers.

"Zoe!" I shouted. I swallowed the lump in my throat. Silence. My rapid breathing slowed to a stop. Anger boiled inside of me. I stood up shouting, "Cons. I said that I did not want to remember!" My voice echoed against the passageways. A humming sound buzzed in response. The humming turned to a howl. A strong gush of wind pushed me down.

Carla…

I got up on my feet. "Cons?"

Carla… he whined. A breeze swept my hair. I turned away.

"I'm dreaming again, aren't I?"

Yes.

"Please Cons, I told you once before, I already know how my family died and I don't care. I'm going back." I said. "Neither you nor my family or some sign is going to stop me."

Your family is not here. He said.

I stopped. "What?"

Carla, they left the maze a long time ago…

I shook my head, "No. That can't be possible. They talk to me."

You don't remember…

"Remember?"

When you first came and failed, you completed the family. Without you, it wasn't complete. Your whole family waited for you and at last you came. They were ready to pass onto the other side, but you refused to go with them…

Parts of my memory came whirling back. The first time I arrived… when I failed and got sent to the center, I found my dead family. They were so happy. *"Carla come with us,"* they pleaded. But I said no. There was a light. I remember how their wounds disappeared. Austin looked at me with sad eyes. *Bye Carla…* I closed my eyes, shaking the memory away.

"No. no. They are still at the center."

Carla please, stop fighting me. You think they are there, but they're not. Remember Carla, remember.

"No…" I shook my head. "No!" I shouted. Covering my ears, I ran. The walls turned white and the ground rumbled. My eyes widened, the walls multiplied in height. They skyrocketed, covering the moon. "No!" I screamed. The ground cracked.

Remember.

I fell on my back, hitting the wall. "Why are you doing this?" I asked.

You need to remember, Carla. This is for your own good.

My breathing increased. The walls coiled around me. Tall broken mirrors replaced the vine covered walls. Faded glass locked onto my eyes and I couldn't look away. *Dad…*

Chapter 5

WITHIN THE BROKEN MIRRORS, I watched how my father sat at a bar in a drunken stupor. His bloodshot eyes watched other men laugh and rejoice. My breathing relaxed.

Do you remember how your father died? echoed Cons's voice.

I closed my eyes, "Yes, he suffered from a heart-attack, he was sent to the hospital and the doctors put him to sleep."

Cons turned silent. *What was the cause of his heart- attack, Carla?* he asked.

Reopening my eyes, I watched the mirror. My father was on the floor. People swarmed while an officer called 911. I sighed "From drinking too much."

The mirror cracked.

It wasn't from the drinks, Carla.

My eyes widened, a flashback of the dark figured man. I gasped and resisted. Cons continued to speak.

Your father suffered from the death of Austin and your mother. He left you alone but, believe it or not, he cared about you. He was going to move on when he found out that you weren't home… you were kidnapped.

"Cons stop." I protested.

You always took nightly walks until you went missing and was never found… he sang sorrowfully. I covered my ears shaking my head violently, refusing to listen.

"Stop!"

You have to remember. he whispered.

"No! I don't want to."

You must.

"I can't." I breathed heavily.

Just remember…

"No!"

The forest… the little girl, Zoe.

"I am not listening!"

There was an axe left on a stump…

My breathing increased. I opened my eyes and a gasp escaped my throat, the maze changed around me.

Remember…

Chapter 6

A RUSH OF WIND went through me. I heard the sound of my own heavy breathing as my heart pounded violently against my rib cage. I was in the forest.

"Don't do it."

I turned around, "What?" In shock, I saw a replica of myself. A mirror? No. The moonlight reflected the fear on her face. I breathed, *that can't be me.*

"Why shouldn't I?"

I jumped at the new voice. I turned back and saw a darkly dressed man, holding onto a terrified little girl's hand.

"Just leave her alone and there will be no trouble."

I turned once again to face myself. They neither saw nor heard me. I watched myself, my eyes filled with fear and determination. I watched how I edged closer to a stump with an axe stuck to it.

"There will be no trouble, huh?" scoffed the man. He narrowed his eyes, knowing what I was about to do. The little girl he held whimpered, her long straight black hair covered her green eyes.

That girl...

I felt myself become one with my past, reenacting that one fateful night.

The man laughed and held the small girl tighter. "I knew you'd come back for her. You are a fool, just like your brother." he said. As he said this, he took a few steps closer. Zoe whimpered.

"I know who you are," I said.

"Do you now?" He smiled showing rows of rotten teeth.

"Yes...and I am not going to let you kill Zoe like you killed Austin." I said.

"I have no idea what you are talking about" he replied.

I lunged for the axe. The man lunged as well, grabbing a hold of me. I pulled out the axe and swung it into his arm. He yelped in pain, letting go of both me and Zoe. I got up and grabbed Zoe. Holding her tight, I ran to get her to safety, but the man, despite his injured arm, grabbed my leg. I lost balance and fell onto the ground. Zoe screamed. I turned on my back, trying to free myself from the man's tight grip. Using his free hand, he pulled out the axe from his arm and raised it high above his head. His face filled with feelings of pain, anger and a strong hatred toward me. I remembered the deep hole he made to bury our bodies. I kicked his face, making him flail backwards in pain. He missed me with the axe. I spotted the hole a few inches away from him and used all of my strength to drag him into it. He was too heavy.

"Zoe help me!" I cried out.

Zoe, being only a little girl, didn't know how. I grunted and managed to push the man into the hole, but he refused to let go of my legs. I screamed as I felt myself falling into the hole with him,

"Zoe!" I screamed.

Zoe overcame her fear and reached for my hands. She stopped, her eyes wide with terror. The axe came crashing down into the side of my chest. She screamed. I winced, my hands clawing the slimy mud.

"Zoe!" I screamed.

My last remaining word echoed as I felt myself plunge into the hole. I felt the pure darkness embrace me and watched as though time moved slowly. The sounds became more muffled. I watched faintly how the red lights of the police sirens flashed in the distance. Zoe cried in terror. I saw her parents running toward her. Her father picked her up, but she wasn't comforted. Her parents didn't notice my dead corpse.

I watched how she screamed. Tears streamed down her face as she tried to reach out to me. Then, everything faded to black. I heard my decreasing heart-beat thump as time slowly returned back to normal. My eyes opened wide as I gasped for air.

"Zoe!" My hands reached out for her, but she was no longer there.

Swallowing the lump in my throat, my eyes adjusted to my family's faces. They stood over me, worried. I pushed myself off the ground and began to relax. I remembered everything. I looked at them and gave them a weak smile. Trembling, I used the rest of my strength to stand up.

Austin was the first to come close to me. "Carla? Are you going to try again?" he asked. His pale blue eyes glistened and his innocent voice quivered. His stare locked onto mine.

I ruffled his golden hair and shook my head. "No Austin, not anymore."

His eyes widened, a new spark of happiness rose from his face.

Turning to my parents, my forced weak smile turned to a small frown. I stared at the ground ashamed. "I'm sorry for trying so hard to escape. I've learned that it is best that I accept my death..." My eyes began to water, recalling what had happened. "I just want to say that, I am sorry for treating you guys so badly, I-I'm sorry for talking back, I'm sorry that I couldn't help you guys when we were all a-al-alive." My voice cracked and I could no longer continue. Tears streamed down my pale face.

I broke into a sob. My body shook from the tears. My family came together and gave me a welcoming hug.

"It's okay, Carla. The important thing is that you did the right thing. You could have saved your own life, but you gave it up for Zoe. We are so proud of you," my mother said.

I sniffled, comforted by her gentle words. I closed my eyes and returned the hug. My tears dried. I no longer felt their presence. I reopened my eyes to no one.

That's right, they are not here.

A soothing cool breeze swept my hair. *Cons.* "Thank you, Cons." I said.

Are you ready to go? he asked in a whisper.

I smiled, "Yes."

Cons turned silent.

"Carla, are you ready to come with us?"

Austin's voice startled me. I turned around. My mouth curled to a smile. His clothes glowed. The blood stains were gone. His frightened eyes glistened with the innocence and purity that he had when he was alive. Another figure came close. My mother. Her eyes, once dead and empty, now were beacons of liveliness. Her hair was straight and her white blue-stained clothes had become a beautiful white gown. My father, who stood behind me, put his hand on my shoulder. I turned to see his magnificent changes. His eyes were no longer sunk into his skull. They shone with that same heavenly glow. He looked like the father and husband that cared for us when we were alive. I looked at them for a moment, afraid and hesitant. *This is it.* I took in a deep breath and smiled.

"Yes, I'm ready."

The soothing breeze swept around me. A rush of color flood into my face. My hands were cleaned and the wound on my chest closed up.

The maze's center broke away. The walls collapsed as the vines withered and died. A blinding light shimmered against my face. A strong gust of wind blew as the walls revealed another world. There were clouds instead of walls and open space filled with animals and plants instead of narrow, insect-infested passageways.

Austin took my hand and lead me into the light. "Welcome home, Carla."

TAKING BABY STEPS
Tuyet Duong

MILLIONS OF PICTURES FLASHED through Celia's mind: her birth, her first steps and her parent's proud excitement, her first bike ride and the scrape that followed, her first day of school, her best friend Tonia, her appointment as captain of the basketball team, and much more. It was like watching a sped up film, only it was about her.

When one neared death, the mind could replay every single memory ever made since birth. Was that what was happening? Was she close to death? Darkness enveloped her, pushing her down. She fell. In front of her, another memory surged forward.

She had been waiting in the car for her brother to come out. Her fingers drummed on the steering wheel, eyes darting between the road and the house.

The sound of skidding and screeching made her whirl around in her seat. Bright lights blinded her. She didn't have enough time to react. The other vehicle slammed into her side of the car, crushing her in. Soon after, she could only hear the distorted shouts for help and the wail of sirens in the distance.

The memory ended and Celia was on the brink of consciousness. She tried to open her eyes, but an invisible forced them shut. She heard parts of muffled conversations.

"Could have died."

"No chance of walking ever again."

"Career over."

"He shouldn't have been drinking and driving."

An unknown amount of time passed before Celia woke again. She pried her eyes open and struggled to prop herself up. She looked around the room. White.

It represented what she felt.

Emptiness.

A lifeless, emotionless void.

She shivered, remembering the snippets she had heard when she had been drifting in and out of consciousness.

She attempted to swing her leg over the bed. She couldn't. She tried again. "Come on," she muttered to herself. She glared down at her leg, commanding it to move. It wouldn't. It stayed there. Still. Limp. Motionless.

Her emotional dam was breached, tears streamed from her eyes. Her emotions, reviving one by one, flooded in. She grabbed the vase of artificial orange tulips on her bedside table and threw it against the wall, screaming.

Never in her entire life had she felt so weak. Never had she felt so useless. So vulnerable.

The tears continued to flow down her cheeks. Her entire body trembled. She buried her head into her pillow and screamed. Breathing became harder and harder as the pillow became more tear-soaked, so she released it and looked up, still crying.

Thousands of question raced through her mind, but one stood out the most. What did she ever do to deserve this fate? She had never hurt anyone. She never lied, never drank, never partied, never caused trouble.

She defined perfection.

Or, at least she did.

Captain of the basketball team, perfect attendance, 4.0 GPA, valedictorian. She was everybody's role model. Now, it was all over. All because someone decided to get behind the wheel, intoxicated.

She wrapped her arms around her body and closed her eyes. The tears had slowed, but continued to stream down her face. Each tear was another one of her accomplishments slipping away from her. Everything she had ever worked for, everything she has ever dreamed of, gone. In just a snap of a finger.

Celia returned home. Her mother helped her through the front door, which closed behind her, trapping her. People crowded around her all day, eyes full of pity.

The wheelchair that imprisoned her stole her smile. She was numb, apathetic. Her life was over before it could even begin. Everything she had dreamed about was gone.

"Celia, do you need anything?" her mother asked.

Celia faced her mother with dead eyes. "My legs."

Her mother looked away, tears building in her eyes. She shook her head. "I'm sorry, Celia."

"Don't," Celia muttered. She faced the window, looking beyond the vast road; a road that she could never take again.

"It may seem like it, but your life isn't over yet. You can still do so much more. Even without your legs." Her mother turned back and gave Celia a sad smile before walking away.

"My life's already over," Celia muttered.

Another face popped into her room.

Her best friend Tonia strolled in, a big grin pasted on her face, as usual. For a moment, everything seemed right in the world. Celia felt like, if Tonia could still smile, things couldn't be that bad. Then, reality reasserted itself. The faint smile that had made its way onto Celia's face faded.

"What are you doing here?"

"I bought donuts." Tonia held up a box and opened it, revealing a dozen different donuts. "Thought they might cheer you up for a while."

Celia's smile didn't reach her eyes. "For a short while, maybe."

Tonia smiled and walked over to her, handing Celia her usual: a glazed donut with red and blue sprinkles. "Want to talk about it?"

Celia shook her head and bit into the donut. "What's there to talk about? Everything's over. My career, my dream, my life. It's all over, Tonia."

"You know, the day my brother had his legs amputated, he felt the same thing," Tonia said.

"He got those fake legs. He's good now."

"Yeah, but it took him a while. The process wasn't easy either." Tonia sighed and looked at Celia. "It's the same for you. It might seem like the end of the world right now, but it's just an option. Whether you turn it into a reality is your choice."

"Tonia, I can never play basketball again. That was my life. Without it, I'm nothing." For the umpteenth time that day, Celia felt tears building.

Tonia placed her hand on top of Celia's. "No, you're not. You can move past that. There are so many people out there in your same condition, but they've made the best of it. Don't use this as an excuse to lose your life. Use it as motivation to continue it."

"Do you really think I can move past this?" Celia asked.

Tonia nodded. "I'm positive you will."

Celia laughed. A few tears ran loose. "Thank you for that."

Tonia kissed her forehead and wrapped her arms around her. "I'm here for you. Remember that."

Celia returned the hug. A few tears escaped her eyes and soaked into Tonia's shirt. Celia pulled away and wiped her face with her sleeve. Tonia's words repeated in her mind. She sighed. "You're right. I can't use this as an excuse. I can only use it as motivation."

She wasn't alright now. Of course not. One conversation couldn't complete turn her life around. However, she wouldn't sulk anymore. She would work hard towards recovery, one baby step at a time.

TO THIS DAY, I CANNOT SLEEP ALONE
Kari Nguyen

I LIVED ALONE IN a one bedroom apartment after my divorce. The place was clean with decent rent and it was one of those rare places that had a doorman so I felt safe. I was alone and loved it. I took the time to focus on my career and things were finally looking up for me.

At the time, I was working pretty late at the office and would often stumble into my apartment, sleep deprived, in the early hours of the morning. More often than not, I would pass out on my bed before waking up a few hours later, 6:30 to 7-ish, to start another day.

I began to notice that in the morning my door would be unlocked. I dismissed this as my sleep-deprived brain thinking that the bed was more appealing than locking the doors. Another thing that I noticed since moving in was that I seem to misplace things more often than I used to. It was mainly little things like my hair brush or nail polish, not enough to be a big deal so much as it was a slight annoyance to my day.

The longer I lived there, the more frequently I seemed to forget to lock the door. At first it was every once in a while, then it seemed to be almost a daily occurrence. More things went missing: pictures, shaving razors, and --most disturbingly-- my underwear. This went on long enough for me to become paranoid.

I took the time at night to make sure the door was locked. I got into the habit of turning the door handle three times after locking it and saying to myself, "It's locked, it's locked, it's locked." Time after time I would wake up and the door would be unlocked. One time, I tried staying up all night to watch the door, but ended up falling asleep.

I decided my mind was not reliable enough to stay up all night, so I invested in a video camera. I went all out and bought the fanciest camera I could get my hands on. One night, I set the camera under a pile of clothes on the floor, facing the door . I locked the door and went to sleep.

When I woke up, my apartment looked normal. Nothing was missing that I could see, so I went to check the tape. I fast-forwarded through hours of footage, not seeing anything. I was just about to give up when I noticed the handle of the door jittering. Then, it slowly crept open. A figure slid through the half-opened door and walked towards the camera. It paused, looking around as if it was listening for something.

Then it walked forward, directly into the camera frame. I paused the camera. The hairs on my arms and neck raised. I was staring into the face of the building's maintenance man. The ginger curly hair. The large mole underneath this chin. I had no doubt who it was. I played the tape a little further. He looked so comfortable as he walked throughout the apartment. Then he headed towards my bedroom, out of the view of the camera.

I called the police, my words incomprehensible through my sobbing. Soon enough, two officers arrived. I told them everything and even showed them the tape. I remember seeing the blood draining from their faces as they watched the video. They promised me that I was safe, and they were going to get the guy.

I needed to lie down, but didn't want to be alone. One of the officers offered to stand outside my apartment door as I took a nap. I laid on the bed, drained. Something felt wrong. I tossed and turned, unable to get comfortable. What was it? Then, a realization washed over me and chilled me to the core.

We watched the tape and saw him enter...but never saw him leave.

I froze, then started to shake. I needed to get out of there. I sat up and looked around the room. No one. Nothing. I swung my legs cautiously over the side of the bed. My feet hit the cold wood. I felt a warm breeze followed by tingling sensations of fingertips on my ankle. I raced out of my apartment as fast as I could to the safety of the officer. He called for back-up. They found the man under my bed clutching a knife and a polaroid camera.

To this day, I cannot sleep alone.

THE TOILET PAPER
Danny Quach

BOB SAUNTERED THROUGH THE automatic glass doors of Metrotonix, grinning from ear to ear. *That job's mine for sure,* he thought. He placed one foot outside of the building.

"Mr. Hills. Please come back inside. The boss wants to see you," said the attendant standing behind the counter near the door.

"Okay. Will do." Bob stepped back and spun around.

Bob strutted back into Metrotonix, heading to the interview room. Workers in lab coats and plain dark suits stared at Bob, smirking and whispering amongst themselves. *What?* He looked down. A foot of toilet paper stuck out from his black pinstripe trousers. His cheeks burned bright red. He dashed to the restroom.

In the restroom, he yanked the toilet paper from his pants. *The boss will never hire me now.* He paced the restroom floor. *How can I salvage the situation?* He stopped. Entering a stall, he pulled out a roll of toilet paper and ran down the hall and into the medical room. Reaching for the top shelf nearest the entrance of the room, he grabbed a bag of blood labeled "Golden Sample."

He unrolled the toilet paper and wrapped some of it around his stomach. *Great idea, me.* Unzipping the blood sample, he smirked to himself. He poured the blood onto his right side and wrapped himself in more toilet paper, careful to leave a visible amount of white dangling from his pants. The right side of his stomach resembled a severe injury covered in white gauze.

He returned into the hall to meet the boss again.

A worker tapped Bob's shoulder. "Hey." He stifled a laugh. "You've got a something sticking out from your pants. Again."

Bob lifted up part of his shirt. "You mean this?" He pointed to the tinted crimson that seeped through the white toilet paper wrapped round his side.

The worker's eyes widened. He grimaced. "Oh. No. Sorry. I just thought... Are you okay?" His co-workers stopped laughing, their faces ashen.

Pulling down his shirt, Bob smiled. "I'm alright. Thanks for asking. I'll be seeing the boss now, if you'll excuse me." He strolled and headed to the boss's office, passing several Metrotonix employees who gave him concerned looks.

Bob knocked on the mahogany door that was labeled with a gold plaque, which read, "Executive Director of Metrotonix." "Bob Hills here, Mr. Michael," he said.

"Come in, Mr. Hills," said the voice of Mr. Michael.

Bob seated himself in the black leather swivel chair facing the boss, a big man with a moustache who sat in a black leather high-back chair.

Mr. Michael glanced at the computer on the left side of his desk. "So, Mr. Hills. I've just received memo that said you had an injury on the side of your body. Is that true?"

Bob nodded, lifting up his shirt to reveal the toilet paper wrapped around his body.

The boss's bushy eyebrows furrowed.. "How did you even get that?"

"Well, I was hiking in the woods the other day, when a grizzly bear attacked me. Its claws dug into my side. I managed to jog a mile from the woods to the local hospital. The doctor said I lost a lot of blood then wrapped me in this gauze. I'm still bleeding a bit, though."

The boss stroked his moustache. "Why did you show up for the interview? Why not stay and recover in the hospital if you're still so injured?"

"I would love this job. As a man who works hard to get what he wants, I couldn't let this little injury get in the way of my pursuits."

Standing up and slamming his palms upon the desk, the boss said, "I like your determination, Hills. You're hired. As of tomorrow, you work for us".

Bob, grinning from ear to ear, rushed to give his new boss a double handshake. "Thank you, Mr. Michael. I'll do my best for Metrotonix."

The boss led Bob outside into the lobby. "Everyone, gather around and meet Bob Hills, our new recruit. He just survived a bear attack but still had the will to come to the job interview. This determined man is what Metrotonix needs."

Most of the workers clapped, but one man who wore glasses and a lab coat said, "Mr. Michael, do you really believe that he survived a bear? He might only be fabricating lies just to make us feel bad for him so we'll give him the job."

The boss looked at the man in glasses and said "That might be true, Phil. But he has wounds to prove it. From now on, he is a part of this company. Why don't we throw a welcoming party for Bob?" The boss turned to the newly appointed recruit. "Why don't you go home for a bit? We'll plan a party for you in the meantime."

Bob nodded and strolled through the automatic glass doors, his chin held high, face beaming.

Two hours later, Bob pranced back through the doors of Metrotonix, a bottle of champagne in his hand. Walking from the lobby towards the cubicles, Bob received glares from all of the employees.

One of the workers shoved him from the back. "Hey. The boss wants to see you." Following from behind, the worker escorted Bob to the office, glaring at Bob's back the entire trip to the mahogany door.

Nothing's sticking out of my pants right now. Did I do something wrong? Bob entered the boss's office, his hands shaking. .

Rising from his chair, the boss walked to the door. He slammed it shut."Bob. We received some news. Not only have you lied to us about the bear, but you also took one of the most important blood samples of human blood that contained something that could've cured cancer." The boss ripped the toilet paper off of Bob. Clear, unblemished skin. No sign of injury. No blood stains. "You lied to us. Why?"

Bob looked at the ground. "Because this morning I had toilet paper hanging out of my pants. I didn't want to look stupid, so I wrapped myself with toilet paper and got one of the blood packs to fake an injury. I didn't know that it was that important. I'm sorry."

The boss approached him and looking him square in the eye, pointed at Bob's chest, the force making him stumble backwards. The boss said, "Look. I hope you realize that we are businessmen. We all make mistakes, but here at Metrotonix, if you make mistakes...You. Will. Pay." Bob trembled.

This was worse than any bear attack.

The boss walked around his table and gripped Bob's shoulder, leading Bob back into the lobby. The boss said, "Look. Just make sure you read what you're putting on yourself, because it could be acid or a cure to cancer. But it's too late now. The past is the past. All we need to worry about is the future."

With the boss still clutching his shoulder, Bob shook, cold beads of sweat running from his forehead. He stuttered. "I-I'm sorry. I didn't know. I'm sorry. I promise I won't do this again. Please forgive me."

The boss smirked. "It's fine. I know that you're sorry, and I know you won't do this again. Because you're fired." The automatic glass door opened. The boss pushed Bob outside. He tripped, hitting his head on the bike rack's outside, which then started bleeding profusely.

The boss laughed and said, "Oh, what happened, Bob? Did something attack you again?"

Bob scurried away as far from Metrotonix as possible.

THE ZOMBIE SURPRISE
Kimberly Viramontes

MAXIE AND JAXON PANTED and wheezed, commanding their legs to run faster. A light shined dimly in the distance. Hope. Just a week ago, they were two normal teens, falling in love and making mistakes. Today, they fought the Zombie Apocalypse, for their lives.

"Maxie, hold on,," Jaxon said. "I can't. Can't run anymore. I need a breather."

"Jesus, are you serious? Jaxon, we're running from zombies. There's no time for breathers," Maxie said.

"I'm sure we're fine," he said. "Just hold on a moment."

Maxie faced the light. She crouched down, huffing. Jaxon screamed, a gut-wrenching scream. She turned around, aiming her gun. *Boom. Boom.* The zombie laid motionless, oozing saliva from its twitching mouth, but the light in Jaxon's eyes had disappeared.

Maxie waited for the tears to come. They didn't. She thought to herself, *I told him to keep going. But no. He insisted that we'd be okay.* She kissed Jaxon's cheek and took his gun.

"Goodbye my love, my little fool."

In less than a mile away, the light shined. She ran. Her heavy footsteps echoed through the streets. Crackle. Behind her, a zombie--by far the ugliest she had seen--loomed. Its ghostly gray skin peeled at odd places. Its yellow teeth snarled. Its nails clawed at her. It licked its lips. Fear tied Maxie in place. The zombie inched closer. It shrieked and lunged at her. Maxie readied her gun and pulled the trigger. Nothing. *Shoot,* she thought, *no bullets.* Zombie hands wrapped around Maxie's neck. Maxie unsheathed her Swiss Army knife from its leather strap and stabbed the zombie's yellow, bloodshot eye. Maxie struck its head with her gun. Thud. The zombie fell.

Maxie began to cry, shocked by another near-death experience. Guilt washed over her. She knew. The whole time she and Jaxon had been running, she only fought for *her* life, never for *their* survival. She continued running. She was almost there.

The sun was about to set when she arrived at the light, a seemingly abandoned shack. She knocked and waited a few minutes. No response. She held her ear close to the door. Footsteps.

"Please. Please let me in. I'm not a zombie. I promise," she said.

"Only a zombie would say that," a boy said.

"Just let me in, kid. I'm still human. Besides, zombies can't speak." Maxie's brow twitched.

"How do I know you're not some mutated zombie freak?"

"Geez, kid. If you don't let me in, you'll be the first one I go after once I *am* some mutated zombie freak."

The door creaked open. A gun greeted Maxie's face, but Maxie sighed, relieved to be inside. She looked at the boy. He stood a head shorter than she did. His face sported a single pimple on one side of his baby face. He looked fourteen at most, four years younger than she. His jet black hair appeared unnatural against his all-white outfit.

"Hey, you're kinda hot," he said.

"Wow, you're kinda annoying. What's your name?" Maxie asked.

"Rill. And is this how you thank your knight in shining armor?"

"What kind of a name is Rill? It sounds stupid. You sound like a lizard."

"You're rude. I let you in and this is how you treat me? You're lucky you're girl. If you weren't--"

"If you didn't open up, I would've knocked the door down. And I'm a girl. So what? You want to hurt me? Do it. I dare you."

"Never mind." He sulked into a corner.

Maxie reached her hand out to pat his head and apologize. She jumped back. Blood had seeped through her shirt. She rolled up a soaking red sleeve and grimaced. There was a deep gash across her arm. *Damn,* she thought, *That zombie must've scratched me.*

Rill hugged his legs, facing the ground.

Maxie needed to escape outside. She knew what happened after a zombie infection. She kicked her gun over to Rill and fumbled with the door. She sweat, struggling to unhinge the heavy door lock.

"What the hell are you doing?" He stood up, ran over to her, and grabbed her by the shoulders.

Idiot, she thought, *Idiot. I gave you the damn gun. Someone else should live this time.*

"Nothing. I want some fresh air," she said. "No offense, but it stinks in here."

"Seriously? You're really that stupid? You want fresh air? We're in the middle of a zombie apocalypse. We don't get to have fresh air."

His response reminded her of someone, but she couldn't remember who. Her mind became cloudy.

"Look, Rill. I think it was a mistake for me to stay here. I think I should go."

"What, are you crazy? No. You're like the first person I've seen since I locked myself in here."

Fool, she thought, *let me go. You don't want me here.*

"No, seriously, I need to get out now," she said.

"Damn it. You're not going anywhere. Stop acting so stupid. You'll be eaten out there. Here you're safe, but just because it stinks a little, do you want to risk your life for some fresh air? Answer me."

Her heartbeat slowed. Her lungs caved inward. Her kidneys ruptured. She wanted to tell Rill to run. Too late. A sharp pain struck her head. She could no longer speak. Her gash stopped bleeding. A nasty scar emerged.

"Are you just going to stand there or are you…." Rill jumped back. Too late. If only he had let her out when she asked. If only he had listened, he wouldn't be caught in this situation. He knew it was too late.

"Hey, are you…. are you okay?" Rill asked.

Maxie's thoughts swirled. She couldn't hear him. The burning intensified, as though acid was eating her alive from the inside out.

Run, she thought.

Her skin peeled off her face in clumps. Her eyes turned yellow and bloodshot. Her teeth, now grimy and razor sharp, decayed. Her nails resembled splintered wood. Her bones broke. She wouldn't need them anymore. Thoughts exploded in her mind.

BLOOD.
KILL.
GUTS.
SPILL.
RED.
RUN.
RUN.

Maxie eyes opened. Whatever just happened, she couldn't recall. She looked at her hands, stained with blood. She licked them. Delicious. At her feet lay Rill's remains. She realized what she had done, what she had become.

Poor, poor Rill, she thought, *should've let me out when you had the chance.*

She chuckled, then doubled over with laughter and patted Rill's back.

Well bud, I guess I was some mutant zombie freak. Better luck next time.

TOUR GUIDE
Brenna Ramirez

"YOU MAY NOTICE A foul odor. For your safety, we ask that you move quickly through this part of the tour," said the hostess.

Her voice had been peaking throughout the nearly two hour tour, and now her eye was twitching. Her lips were pulled to show an unnaturally large and stiff smile that did not reach her eyes.

The young child in the front of the group had been asking question after question throughout the entire tour, and someone had yet to claim him. Though, seeing how he's mine to claim, I refused to say anything. While I felt bad for letting my little brother run rampant for the whole tour, this was the first time I hadn't had to keep a constant eye on him in almost a month. Eli isn't a bad kid, honest, he just gets stir crazy. His constant bouncing around and machine gun mouth are a lot to handle.

"What makes the smell?" Eli asked as he leaned over the railing.

Vats of vile green goop, the source of the smell, sat below us and I had to hold myself back from rushing forward to pull Eli from his perch. The hostess placed her hand on Eli's shoulder, gently guiding him away from the railing. I definitely had to give her props for not snapping at Eli like other tour guides have done in the past.

"The combination of chemicals used to produce the energy source for hover crafts is quite toxic, if not disposed of correctly. This room is where it is stored. It is also the reason we should keep moving." she said with a soft smile.

Eli looked up at her in awe, his brown eyes wide and innocent under dusty curls. I could see him cataloging the new information as she spoke, excitement flashing behind his eyes.

"Cool." He beamed as though she had presented him the world instead of a simple answer.

The hostess looked a little taken back by his obvious wonder and took a moment to fully regain her professionalism. Through the rest of the tour she took a little more time to answer Eli's questions, spending more time at parts that enthralled him. By the end of the excursion, she had become enamored by Eli's innocent naivety instead of simply being annoyed.

Although watching her interact with Eli was great, I couldn't help but hear the other people in the tour group grumble about how irresponsible it was for a parent to let their child come here on his own. They kept muttering about how he needed a good walloping to straighten him out. I waited for those people to wonder off before I caught up to Eli in the gift shop.

He was looking at books about hover crafts that looked like they were written for college students. The one in his hands, *Hover Boards In Modern Times*, had a big red sticker on the cover that announced a thirty percent sale. I smiled before resting a hand on the top of his head. He turned to look up at me. A grin plastered on his tanned face.

"You have fun, kiddo?" I asked.

His grin grew even more as he launched into his favorite parts of the tour, which sounded like everything. His voice grew in volume as he got more excited. I could feel the looks being sent our way and ignored them. This was our fun day and I was not going to dampen Eli's mood. I waited for a lull in his run-on sentence before interrupting.

"Is this what you want?" I asked, taking the book from his hands.

"Yeah! It's all about the creator of the hover board and how she influenced transportation today," he said. "It's on sale, so that's cool."

I laughed at his last statement and put an arm around his shoulders, directing him to the counter to pay. The cashier's eyebrow rose at Eli's selection, but he didn't say anything other than wishing us a good day. Eli thanked him eagerly as he was handed the newest edition to his growing library.

"The usual for dinner?" I asked, willing the air conditioner to work in the crappy little car that was our transportation.

"Yeah," Eli said, already nose deep in his book.

Getting Eli out of his book was the hardest part of the day. Only the arrival of our food could accomplish that feat.

"Thanks Marg," I said as the older woman set down our food.

A woman on the plump side of the spectrum, Marg, had been a staple at The Burger Joint longer than the joint itself. Her soulful eyes were surrounded by laugh and frown lines alike, and her hair was never out of place from its militaristic bun. She'd kept an eye out for Eli and I ever since we'd been on our own, helping us out whenever she could.

"No problem, pumpkin. If you need anything else, you just let me know," she said.

She picked the book from Eli's hands, marked his place with a napkin, and pushed his plate closer to him. For a moment, he looked lost, as if he was still reading the book that now lay closed next to him. He recovered quickly and focused on the burger and fries in front of him.

"Thanks Marg," he said through a mouth full of food.

"Don't speak with your mouth full." She tugged at his ear before walking back to the kitchen.

I watched for a while as Eli ate, enjoying the silence that so rarely accompanied the time spent with him. The instant I saw his eyes light up, I knew the silence had ended.

"Veronica!" he yelled.

The bustle of the dinner hushed for moment before picking back up again. I turned to see the tour guide from earlier standing in the entry way. Her pristine skirt and blouse had been replaced by jeans and a tank top, her perfect auburn curls now in a frizzy ponytail. Eli was up and out of the booth before I could process what had happened. She looked surprised to see him, but gave him the same soft smile she had given him during the tour. Then, she shook her head 'no.' As always, he didn't listen and pulled her toward the booth.

"Cassidy, this is Veronica," Eli said. "She was the one who led the tour earlier. Isn't she pretty?"

I choked on my food, looking up at her with an apologetic look, hoping that Eli hadn't gone too far. She smiled back at me.

"Can she join us for dinner?" Eli asked.

"Eli, sweetie, I'm sure she's had a long day," I said. "She probably just wants to go home."

He still held her hand even as the excitement drained from his face.

I felt bad, but I didn't want the girl to feel obligated to stay if she had other plans.

"It's okay, I wasn't in a rush to get home," she said.

His face lit back up, and he made room for her to sit next to him on his side of the booth. I flagged Marg down, and Veronica placed her order.

Eli switched between rambling off questions and taking bites of food, pausing every now and then to breathe. Veronica, for the most part, was able to keep up with him, answering questions he still had about the factory's production as well as some questions about the book he had bought in the gift shop.

"I like to read the books we get in the gift shop when I get a chance," Veronica said. "The company owner is actually coming out with a new one soon. If you like this one, I'm sure you'll like some of her other books."

Eli looked at me. I shrugged. I knew he was already calculating how much money he would need for a brand new book.

"We'll see," I said.

"Alright, everybody," Marg said, "we're closing up soon so I need ya'll to start heading out."

I went to grab my wallet, only to have Marg stop me.

"On the house tonight, pumpkin. You too, sugar," she said to Veronica.

"Oh, no. I couldn't," Veronica said, trying to leave money for the food.

"Sugar, I ain't takin' your money, not when you're making that one smile like he is," Marg said.

We all looked back at Eli, who was by now nose deep in the book again.

Veronica smiled and nodded. "Thank you."

"So, why didn't you say anything to him during the tour?"

We walked down the sidewalk to Veronica's bus stop. Hover crafts cruised along the streets, creating a slight air current on the sidewalk. The night, though cool, was not cold like it would be in a few more weeks. Eli walked a few feet in front of us, still buried in the book.

Veronica's question was a good one, but not one that I had ever had to answer before. No one had ever noticed that Eli and I were together when I took him out for trips and tours. We look so vastly different from each other that no one had ever suspected it.

"Ever since I've had custody of him, about a year or so now, I haven't had a whole lot of time to myself," I said. "The tours that I take him on are somewhere that I don't have to worry about keeping at eye on him all the time. I would just get in his way if I tried to keep hold of him during one anyway. I only step in if I have to."

Veronica nodded. "He seems like a good kid."

"He's the best. I couldn't ask for a better little brother," I said.

The rest of the walk was spent in comfortable silence, the only noise from the sterile city came from the constant hum of the technology that surrounded us. Reaching the bus stop was more of a disappointment than I had expected. Veronica was the first person I had had a real conversation with in a long time. As smart as Eli was, and as much as I loved him, he was still only twelve and not much of a conversationalist when it didn't concern a subject he was interested in. At work, conversations were pretty much limited to the people whose hair I was cutting.

"Well, it was really nice meeting you," I said, holding out my hand.

"Yeah, it was," Veronica said.

Her hand was warm and soft, lingering in mine a little longer than what would be considered a normal handshake. Warm brown eyes smiled at me and I found it harder and harder to swallow.

"Do I get to say bye now?" Eli asked.

I was shocked back to reality, dropping Veronica's hand. I felt my cheeks grow warm and cleared my throat.

"Yeah, of course," I said.

Eli hugged Veronica around the waist, his head only coming up to just under her chest, mumbling about how much he had enjoyed the day. Veronica ruffled his hair, but her eyes were still on me.

"Yeah, today was really nice," she said.

My cheeks grew warmer. She was still smiling at me. It had been so long since I had been in this situation, and I had no idea what the proper response was. My hands grew sweaty. Somewhere in my mind I knew that she was telling me that she was interested, but, for the most part, my brain wasn't functioning.

"Would, ah, would you like to do it again sometime? Maybe?" I heard myself say.

I heard Eli make a sound that I assumed was an agreement, and mentally kicked myself for forgetting that he was there. Veronica's smile grew into a grin, making my brain short circuit again.

"Yeah, I'll give you my number," she said.

I watched as she pulled out a pen from her purse.

"Here, you can write it in this," Eli said, holding his book open to one of the empty pages at the front.

"You sure?" she asked.

He nodded excitedly, practically shoving it into her hands. Her hand moved quickly as the bus stopped beside us. The book snapped shut, and she handed it to me, her smile still present.

"I'll be seeing you," she said.

"Yeah, you will," I said, my brain finally finding the ability to speak again.

She climbed into the bus, and it left a few moments later. I looked down to the book in my hands before opening it slowly. There it was, her name and number in loopy handwriting.

Veronica Right.

My fingers trailed over the ink, memorizing the numbers.

"Can we go back to the car now that you've got a date?" Eli asked.

"You can hush," I said, closing the book. I slung an arm around his shoulders, pointing us in the direction of the car.

"But, you did get a date, right? Or at least a strong possibility of a date?" he asked.

Large brown eyes were looking up at me with hope and curiosity. His tanned face was littered with freckles that reminded me so much of our father. Hints of his mother peaked through in the shape of his nose and the curl in his hair, but he was mostly Aiden Garrison. Alissa was kind, and I had liked her when she had married my father. A year later, Alissa was expecting and then there was Eli.

Looking at him now, I remembered looking after him as a toddler. His eyes had never lost the look of wonder. He kept it, even after the plane crash.

"We'll see," I said.

His face split into a giant grin as we came up to our car. I ignored his look until I felt the car start to hover tentatively.

"What?" I asked.

"Whenever you say 'we'll see' it's always a yes. You're gonna ask her out, and you're gonna go on a date, and it'll be great because she's great and you're great, and then I'll get to see her, and--"

I held a hand up to his face. "Whoa there little man. Relax. Take a breath. I haven't even called her yet," I said, bringing my hand back to the wheel.

"But you will," he said.

"Did you plan the whole thing?" I asked.

"Plan what?" Eli asked.

He was unpacking a box full of dishes, placing them on a shelf that was too high for me. He was doing it on purpose, but considering that both he and Veronica could reach them, I had no say in whether they would be moved.

"This. Me and Veronica. Everything."

"I have no idea what you're talking about," he said, avoiding my eyes.

I threw a pillow at him, hitting him square in the chest. He fell against the counter dramatically while pretending to gasp for air. I walked over to where he was now lying on the floor.

He had turned into a lanky seventeen year old without my noticing and was now starting to fill out in his chest and shoulders. Dirty blond hair curled around his face. He would need a haircut soon. I would have to find my scissors.

I sat on his chest, and he groaned.

"God, what have you been eating? You weigh a ton," he said.

"Oh hush, you're fine. Now answer my question."

He rolled to the side, dislodging me from my perch and onto the tiled floor. He leaned against the cabinets, resting his arms on his knees.

"Are you asking if I, at the age of twelve, set you up with a tour guide on purpose, thinking that you would end up going steady with her and eventually propose to her?" he asked.

I shoved the pillow in his face, "Could you maybe keep that last bit quiet? I haven't even gotten the ring yet."

"Oh, you know she's going to say yes with or without a ring," he said. "But maybe I did let it slip where our favorite diner was and that my sister was single."

"How did you even know she was into girls?" I asked.

"Intuition."

I raised an eyebrow.

"Okay, so maybe I did some digging into who would lead the tour, and at what time, and just so happened to find Veronica."

"Eli!"

"What? You hadn't even had a date since you'd taken me in after Mom and Dad died. You needed someone to make you happy." Eli looked away from me then, brushing his hair to one side, "I didn't want you to not have a life because of me. I didn't want to be a burden."

I had him in my arms before he could protest, hugging him tighter than ever. The position wasn't the most comfortable, as the hard tile pressed into my knees, but I didn't care. Feeling his head tucked into my neck like when he was little was well worth it.

"Am I interrupting a moment?"

We both turned to see Veronica, a box in her hands, smiling down at us. Her hair was pulled back in a messy braid, showing off her beautiful dark eyes. She took the hand I held out, coming to sit on the floor with us. She kissed me, nothing more than a quick brush of lips, but my stomach still did flips nonetheless.

Looking between them made it easy to see a future spread out in front of us. Eli would go off to college, Veronica and I would open our own salon; she on the books and me as the lead stylist, all of us happy. Maybe one day we would buy a house, who knows, maybe we would get a cat. Right now though, it was just nice to be there, in our small apartment with each other.

Us against the world.

POETRY

BIRDIE

The girl in the white dress,
staring in a mirror-
her hair all up in knots
(and her stomach no better).
The glass reflects
beauty and
grace,
but her heart is sinking;
it breaks and
breaks.

Sadie Adams

FIRELIGHTS

If you really do leave... Let's just say:
It'd be as if you took my firelights away.
The firelights that once had me guided,
The warmth they generously provided
Without them, I would be deprived.
I cannot see, no matter how hard I try.
My need denies all common sense,
But I'd choose not to give you up, no matter the expense.
You are the firelight that shines brighter than any sun.
Besides you to be my firelight, there is none.
Without a firelight, my vision will have no hue.
Bound to only see how much I miss you.
So if you really do leave, dimming would be my day
Because you will have stolen my firelight away.

Monica Van

BRIGHTER THAN A TELEVISION

Momma gave me a talk yesterday.
She said, "The TV is bright, but never more than a sun during daylight,"
so she took me out on a walk.
We ate at the park and stared at the sky;
at first, it was boring, but then, the clouds came alive.

I saw a white phoenix with a tail big and wide,
next to a canary rushing to race alongside.
The eyes of the little bird filled with envy and desire,
chasing the beautiful phoenix whose feathers he knew he couldn't dream to acquire.
Red and orange, embellished with flames that brought him higher,
the poor little canary had nothing to admire.

Suddenly then, the canary slowed down.
He couldn't continue anymore.
But the phoenix still went higher.

I watched as the canary pushed his little wings back up,
But he was smaller, weaker, and couldn't live up.
Suddenly despaired, the canary rushed tears down after,
Until he looked behind him, and saw that he'd grown a tail himself that lit on fire.

The canary, now a phoenix, followed the other,
and the two birds drifted in the distance, and the clouds reshaped one another.

Mother nudged me one more time, "Honey, it's time to rise."
Grudgingly, I got up, and told her twice,
"Momma, can we go back to the park another time?"

Jennifer Chau

Richard Trejo

DARKNESS OF THE MINDS

Darkness swarms us
Light fades from us
The ending is nearing,
But my mind is elsewhere.

I relive my memories
Relive my choices
Walking my same paths,
Wanting to change the past.

Feeling the joy after winning,
the sadness of her passing
the regret when I left my home,
the confusion that is my life.

Memories are good to collect,
But a burden to relive.
Fun to see,
Painful to react.

Now is the end,
My time is up,
The time for others is now.
All I can do, is watch them struggle.

Richard Trejo

DEPRESSION CAN TURN YOUR LIFE UPSIDE DOWN

I love life.
I could say
I miss the days when
I cried and declared

The world is a horrible place

But that's not true.
You can see good all around
If you care to look.
People always tell me

It's all in my mind
And
I made myself feel depressed.
I used to believe that

Life is a nightmare.

That is completely wrong.

Depression is not a real sickness.
They were right when they said
You'll never hear me say

I hate life.*

Dawn Pham

Depression can turn your life upside down so, please read the poem from the bottom up.

EYES LIKE A GALAXY

You're a metaphor
written in ink,
drifting through
space,
drifting through
the sea.

I've written you down
in so many ways,
but my heart never
seems to be at bay.

I can't conquer
this
restless head-

I guess I'll just
wander,
search for your bed.

Sadie Adams

FAMILY

I took my dignity
Looked up the word 'family' in the Webster's Dictionary
"A group of people who are related to each other"
Related to me was mother and father
Why didn't it feel like a family?

The realization hit me:
The word family
Is not only a noun.
Family should be a safe sound
Family should give you a warm feeling
To say it's just a noun would not be as real
Family is not only those related to you
Rather family is those who care, too
Family is there
When present, you feel the warmth everywhere
Family does not only mean the same DNA
Family actually remembers your birthday
Family doesn't just mean the same genes
Family remembers the small things
Family does not just mean blood
Family is supposed to be full of unconditional love.

Gina Nguyen

FOCUS

I could've sworn
I knew that there would be a thorn
I just don't understand why
When it hit me, I was still so surprised
Acting hurt, tears pouring out of my eyes
I planned every precaution
Or so I thought I did

Every part of me was put up for auction
What will be the highest bid?
Waiting to know my value
Self-worth in the hands of a few
Of those who don't know me

Pass or fail
Is like heads or tails
Your knowledge and interest
only depends on the subject
Sometimes knowledge is taught
Or expected to learn
Some knowledge or not
But those are the ones that the students yearn
Injecting information
Rejecting lack of cooperation
The system came from what it was supposed to be,
Educating people from mathematics to integrity
Now to building people, or shall I say robots
To entering competitions
Facing rejection
While watching others praise a paper that states acceptance
To only face another challenge

It sends a great message of never giving up and working hard
But when will they stop to admit that they've gone too far
Students are crying and stressing
Lack of focus is blamed on the minds of the young

They despise the students expressing,
they stop us before our tongues touch the roofs of our mouths
They tell us they want the best
Well, then stop giving us these tests

Everything must be ranked
Nothing is ever just blank
From tests to students to school to environment
Have they lost the thought of what education meant?
We lose focus during the day
Due to these standards and expectations that we're cramming for at night
While the education system lost their focus by only seeing how we obey
To THEIR steps of how to make our future bright.

Gina Nguyen

PICTURE FRAME

picture frame
hold me tight,
capture a memory
and make it
alright

one moment in
time-
loving, all together

picture frame,
please hold these lies.

Sadie Adams

PARADIGM OF A LADY

"Play with your dolls
Don't dirty your dress
These are the things that girls do best.
Dab light with your napkin
Speak soft when answering
These are traits you need be mastering.
Your hair in curls
Gold, long, and shining.
You are a girl, you need no minding.
Your opinions matter not,
I tell you what to do.
What matters to girls?
What's there to pursue?"

They know not
Of these meaningless pebbles
I scoop them, throw them
For I am a rebel

My hair is short, ragged, and dry
I shout when I speak
I need no why.
My knees are skinned,
My knuckles are bruised
I am a girl
But I will not be used

I have my opinions,
My views,
Myself
I am no doll.
I don't belong on a shelf.

Alexandra Quang

Emmanuel Ramirez

POETRY THOUGHTS

I don't know what it is about poetry…
It sets me free,
Lets me be me,
Forces me to see
Another side of my creativity,
my fullest ability.

It's like an addiction
Of my imagination.
Line after line
Rhyme after rhyme
Pen in motion
Of pouring emotion
Until I've written what needs to be spoken.

Emanuel Ramirez

THE SKY

The sky is a paradise.
It's so big and blue.
What's up there is a surprise,
So it's mysterious too!

There's a secret that Mommy told me,
There's a "heaven" in the sky.
Angels live there, happy and free,
But first they have to die.

Mommy always smiles sadly
When she looks up above.
She must be thinking of Daddy,
The man she lost but still loves.

Daddy is an angel, you know.
He lives up in the sky.
He crashed so he had to go.
He never even said goodbye.

I hope he's living happily,
In the paradise of blue.
I hope he never forgets me.
One day, I'll be up there too.

Dawn Pham

SHADOW SPEARS

Shadows stride alongside me,
Tempting me to forsake light for eternity.
"To the world, you are nothing," say they,
"Join us and them, betray."
"Nai," the other one says,
"It is you who's been betrayed.
Loyal to light you have been.
But who are you once you've sinned?
Nothing. Cast to the street.
Groveling beneath light's feet.
For what, you beg?
A little mercy is all you plea.
But how does light see thee?
Nothing. But a stained, disturbing flea.
Why, then, must you waste your efforts?
Fighting for the light
that recognizes not your merit.
Come, I say. Fight for us, I say.
Light does not want you anyway."

Monica Van

PLAYS

A NIGHT AT THE PIZZERIA
Zachary King

CHARACTERS

CHARLIE, *a newly-trained night guard. Tonight's his first night on the job.*
MASON, *the main animatronic. Wears a monkey suit. Holds a microphone and sings during the daytime.*
ELLIS, *an animatronic that holds a bass guitar. Wears an elephant suit.*
SWEET PEA, *animatronic that holds an electric guitar. Wears a parrot suit.*

(NOTE: *Animatronics never speak, only move when lights are off, and they always smile. It would also be safer for* CHARLIE *to remain still while the lights are off.*)

Inside office. Night.
(*Lights on.* MASON, ELLIS, *and* SWEET PEA *are on center stage, completely motionless, smiling. Some chairs and tables are arranged in front of them with party decorations thrown about the room. Enter* CHARLIE, *stage Right.*)

CHARLIE (*Holding clipboard, pacing*): Alright, inventory check. Clipboard? Check. Pencil? Check. Nightstick? Check. Flashlight? Check. Handsome new watchman in a stuffy uniform? Check. Three of the creepiest puppets ever witnessed? (*Looks at animatronics, shudders*) Sadly, check. Alright, piece of cake! Just gotta stay awake 'til six, then get the easiest fifty bucks ever made! This is gonna be nice.

(*Lights begin to flicker,* Charlie *drops the clipboard and pencil.*)

CHARLIE: Damn wiring in this place! Need to hire an electrician or somethin'. Well, better make the most of this. After all, who'd rob a pizza place? (*He sits, pulls phone out, and starts playing games.*)

(*Lights out momentarily. Back on, all characters looking at* Charlie, *still smiling.*
CHARLIE *turns to them and gasps.*)

CHARLIE (*Shouting to offstage*): Hey! Who's back there? That ain't funny! (*Beat.*) Come on out and I might not hurt you. (*Beat. Stands*) Alright, that's it! (*Stomps offstage*)

(*Lights off before he exits*)

CHARLIE: Oh, for the love o-

(Lights back on. All eyes on CHARLIE *again, he glances at them quickly)*

CHARLIE *(Nervously)*: I'm not afraid of you. Get out of the electronics room, now! *(He exits)* *(Offstage)* Where are you? Come on out. I ain't got all night. *(Enters)* Must've ran off. Ah, well. Back to my Flappy Bird.

(Lights off. All animatronics drop their instruments. MASON *takes a step forward.* ELLIS *and* SWEET PEA *now face* CHARLIE. *Lights on.)*

CHARLIE: H-hey, guys, how's it going? Please get back on stage…

(Lights off. All animatronics return to their original positions and pick up instruments. Lights on.)

CHARLIE: Wow, I must be insane. Talking to robots, like they're gonna respond. *(Approaches* MASON, *knocks on head.)* Hey, MASON, you got a screw loose or some-thin'? *(Moves to* ELLIS) Aw, looks like ELLIS broke a string. *(Plucks string. Moves to* SWEET PEA) Hey Sweet thing, you doin' anything later?

(Lights off. SWEET PEA *is now gone; others look at* CHARLIE. *Lights on.)*

CHARLIE: Guess she got cold feet. *(Looks back)* What's the matter? You two get-tin' jealous? Of course not, look at you! Happy as can be. *(Flicks* MASON's *cheek. Looks at watch while walking Downstage)* 2 a.m. Only four more hours until I get my cool fifty!

(Lights off. SWEET PEA *is back, holding a fire axe. Animatronics surround* CHARLIE, SWEET PEA *raises the Axe. Lights on.)*

CHARLIE *(Stuttering nervously)*: Okay, you guys. Calm down. *(Walks out of the circle)* You know I was just joking, right? I didn't mean any of that "Jealous" business. It was just for fun! You know? Just for fun.

(Lights off)

CHARLIE: Oh, no. Please!

(They return to their original positions and pick up instruments. The fire axe is now gone. Lights on.)

CHARLIE *(Absolute panic)*: Look, I dunno what you want from me. Money? Re-pairs? Blood? Tell me! *(Beat, head in his hands)* Look at you CHARLIE. Look at you! You're goin' nuts. These things ain't movin', they're bolted to the floor! They don't even have brains. They're just a bunch of servos and hydraulics and stuff. Just calm down. Take a deep breath, and relax. (*Deep breath, lights off before he can exhale*)

(*Animatronics surround* CHARLIE *again. Lights on*)

CHARLIE: (*Shouting*) I'm gettin' outta here! This ain't worth fifty bucks!

(*Lights off.* CHARLIE *screams, then lies on the floor, dead.* MASON *has a hand over his torso and all look down at* CHARLIE. *Lights on*)
(*Lights fade off, animatronics jerk heads towards audience just before full black out*)

DREAMS
Nicole Le

CHARACTERS

AYUMU, *better known as "Baku," a spirit, that eats children's nightmares for them when they ask. Other bakus only eat nightmares, like they should; however, Ayumu tends to steal dreams throughout his contracts with children. He is suave and good at speaking. He wears a nice suit, though with more than black and white. He could look like a dark dream, with yellows and purples. He also holds a cane with a tapir head.*

JAY, *an innocent, 12-year-old boy. His best friend is Kei. He would trust anyone's words, so long as he doesn't have a previous relationship with them. He wears a T-shirt and shorts generally. At night he wears a tank top and shorts. He tends to get into a lot of fights, not out of anger, but out of testing himself.*

DREAM JAY, *the Dream version of Jay. He wears a similar outfit to Jay; however, it is in bright neon colors.*

KEI, *a 12-year-old boy, best friends with Jay. He is not as innocent as Jay, and is skeptical of everyone. He wears a jacket with jeans. A black T-shirt is optimal. He also fights along with Jay.*

DREAM KEI, *the dream version of Kei. He wears clothes like real Kei; however, it is in bright neon colors.*

ELL, *Kei and Jay's mentor. He wears a turtleneck and semi tight pants. He is a young man. Ell is greatly respected by Kei and Jay, although Jay likes him more. He is very serious, but still lax with the kids.*

DREAM ELL, *the Dream Version of Ell. He wears similar clothes; however, it is in bright neon colors.*

DREAM FIGHTER, *really buff with a muscle tank.*

Scene 1
In the empty streets in the evening.

(KEI *and* JAY *walk together down the street,* KEI *slightly ahead of* JAY)

KEI *(walking backwards, looking towards* JAY): Jay… Jay… JAY!
JAY: Huh?! Oh, uh, hey. Yeah, what is it, Kei?
KEI *(stops in the middle of the stage)*: Geez, are you okay? You haven't been yourself lately.
JAY: What? It's nothing, you shouldn't worry about it. *(He shoos* KEI *away.)*
KEI: Hmm? *(stares at* JAY *for five seconds.)* Yeah, you're not okay. What is it?
JAY: Like I'd tell you!

177

(They chase each other around the stage, yelling appropriate things for the situation. KEI catches JAY around the waist, holding him in place.)

KEI: Alright, tell me!

JAY (shouts): Okay okay! Jeez, put me down! *(Is put down)* Okay, so it's not anything important. It's just uh. *(Stares at KEI)* I've been having bad dreams. Nightmares, I guess?

(Enter AYUMU downstage, behind the curtains. KEI and JAY do not notice him.)

KEI: Oh, you know you can talk to me about those, right? Because, we're friends, right?

JAY: Huh? Of course we're friends! It's just a little embarrassing, since they're just dreams. I mean, it's about that thing that happened last week…

(KEI looks towards the floor and says nothing.)

JAY: Uh, well. Okay. I'm gonna go home now. *(He shrugs and exits stage left.)*

KEI: Bye! See you tomorrow. *(walks around, almost in place.)* Did losing that fight last week really do that much to him? I mean, I guess, I was sort of scared too. Thank god Ell stepped in. *(exit stage)*

AYUMU *(slowly walks downstage center)*: That child is having nightmares… Jay, was it? Well, it seems I've found my next… target. *(He darkly laughs and exit stage)*

(The lights dim.)

Scene 2
Empty street. Night.

JAY *(walks back and forth on stage)*: I *live* here. Where's my house? Was this road always like this?

(JAY peers down stage right, AYUMU walks behind JAY. JAY turns around and sees AYUMU. He jumps back and gets into a fighting position. AYUMU stands defensively. JAY steps forward and threw punches at AYUMU. AYUMU dodges all the punches. JAY kicks but was blocked and forced to stumble backwards.)

AYUMU: Okay. Do you always fight anyone you come across?

JAY: There's no one on this road, I'm trying to get home, and you snuck up on me.

AYUMU: Reasonable. Should we start over? *(extends his hand out for a handshake.)* Baku.

JAY *(slowly reaches his hand out and shakes hands with AYUMU)*: Jay. Is Baku your name? It's a weird one.

AYUMU *(hesitantly)*: Yes, yes it is. It's nice to meet you, Jay.

JAY: It's nice to meet you too. But, uh, why'd you talk to me? Especially at night, and, well, you saw how I reacted.

AYUMU: Well, *(circles around* JAY *as he talks, and stops walking once he is stage right of* JAY. *Leans on his cane as he stays stage right.)* A little birdie told me, that you were having bad dreams, more commonly known as nightmares.

JAY: You talk to birds?

AYUMU: No. I'm what you would call a dream eater. And, I can eat your nightmares, if you want me to. All I need is your name, which I have, and a pinky promise. *(sticks out his pinky finger.)*

JAY *(almost places his pinky in* AYUMU's, *but pulls back last second)*: Sorry, I just realized, I really don't know you. Plus, Kei would probably be mad if I made a contract with someone I barely met.

AYUMU: *(Pause.)* Understandable. Well, if you need me, just call "Baku," okay? *(He bows and points upstage to* JAY's *balcony. Discreetly exits)*

JAY: Ah, my house! *(looks around to find that* AYUMU *has already left. He shrugs and climbs up his balcony to get home.)*

Scene 3
Jay's room. Night.

*(*JAY *throws the blanket off the bed, located upstage, and sits in bed. He looks around before falling into bed and into sleep. Light change to many colors to stimulate dream. Enter DREAM JAY, standing stage center left slightly, and DREAM FIGHTER, standing stage center right slightly. Enter other DREAM EXTRAS, surrounding DREAM JAY and DREAM FIGHTER)*

DREAM EXTRAS *(in unison)*: Fight! Fight! Fight!

DREAM JAY: Gladly!

(DREAM FIGHTER puts his hand up and does a "Come at me" motion. The DREAM EXTRAS begin cheering, and making certain noises appropriate for the fight that will ensue. DREAM FIGHTER expertly throws punches and kicks, similar to kickboxing. DREAM JAY dodges the first few punches before getting kneed in the gut. He falls to his knees. As DREAM FIGHTER approaches the down DREAM JAY, DREAM JAY looks up to DREAM FIGHTER's face. The DREAM EXTRAS join in on the laughter. As DREAM JAY slowly gets up to only stay sitting, the laughter dies down)

DREAM FIGHTER: Eh? So you can still get up?

DREAM JAY: Ugh…

DREAM FIGHTER: Huh? Was that something? Speak up!

DREAM JAY: B-Baku! Please… Save me…

AYUMU: *(offstage)* Gladly! *(AYUMU rushes in and flawlessly beats DREAM FIGHTER with his cane. The way that AYUMU fights is very elegant and fluid. Once DREAM FIGHTER is on the ground, AYUMU looks toward all DREAM EXTRAS and smiles at them. They stay still in place.* AYUMU *picks up* DREAM JAY *from off the ground.)* Wake up, dear.

Scene 4
Inside JAY's bedroom. Night.

JAY: *(Jolts up in bed.)* Ah! *(Sees* AYUMU *in his bed and screams.)*
AYUMU: Have any nice dreams?
JAY: *(Fumbles with sheets and struggles to gets out of the bed. He does eventually and ends up a bit away from the bed.)* Y-you were there! You know what it was like.
AYUMU: I suppose that's true. *(Rolls his shoulders.)*
JAY: Oh? Are you alright? Are you tired?
AYUMU: Just a little. Had to take some extra steps to get into your dream. But you called me, even though it's only been a few hours since I last talked to you. Can I assume...
JAY: I-I have questions first. Can.... Can you do the thing you did tonight every night?
AYUMU: Even better, I can prevent those sort of dreams from even happening. Or, at least you won't see them.
JAY: What do you even get from this?
AYUMU: Hmm? Oh, nightmares are how I eat. I'm a dream eater, remember?
JAY: So... You work for food?
AYUMU: Yes, generally. I'm a Japanese spirit. Don't think about it too much.

JAY *(gets slightly closer)* So, I won't see these... nightmares anymore?
AYUMU *(gets slightly closer)*: Nope.
JAY *(gets slightly closer)*: And you just need it for food?
AYUMU *(gets slightly closer)*: Yup.
JAY *(gets slightly closer)*: So we can just seal the deal.
AYUMU: Yes! *(*AYUMU *clasps both of* JAY's *hands into his.)* Ahaha, yes... *(stands)* You just have to promise *(brings out his pinky finger)* that I'm allowed to take your nightmares when they pop up. And, you have to say your name in the promise.
JAY: I, Jay, promise... promise to let you take my nightmares when they pop up. *(He curls his pinky with* AYUMU's.)*
AYUMU: Sealed with a promise of pinkies... Thank you. Have a good night's rest, sunrise will be in a couple of hours. *(He bows and exits)*

Scene 5
Outside on the street. Day

KEI *(*KEI *is ahead of* JAY *and looking back towards him as he walks.)*: Jay... Jay... Jay! *(He stops in his tracks.)*
JAY: Huh? Yeah?
KEI: Are you still having those dreams or something? It's been like, two weeks

since I last heard about them. Don't tell me you're keeping them secrets from me again--

JAY: What? No! In fact, I'm actually having great dreams now.

KEI: So, you already got over losing that fight?

JAY: *(Pause.)* Y-yes?

KEI: So you didn't, but you've just been on a lucky streak?

JAY: *(Pause.)* Y-yes?

KEI: Ah, so you have a different means of avoiding nightmares. How?

JAY: Uh… Um. I know this guy… He can eat dreams and stuff.

KEI: What.

JAY: Well, I mean, I guess I can call him right now, for it to make sense.

KEI: Please do.

JAY: Okay, Baku!

(Enter AYUMU.)

AYUMU: Good evening, Jay. And hello… *(He examines KEI.)*

JAY: That's Kei.

AYUMU: Oh, yes. That one.

KEI: What's that supposed to mean?

JAY: Ah, I think it's because I talk and dream about you a lot.

KEI: Huh… How'd you even get here?

AYUMU: I am a spirit. I have that sort of power. Just call me when you need me. Mm, do you need your nightmares eaten, Kei? *(He wraps an arm around KEI)*

KEI *(He pushes AYUMU's hand off of him.)*: Uh… How does that work? You eating dreams, I mean.

AYUMU: It's just as it sounds. I eat dreams when a person wants me to.

KEI: That's it?

AYUMU *(He nods his head.)*: Ah, if you're done, the two of you should get home. I can walk Jay home if he wants. *(He gets closer to JAY.)*

JAY: Thanks--

KEI: You'll just see him tonight, right? *(KEI gets between AYUMU and JAY.)* You can see him then. Plus, we're right here anyway. *(He points to the balcony that is upstage right.)*

AYUMU *(Pauses.)*: You're right. I'll see to do that then. *(He leaves stage right.)*

JAY: Bye! Huh, didn't realize we were already at my house. Well, see you tomorrow, Kei. Stay safe on your way home, yeah? *(He climbs up his balcony and back into his house.)*

KEI *(As JAY climbs up his balcony.)*: Yeah, see ya! *(Once JAY is out of sight.)* Like hell that dude is only eating dreams. *(KEI exits stage left.)*

Scene 6
ELL's office.

(ELL at his desk. KEI enters, rushing in towards ELL's desk.)

KEI: Ell!

ELL: Good evening, Kei. Should you not be at home? It is very late.

KEI: You know how much I hate it there.

ELL: Yes, but you should go home. The last time you stayed here, your older brother broke down my door and threatened to kill me for taking you away from your family. I did not even know you were here.

KEI: Okay, okay. Jeez. But I have a question first.

ELL: Please make it quick.

KEI: So, I know you're all into the creature, monster, and spirit hunting. Have you heard of some sort of dream eater spirit?

ELL: Mmh. *(picks up the thick book.)* I believe it is called baku...

KEI: Yes, that!

ELL: Oh? I am glad for your enthusiasm, but I am your fighting mentor. Why do you wish to know of these spirits? You showed no interest before.

KEI: I met a guy. Can you just read more from the book?

ELL *(Pauses.)*: Alright. It is all in Japanese, so this may or may not be accurate. 'The baku is a Japanese spirit who comes and eats dreams and nightmares. It can be summoned by anyone, but people should only do so sparingly, because if a baku does not feel full, it will feast on that person's hopes and dreams.'

KEI: Hopes and dreams...? Shiz! Oh my god... *(He covers his face with his hands.)*

ELL: Kei, what is wrong? Is it Jay?

KEI: Did I really make it that obvious?

ELL: You care for your friends. I can guess that Jay has made contact with a baku? If that is the case, I will say this. I do not know how baku works exactly. However, I do know that to Japanese spirits, names are very important.

KEI: Names, huh? *(ELL nods.)* Thanks, Ell! *(exits.)*

Scene 7
In JAY's bedroom. Night.

JAY *(lies in bed. gets up and sighs.)* Hmm... The dreams won't get bad, because Baku is here for me? Right? *(He shrugs and lies back down.)*

(Enter DREAM JAY.)

DREAM JAY: Ah. There's no one here. *(Enter DREAM ELL from stage right. DREAM JAY looks stage right.)* Oh, Master Ell!

DREAM ELL: Why do you call me that?

DREAM JAY: What? The Master part? That's always how I greet you, Ell--

DREAM ELL: No. Why do you still call me Master?

DREAM JAY: What--

DREAM ELL: After that loss? You should get out of my sight!

DREAM JAY: Wait--

(Enter DREAM KEI. *He's just walking and listening to music.)*

DREAM JAY: Kei! Kei!
DREAM KEI: What? *(He takes out one earbud.)* Oh, it's you. Man, I don't even want to talk to you. *(He begins to leave.)*
DREAM JAY: W-wait! *(He grabs* DREAM KEI *by the shoulder.)* Why?
DREAM KEI: Why? Why? Because of that fight a couple weeks ago! Why would I be friends with such a loser like you?
DREAM JAY: Wait, I thought you didn't care about that!
DREAM KEI: I was just lying for your sake. Honestly, it's hard to keep up an act for so long. I didn't want to see you cry home to your Aunty Em. You're really such a loser, you know? *(He laughs.)*

*(*DREAM ELL *joins in the laughter. Enter* DREAM EXTRAS *slowly surrounding* DREAM JAY *while laughing. Please don't cover* JAY *who is in bed.)*

DREAM JAY: H-huh? Ah... Huh? *(He is pushed to the ground by* DREAM KEI.*)* No... B-baku... Baku, please help...

(Enter AYUMU *who walks over to the sleeping* JAY *in bed.)*

AYUMU: I'm here... *(He touches sleeping* JAY's *forehead.)*

(All DREAM CHARACTERS *scatter off the stage.)*

JAY: AH! *(He jumps up in bed.)* Baku!
AYUMU: Yes?
JAY: That dream... Why did I see it this time?
AYUMU: Due to deep psychological reasons, your brain must've put up a formidable barrier to make sure no one would learn your secrets. It's only logical to create stronger bonds between me and you, mh?
JAY: Uhhh...
AYUMU: Dreams got stronger. Let's also make a stronger promise.
JAY: Oh. So you have your limits, also?
AYUMU: Yes. So, do you want to make another promise?
JAY: Yes! It worked well last time. *(He sticks his hand out for a pinky promise.)*
AYUMU: Ah, it's a little different this time. It's sealed with a kiss.
JAY: Kiss?! I'm a twelve-year-old boy!
AYUMU: No, no, it can be anywhere. Like so. *(He kisses* JAY's *hand.)*
JAY: Ah... Okay... Still a little awkward. *(He reluctantly then hastily kisses* AYUMU *on the cheek and then falls over and buries himself into his pillow. Muffled and through his pillow.)* I, Jay, allow you to eat my... Dreams? Yeah, dreams from now on.

AYUMU *(He enjoys this decision, and his noises may come off as gross. He coughs and corrects himself.)* Thank you. You will… Let's see what will happen, yes?

JAY: Yeah. Hey, Baku? You make weird noises sometimes.

AYUMU: And that I do. Sweet dreams, Jay.

Scene 8

Outside in the street. Day.

KEI: So Jay… How was last night? With Baku, you know?

JAY *(absent-mindedly)*: Uh… It was fine, really… Like I had a horrible nightmare… then, I made another promise with him to get rid of that nightmare… That sort of thing.

KEI: Another promise?

JAY: Yeah… This time sealed with a kiss rather than a seal with pinkies…

KEI: K-kiss?!

JAY: Yeah. Just on the cheek.

KEI: Oh. Oh thank god. Don't leave out information like that. Baku looks like an adult you know. *(He pauses to think.)* He's probably a lot older than that actually…

JAY: Yeah…? Probably…

KEI: So, you did make another promise with him?

JAY: Mmh.

KEI: Do you remember what you said?

JAY: Pretty much the same thing… He can eat my dreams… Mmh.

KEI: Your… dreams, this time? *(He inspects JAY, turning him around every now and then. JAY just goes with it. He clasps JAY's face into his hands.)* Jay, do you still want to do that thing?

JAY: That thing…?

KEI: Yes, the most important thing to you!

JAY: The most important thing…?

KEI: Finding your dad! You know, Ji!

JAY: Yeah… I mean, I guess I should.

KEI: You guess? You guess?! Oh my god… *(He begins pacing around the stage.)* No, ugh, this is, ahhhhg! Why don't you want to find Ji anymore?

JAY: I don't… really see the point of it anymore.

KEI: Huh?! You! This is the only reason you wanted to have Ell train you, remember? You needed to get stronger to find your dad and… This was the only reason I met you. Ugh! *(He sits on the floor dejectedly.)* No, I shouldn't get mad at you. This is all Baku's fault!

JAY: Huh…? Huh? Baku? Why is this Baku's fault?

KEI: What?

JAY: What do you mean, "what?" You just said this was Baku's fault.

KEI: Well, it is!

JAY: All, Baku has been doing was taking my nightmares away from me.

KEI: Are you sure? It's only been last night since you made that promise, right? Why are you acting so differently already? Surely, you've noticed the change by now.

JAY: I'm acting perfectly fine.

KEI: No, you were totally out of it until I mentioned Baku.

JAY: Why do you hate Baku so much?

KEI: Don't change the subject. And I don't hate him, I'm just suspicious of him.

JAY: What made you so suspicious?

KEI: How could you be so naive? He's just a suspicious man, with suspicious powers, with what seems to be zero motive.

JAY: He needs to eat.

KEI: And why did it have to be you? He could've picked someone else; you could've easily refused. Did you just assume you could've taken him on if something went bad along the way? Honestly, your naivety is why you started having bad dreams in the first place. Did you think you could've taken on that guy back then?

JAY *(quietly)* W-wait... You... Actually thought that...?

KEI: H-huh?

JAY: I thought... that only happened... in my dreams... I didn't think...

KEI: Wait, Jay, no!

JAY: Does that mean... You don't actually care...?

KEI: Hey, wait--

JAY: I guess... That would make sense. You're just that type of person. You're lucky, you know? You don't have to care... *(walks away. exits)*

AYUMU *(Offstage)*: Oh? Is something wrong? *(Enter AYUMU.)* Mmh? A fight with your friend? Should I even call you friends now?

KEI *(He doesn't look at AYUMU at all.)* We're still friends... This is... fine. We'll make up... That's how it always is...

AYUMU: Really, now? After all that? What are you going to do?

KEI: ... I'll stop you.

AYUMU: How?

KEI: I'll find a way.

AYUMU: Really?

KEI: Yes. *(He looks up at AYUMU.)* For sure.

AYUMU: I admire your confidence. But... *(He gets close to KEI.)* How do you plan to do that? What is your "way?"

KEI: *(He attempts to step back, but steels himself to stay in place.)* I'll end it now... Let's play a game.

AYUMU: A game? Oh, do tell.

KEI: ... We should go over the rules first.

AYUMU: Smart. You make them. *(He leans back on his cane.)*

KEI: We'll... Throw some dice. *(He pulls dice from his jacket pocket.)*

AYUMU: Do you always have dice on you?

KEI: ... It's for figuring out the loser in a tie.

AYUMU: Are you saying we're equal?

KEI *(Ignores the question.)*: So I'll let you pick what sides you want. If a person loses, they lose one of the sides they own, and it goes to the winner for that round. The winner overall will be the one who gets all six sides first, or the person who gets the single number they own. Meaning, if one of us had five out of six sides, but if the die lands on the one side that person does not own, then the other wins.

AYUMU: Okay, I get what you're saying. Now, what am I going to get once I win?

KEI: My hopes and dreams. You can go straight for them.

AYUMU: Mmm? But, what kind do you even have...?

KEI: Find out when you win.

AYUMU: Okay. What do you want after all this, assuming you win?

KEI: Find out when you lose.

AYUMU *(chuckles)*: Alright. Shall we start then?

KEI: Pinky promise first, so you don't get out of this deal. *(He sticks his pinky finger toward AYUMU.)*

AYUMU: Oh. Precautions. You *are* that type of boy. *(He reaches forward and curls his pinky towards KEI's.)*

KEI: *(He quickly takes his hand away from AYUMU and wipes it off.)* What sides do you want?

AYUMU: Six... Five... and four.

KEI: Alright then. *(He throws the die.)* Six. You get a side. Which one do you want?

AYUMU: Three.

KEI *(throws the die)*: You get another side.

AYUMU: Two.

KEI: *(hesitates, then reaches back into his pocket.)* How about I add another dice? *(takes another die out of his pocket.)* If either one of them lands on your numbers, then you still win.

AYUMU: I still have the same chances, but I don't see why not. It'll entertain you, right?

KEI: Haha, yeah, thanks. *(nonchalantly throws the dice towards AYUMU.)*

AYUMU: They're... both ones. *(Loud MMMMMMM-ing sounds.)* How?

KEI *(He shrugs and makes an "I'unno" noise.)*

AYUMU: Okay, what do you want...? I can--

KEI: Tell me your name.

AYUMU: What—

KEI: Your actual name. I know it isn't Baku.

AYUMU: It's... It's Ayumu.

KEI: Ayumu.

AYUMU: Ugh... A name I abandoned long ago...

KEI: Yeah, yeah, Ayumu. Listen to me. You must leave this town and never come back, but only after my next commands. You can't take the dreams of anyone from this town ever again. And, uh... Right. Give back Jay's hopes and dreams.

AYUMU: Fine, brat. Here, just give him this. *(holds out a bag of an unknown material.)*

KEI: What is it?

AYUMU: It's Jay's hopes and dreams, or what's left of them anyway. I didn't eat all of them yet, but I'm afraid I can't give back the ones I have eaten.

KEI: How do I give them back to Jay?

AYUMU: Do you not know how to eat?

KEI: Right, then. It'll have to do for now. Now get out of here!

(AYUMU exits)

Scene 9
Outside in the streets. Day.

(JAY sits on the sidewalk)

KEI *(running in)* Jay! Jay! Here, take this! *(gives the bag to JAY)*

JAY: It's a bag of flour?

KEI: It's not flour. It's your hopes and dreams. Here, just eat it.

JAY: If you say so… *(pours the contents into mouth, then coughs)*

KEI: Now then, what is the most important thing in the *entire world* to you, Jay?

JAY: I... I... I need to find my dad.

KEI: *(Hugs JAY)* I knew I could get the real you back! I just knew it!

JAY: Hey, whoa! You never hug me. Hey, how did you get myself back?

KEI: I won them in a bet.

JAY: From Baku?

KEI: Yes, and his name is Ayumu, in case he ever comes back. Which he really shouldn't.

JAY: But what about my nightmares?

KEI: I can help you through those, bro. It's what friends are for.

THE LORD'S BANQUET
Thong Pham

CHARACTERS

BLAKE COLLINS, *a man in his late 20's*
SHEILA WATERS, *a woman in her mid 20's. Blake's longtime girlfriend*
LORD BRADLEY, *a man in his 40's. Extremely wealthy eccentric*
CASSANDRA CROWE, *a woman in her late 20's. Kevin's wife*
KEVIN CROWE, *a man in his early 30's. Cassandra's husband*
SAMUEL DEAN, *a man in his late 20's. Has a limp leg*
BRIANNE T. HART, *a woman in her early 20's. Lord Bradley's maid.*
JAMIE LANCASTER, *Lord Bradley's personal assistant.*

Scene 1

BLAKE'S living room, early Sunday morning.

BLAKE (*Offstage to the left*): All right, all right! I'm coming! (*enters from the left and storms across his living room to unbolt the lock*) This better not be some serial killer interrupting my beauty sleep. (*unlatches and opens door*) This better be good. I was in the middle of the most wonderful dream.

JAMIE (*rummages through bag*): You've got mail.

BLAKE (*scoffs*): Mail? On a Sunday? This must be prank. Or an elaborate marketing campaign. Either way, I'm not interested. Good day to you. (*attempts to close the door*)

JAMIE (*Stops the door*): Please, sir. This is no joke. I request that you take this letter. It is of the utmost importance. (*hands BLAKE the letter*)

BLAKE: Fine, I'll indulge you. (*rips open the envelope and skims over it*) Who is this Lord Bradley? Does he always send early morning love letters to people?

JAMIE: Lord Bradley is one of the most distinguished citizens of our time, sir. He has more money than he knows what to do with. That's why he likes to give back to the community on occasion.

BLAKE (*still skimming the letter*): A banquet? Tomorrow at noon? This guy is crazy. I don't even know who he is.

JAMIE: You may not, but I think there's someone who does. Someone you're quite intimate with.

BLAKE: Who? My mother? She's dead. (BLAKE'S *eyes go wide*) No. Way. Commissioner Lynch? Commissioner James Lynch?

JAMIE: The one and only. He is your boss, isn't he?

BLAKE: Well, this *is* his signature, but (*looks up from letter*) signatures can be forged.

JAMIE(*chuckling*): I was told of your keen intellect, Mr. Collins I see you live up to it.

BLAKE: So then, you know my name. You know my work. You even know where I live. Frankly, this is all very suspicious.

JAMIE: I am aware of how it seems, Mr. Collins. My words may carry little weight to you, but this is legitimate. There are plenty of charitable billionaires in the world who just want to give back

BLAKE: And there are plenty of arsonists, thieves, and murderers in the world. Your point being?

JAMIE: Mr. Collins, believe me or not, you have nothing to lose. With your skills, if anything is amiss, you can do what you do best. But if you should refuse to come, you'll be losing out on an experience of a lifetime, good or bad.

BLAKE: I've had my share of life experiences, thank you.

JAMIE: Please, Mr. Collins. Do not dismiss this so easily. It would be a shame to let the food go to waste. This is in your honor, after all.

BLAKE: My honor?

JAMIE: Finish the letter.

BLAKE (reading out loud from the letter): "After much discussion with Commissioner Lynch, we have decided that this banquet is in your honor. Your work on the McKenzie murders was the epitome of skill and knowledge in your field. Therefore, when we have ate our fill, the Commissioner and I will award you the Gilded Holmes Laurel in recognition of your success." (*trying to hide his joy*) The Gilded Holmes Laurel...

JAMIE: A big deal?

BLAKE: Very. A distinguished commissioner has to submit a recommendation to the board. Then, they go into months of scrutinizing the awardee in question. Then, there comes the paperwork. And more paperwork. It's quite tedious. Also risky. By submitting a recommendation, a commissioner could lost all credibility if it doesn't pan out. This is- this is insane. Me- getting the Laurel.

JAMIE: An opportunity too good to pass up. (*pulls out some papers from bag*) I have the official documents here, if you are understandably in doubt. The seal and signatures of the board should all be there. And before you go on about forgery again, think of this. There is no reason to go through so many hurdles to scam you. Faking the signatures of these people is highly illegal. It would be safer to just break into your house. We do not want your money, Mr. Collins. We simply want you to get what you deserve. To get what is rightfully yours. You don't have to live with the fact that your case was overshadowed by a story about celebrities eating lunch anymore.

BLAKE: It would be shame to let that food be wasted. But tomorrow at noon is much too early for me. I don't have a proper suit for this. I don't even know where it's being held.

JAMIE All taken care of. (*pulls out a package from bag and tosses it to* BLAKE) One hand-stitched, Italian silk tuxedo, complete with bowtie. Also, a limo will take you to the mansion. No need to spend money on gas.

BLAKE: This is a bit too good to pass on, now.

JAMIE: I'm glad you feel that way. We'll be seeing you tomorrow then?

BLAKE: Wait. (*face palms*) I have a date with my girlfriend tomorrow.

JAMIE: Bring her. There's always room at Lord Bradley's mansion. (*glances at watch*) Oh! Would you look at the time. I must be going be going. Errands to run, places to be. Farewell, Mr. Collins. (*exits right*)

BLAKE: (*stares at letter for a few moments*) I deserve a treat. This will be my night. Now, back to sleep.

(*exits left*)

Scene 2

Inside a large limousine. Afternoon.

(JAMIE *is sitting at the driver's seat, hands on the wheel, dressed in a neat outfit.* BLAKE *and* SHEILA *are seated next to each other near the back.* BLAKE *has on the tuxedo he'd received the night before, and* SHEILA *has on a beautiful red dress.*)

BLAKE: Well, the limo is real. The suit too, as far as I'm aware. This might be worthwhile after all.

JAMIE: Glad to hear that, Mr. Collins. It will be even better once we arrive.

SHEILA: You aren't one to be so gullible, you know. Losing your touch, old man?

BLAKE: Don't be crass. This is for me. I'm finally being recognized for my work. And I've done my research. Lord Bradley is real, that's for sure. And he is very, very, VERY wealthy.

SHEILA: That's it? Eh, C minus. You confirmed he exists. Not much else.

JAMIE: Lord Bradley is a private man. He isn't particularly fond of photographers taking pictures of him showering.

SHEILA: There should be more to go off of, though. Like, how he got rich. His contributions to society. His business. Blake, do you even know his first name?

BLAKE (*shrugs*): I didn't come across anything.

JAMIE (with a perfectly straight face): His first name is Lord.

(BLAKE *and* SHEILA *stare at* JAMIE *for few moments before bursting into laughter*)

BLAKE (*whispering to* SHEILA) I think he's serious.

SHEILA (*to* BLAKE) We have quite the character on our hands. He's just your type.

BLAKE: You are the only one for me.

SHEILA: You just like the dress. (*leans in for a kiss but the limo suddenly stops, causing* BLAKE *and* SHEILA *to bump heads*)

JAMIE: Apologies for the interruption. We will be making a quick stop.

SHEILA (*rubbing head*): A warning would've been nice.

JAMIE (*presses a button, opening the limo door*) Please, be nice to our new guest.

SAMUEL (*enters*): You weren't lying about the limo, at least.

JAMIE: Have a seat anywhere you want.

SAMUEL: Will do. (*limps over to where* BLAKE *and* SHEILA *are and sits opposite them*) Hello there. (Extends hand towards BLAKE) Samuel Dean. Just Sam is fine.

BLAKE (*shakes hand*): Blake Collins. This is my girlfriend, Sheila.

SHEILA (*gives a small wave*) Hi.

BLAKE: She can be jerk sometimes, so be prepared.

SHEILA: Oh, I'm sorry. It's not my fault no one loves you.

BLAKE: Case proven. (*wraps arm around* SHEILA)

SAMUEL (*laughs*) You two seem alright. You here for the banquet too?

BLAKE: We are. Did you also get the invitation Sunday morning?

SAMUEL: Early Sunday morning, actually. With all that money, you would think he could afford to have good manners. An email would have been better.

JAMIE: Lord Bradley thinks hand-delivered letters are more personal. More intimate. Would any of you have even replied to an email?

BLAKE: Good point. That doesn't make it any less creepy or annoying.

SAMUEL: He's right. A little bit of tact doesn't hurt. Quite the opposite actually. How's your arm by the way, errrr...

JAMIE: Jamie. And my arm still aches, no thanks to you. I'm afraid it might cause me to miss a cliffside turn.

SAMUEL: Sorry about that, Jamie. A man needs his sleep.

JAMIE: I'll keep that in mind at the estate.

(*the group sits in silence for a few moments*)

SHEILA: So you got any food here? I'm starving.

BLAKE: I thought you brought snacks?

SHEILA: Oh, how awful of me for forgetting. If I only had more than an hour to get ready.

BLAKE: Why would anyone need that long to get ready?

SHEILA (*exasperated*): Men.

SAMUEL: Hey! That was uncalled for. Not all guys are like that. Just Blake.

BLAKE: I thought we were friends. (*sheds a fake tear*)

SHEILA: Seriously though, is there food on this thing?

JAMIE: Check under the table.

SHEILA: Thank you. (*reaches under table and opens a cabinet*) Dried fruit. Wonderful.

JAMIE: There are also rare truffles and caviar if you so desire.

SHEILA: Never mind then. Anything to drink?

JAMIE: On the other side.

SAMUEL: I got it. (*opens cabinet and takes out a bottle of wine along with a corkscrew*) 1983. Not bad.

JAMIE: Glasses are at the back.

SAMUEL: Open this for me. (*hands BLAKE the wine and corkscrew and goes to the far left*)

BLAKE (*opens the bottle and sniffs it*): A good year.

(SAMUEL *comes back with three glasses and hands them to BLAKE and SHEILA*)

JAMIE: Try not to drink too much. We're still hours away from the estate.

BLAKE (pours wine in each glass) To new friends. (*raises glass*)

SHEILA & SAMUEL: To new friends. (*touch glasses with BLAKE*)

(*Everyone drinks*)

BLAKE: I'm sorry if this is rude, but what happened to your leg? My curiosity is getting the best of me.

SAMUEL: This old thing? (*pounds limp leg*) Ah, it's nothing. Got it in an accident.

SHEILA: What kind?

SAMUEL: Car accident. I was driving my Impala along the street when this guy, Randall Ortiz, came outta nowhere.

SHEILA: Oh my God.

SAMUEL: It's not that bad, really. At least I can still walk. Any more questions you two want answered?

BLAKE: We're good. Let's not dampen the mood anymore. We're supposed to be having fun. (*refills glasses*)

SAMUEL (*raises glass*): I'll drink to that. To good times ahead!

BLAKE & SHEILA: To good times. (touch glasses)

Scene 3

Inside foyer of BRADLEY's mansion. Evening.

(BLAKE *and* SHEILA *are admiring the busts and paintings. They are the only two there at the moment.*)

SHEILA: This guy is loaded. He pays thousands to put people's heads in his mansion.

BLAKE: I know right? Look at this one over here. (points to *Starry Night* on the wall) It seems like the real deal, not some shabby replica.

SHEILA (*giggles*): You mean the one currently in the Museum of Modern Art? The one we saw last Summer?

BLAKE: Whatever, nerd.

SHEILA (*audibly smirks*): You were the one who wanted to go there. Just saying, geek.

BLAKE: Excuse me, but who invited you here? That's right.

SHEILA: You're going to throw me out? Leave me alone on the streets to be preyed on by terrible monsters?

BLAKE: *You're* a terrible monster.

SHEILA (*grins widely*): I know.

BLAKE: But at least you're a cute monster. *(kisses* SHEILA)

(footsteps can be heard offstage to the right)

CASSANDRA (*offstage*): Oh. My. God. This place is amazing, Kevin. The wood-work is marvellous.

KEVIN (*out of breath*): That's nice, dear.

CASSANDRA (*enters right*): The decor has a very... soothing atmosphere. (*notices* BLAKE *and* SHEILA) Oh! Honey, come quickly! There are other guests here.

(KEVIN *enters right, overburdened with many assortments of bags and purses*)

CASSANDRA: It's so nice to meet you both! I'm Cassandra. Cassandra Crowe. That's my husband, Kevin.

KEVIN (*has great difficulty standing upright*): A pleasure. (*smiles weakly*)

CASSANDRA (*very quickly*): Kevin and I just got off *the* longest ride ever. It's was quite nice of Mr. Bradley to invite us, but did it have to be so far away? God, I need a bed. It's all so horribly tiring. You two must be feeling the same. Or did your ride here go smoother? I'm going to have a word with that girl later. We didn't even have steak on the way here! No built in grill, apparently! Can't you believe that? Oh, where my manners? I don't even know your names.

BLAKE: I'm Blake.

SHEILA: Sheila.

CASSANDRA: What a pretty name. Sheila. Sheeeiilllaaa. Rolls off the tongue beautifully. Right, Kevin?

KEVIN: Absolutely, dear.

CASSANDRA: Blake is a nice name too.

BLAKE (*hesitantly*): Thank you?

CASSANDRA: Blake. Short and to the point. Yet not so rough. A smooth motion followed with a strong finish. And then there's my name. Cassandra. What a mouthful. I could shorten it to Cass and Sandra, but I don't know. It just isn't me. It's long-winded, but Cass and Sandra just don't work for me. Too short. Not enough emphasis on certain parts. Or maybe it's just nicknames in general. It's like you're losing a part of yourself when you shorten your name. You don't get the whole story. Unfortunately, really. There are such nice nicknames out there.

SHEILA: That's, um, an interesting thought. I--

CASSANDRA: And then there's you, Kevin. You're simple.

(SHEILA *rolls eyes*)

CASSANDRA: It does a good enough job. A decent name. Nothing fancy or strange or dazzling. Simple. Normal. Maybe's that's a good thing. But then again, there are a million Kevins. A Kevin here, a Kevin there. Kevins of all kinds. But would a rose smell just as sweet called by any other name? Probably, yes. Shakespeare is outdated anyway.

BLAKE (*to* SHEILA): She has better dialogue than Hamlet or Macbeth.

CASSANDRA: It's getting late. I think Kevin and I are going to turn in for the night. It was a wonderful conversation, Blake, Sheila. We'll be seeing each other again soon.

(CASSANDRA & KEVIN *exit left*)

BLAKE (*gives* SHEILA *a puzzled look*): That was a conversation.

(SHEILA *shrugs*)

BRIANNE (*enters right*): I see you've met the other guests. Quite a mouthful that one is. And her poor husband.

BLAKE: That's an understatement. I would kill myself if I were him.

SHEILA: I would kill *her*.

BRIANNE: I am Brianne. I will be serving you this evening. Pleased to make your acquaintances, Blake and Sheila. (*bows*)

BLAKE: Did Lord Bradley give all his workers our names?

BRIANNE: Just me and Jamie. But we're the only ones in Lord Bradley's service, so technically, yes. All his servants know your names.

SHEILA: Only two? With this estate, he needs at least a dozen, if not more.

BRIANNE: He values his privacy. He's not one to be around people all the time.

SHEILA (*to* BLAKE): And just like that, he's creepy again.

BRIANNE: Let me show you to your room. I'm sure you both want a comfy bed after that long ride.

BLAKE: One moment, please.

BRIANNE: Yes? How can I be of service?

BLAKE: Is the Commissioner here yet? I want to thank him for the nomination.

BRIANNE: I'm afraid to say that Commissioner Lynch will not be attending this evening. Fallen sick with the flu.

SHEILA (*to* BLAKE): Shady.

BLAKE: Oh. That's… unexpected.

BRIANNE: Don't think too much off it. You've had a long ride. Try to get some rest. Now, follow me. (*exits left*)

BLAKE (*shrugs*): We're already here. Not much to be done.

Scene 4
Inside dining room of LORD BRADLEY's *mansion. Evening.* BLAKE *and* SHEILA *are sitting next to each other on one side of the table.* JAMIE *is setting up plates and such.*

BLAKE: We're finally going to meet our eponymous host.

SHEILA: About time. A face to put to this madness.

BLAKE: I wonder what he looks like. Strange to say, I never gave it much thought until now.

SHEILA: I see a hideous beast that eats the bones of men and ferries women away into the night. Oh wait, that's you.

BLAKE: Well that would be better than the cruel mistress responsible for that beast.

JAMIE: Don't get too excited now. He's just a man. You would only be setting yourself up for disappointment.

SHEILA: It's not just the look. It's the idea of him. I want to believe there's more to Lord Bradley than the image of a creepy old man.

JAMIE: Oh, I wouldn't be worried about that. It would be the least of your concerns. There's much more to Lord Bradley than you could know.

BLAKE: These cryptic hints aren't helping.

JAMIE: It matters not. He will be here soon. In fact, I'm going to get him right now. (*exits left*)

(CASSANDRA & KEVIN *enter right.* CASSANDRA *is a little unsteady*)

SHEILA (*to* BLAKE): Oh God, not again.

CASSANDRA (*groggily*): Lovely friends! It's so wonderful to see you again. I feared that our paths may never cross once more. But the fates have brought us together again. (*cups* SHEILA'S *face*) To you again, sweet Sheila.

(SHEILA *groans and* BLAKE *stifles laughter*)

KEVIN: Come along now, dear. Let's take our seats.

(KEVIN *leads* CASSANDRA *to the other side and they sit*)

KEVIN: Sorry about that. Getting her drunk as the only way she'd shut up. Even I can only take so much.

BLAKE: Oh no, don't sweat it. I prefer this version. Much more enjoyable to be around.

CASSANDRA (*mumbling to herself*): Friends, Romans, countrymen. Swear not by the moon, the inconstant moon...(*the rest is inaudible gibberish*)

KEVIN: I'm especially sorry for ruining that...moment between you two, Sheila.

SHEILA: Oh heavens, no. Thank you for rescuing me from that dire fate.

SAMUEL (*enters right*): I hope I'm not late for the party. (*takes seat at one end of the table*)

BLAKE: No, but you just missed a very interesting exchange.

SAMUEL: What a shame. (*looks at* CASSANDRA, *still mumbling gibberish*) At least she's finally quiet.

KEVIN: Imagine waking up to talking every single day.

SAMUEL: My condolences.

KEVIN: It's not so bad after a few years. I think it's why I fell in love with her in the first place. It's mysteriously endearing. We may be at odds sometimes, and I may get fed up, but I love her all the same.

(BLAKE & SHEILA *give each other a knowing look and a smile*)

JAMIE (*enters left*): And now, our prestigious host, ladies and gentlemen. The man behind the curtain, Lord Bradley.

LORD BRADLEY (*enters left, wearing unkempt clothes*): Ah, it's a pleasure to finally meet you all. (*takes seat at final chair*) Mr. and Mr. Crowe. Mr. Dean. Ms. Waters. And you, Mr. Collis. (*spreads arms*) Welcome to Bradley Manor.

SHEILA (*to BLAKE*): He looks sane enough.

BLAKE (*to SHEILA*): Yeah, but something feels off…

LORD BRADLEY: I think I've kept you here long enough. I'll have plenty of time to talk, but let us now dine. (*claps hands*)

BRIANNE (*enter left carrying a covered plate*): A feast fit for a king. (*sets plate on table*)

LORD BRADLEY: Thank you, Brianne. (*lifts cover*) Stuffed pig. It smells amazing, wouldn't you all agree?

SAMUEL: We came all the way here for bacon?

LORD BRADLEY (*creepy laughter*): Of course not, Mr. Dean. This is just the appetizer. The main course will come after. Jamie? If you'll please.

(JAMIE *nods and exits left. Returns with a bottle, a corkscrew and large knife*)

LORD BRADLEY: If you don't like pork, how about some pomegranate wine to win you over?

(JAMIE *opens bottle with corkscrew and pours it into everyone's glass. Everyone sits down and drinks from their glasses*)

SAMUEL: Not bad.

CASSANDRA: Exquisite, like a midsummer night's dream.

SHEILA: Almost as good as the two dollar liqueur I buy.

BLAKE: You mean the one *I* buy.

KEVIN: It has a tang that excites the senses.

LORD BRADLEY: It's a 1944 brew from Greece. One of the finest in my collection. And the pig isn't just from some unknown farm. No. This swine was bred and raised to be slaughtered by the most talented curators of meats. Jamie, the knife. (*takes knife from* JAMIE) Now watch. (*carves up the pig*) See how the blade cuts the soft, succulent flesh so effortlessly. The juices seep out at the barest touch. The moist pink ready to be devoured.

SHEILA (*to* BLAKE): Uh yeah, this guy is not okay.

LORD BRADLEY (*creepy laughter*): What a fine meal we are going to have. So tender. I can wait no longer.

(JAMIE *exits left and* BRIANNE *exits right*)

LORD BRADLEY: I daresay, this is a feast worth dying for. (*the lights flicker before going off*)

SHEILA: What was that? (*shuffling and a woman's scream can be heard*)

(the lights come on and CASSANDRA is slump over the table covered in blood)

(BLAKE, SHEILA, KEVIN, & SAMUEL *shout and gasp, then stand.*)

KEVIN: Cassandra! (*shakes her lifeless body*)

BLAKE (*puts* SHEILA *behind him*): I knew it! I knew something was off!

LORD BRADLEY (*perfectly calm while covered in blood*): Darn right something is off. A woman was killed. There's a murderer in this room.

BLAKE: Are you serious right now?

LORD BRADLEY: I'm absolutely serious. We need to find the killer. Personally, I think it's Kevin.

KEVIN: What?!

LORD BRADLEY: You know what you did. I heard you complaining about how annoying she was.

KEVIN: I loved Cassandra! I would never harm her!

BLAKE: Something tells me it wasn't Kevin.

LORD BRADLEY: He's obviously trying to pull a fast one on you, Mr. Collins. Don't be fooled by his clandestine wiles. Arrest him! (*points a bloody knife at* KEVIN)

BLAKE: I can see the knife, Lord Bradley.

LORD BRADLEY (*hides knife behind his back*): What knife?

SAMUEL: This can't be real.

BLAKE: You're also covered in blood.

LORD BRADLEY: What? Nonsense. It's just...paint. Yeah, it's red paint.

BLAKE: You got yourself covered in paint in the middle of a dinner party?

LORD BRADLEY: The food inspires me to do some painting.

SHEILA: This is ridiculous! Just arrest him already, Blake.

BLAKE: You're right. Lord Bradley, put the knife down and get on your knees.

LORD BRADLEY: But I've done nothing wrong! You can't do this! This is oppression, I tell you. Total fascism!

BLAKE: Enough games! I know you murdered Cassandra.

LORD BRADLEY (*gets on his feet*): So you've figured it out. Bravo, detective. Bravo.

BLAKE: The blood is literally on your hands. Now get down on your knees.

LORD BRADLEY: I don't think you're in a position to be giving orders. I do, after all, have a knife. (*brandishes knife*)

BLAKE: Well guess what? I thought something might happen. (*reaches into his pockets*) So I brought my gun. (*pulls out pistol and aims it at* LORD BRADLEY) Put the knife down and get on your knees!

LORD BRADLEY: So you do. That is indeed a gun in your hands. Wait, you brought a gun to my banquet?

BLAKE: Put. The. Knife. Down.

LORD BRADLEY: That is very poor etiquette, Mr. Collins. And your tone of voice isn't all that pleasant either.

BLAKE (*fires a warning shot into the air*): I have had enough of you. Put it down or I *will* open fire.

LORD BRADLEY: Haven't you already? Fine, you win. (*tosses knife behind him*) There's one thing you should know though. (*reaches into pockets*) I ALSO BROUGHT MY OWN GUN!

BLAKE: GET DOWN! (*the lights go out again and gunshots and screams are heard*) (*when the lights come on again,* KEVIN *is on the floor dead, and* LORD BRADLEY *is nowhere to be seen*)

BLAKE (*under his breath*): Damnit. He got away. (*addressing everyone else*) Everybody good?

SHEILA: I-I'm alright.

SAMUEL: Still kicking I guess. Can't say the same for Kevin.

BLAKE (*slams table*): He didn't deserve this. *They* didn't deserve this...

SHEILA (*places hand on* BLAKE'S *shoulder*): You did everything you could...

BLAKE: And it wasn't enough.

SAMUEL: None of that matters now. We're still stuck in this place with a delusional psychopath and his lackeys.

BLAKE: You're right. Let's get out of here. (*everyone starts to exit left, with* SAMUEL *trailing behind*)

(*as* BLAKE *and* SHEILA *cross the doorway, it closes and locks* SAMUEL *inside*)

BLAKE (*pounding door furiously*): Sam! Sam!

SAMUEL: I'm ok. Don't worry. I can go another.

BLAKE: No, we need to stay together. Stand back. I'll blow the lock open. (*readies gun*)

LORD BRADLEY (*offstage*): I wouldn't do that, Mr. Collins. (*enters right*) That door is reinforced to the point that it can stop a 50 caliber sniper rifle. Your bullets will bounce right off.

(*picks up knife he tossed earlier*)

BLAKE: Scum!

LORD BRADLEY: How rude of you, good sir! You offend my honor!

BLAKE: You're right. Calling you scum is an insult to all the other scums in the world, and I've met plenty.

LORD BRADLEY: Very well. Call me whatever you want. In the end, I am in control, Blake. You don't mind if I call you Blake, do you? I feel like we've really bonded over that exchange of gunfire. (*starts walking to the other side*)

BLAKE: I will get you, no matter what.

LORD BRADLEY: An empty threat at best. I'll indulge you for now though.

BLAKE: Oh, *you're* indulging me? You, with your idiotic ramblings and theatrics.

LORD BRADLEY (*laughs*): You're in *my* mansion, remember? Now if you'll excuse me, Sammy and I need to talk. (*stops a few feet away from* SAMUEL)

BLAKE: Don't you dare--

SAMUEL: Enough, Blake. There's nothing you can do for me.

BLAKE: But--

SAMUEL: You've been a good friend to me the short time we've known each other. Both you and Sheila have. That's more than I've ever asked for.

SHEILA: Sam...

BLAKE: I can't leave you to die!

SAMUEL: I'm already dead. I'm only still talking to you because he's allowing me to.

LORD BRADLEY: This guy is pretty smart. You should listen to him more after this. Well, listen to as much as a corpse can say.

SAMUEL: Go! Get out of here! Save yourselves!

BLAKE: We won't forget you, Sam. Lord Bradley will get justice for this.(*exits left with* SHEILA)

LORD BRADLEY: Now that we're alone, let's have some fun. (*twirls knife*)

SAMUEL: Do your worse. I'm not afraid of you.

LORD BRADLEY: That's expected, given your history.

SAMUEL:...

LORD BRADLEY: Don't act so surprised. I did my homework. And my, you have quite the history.

SAMUEL: You know nothing about me. Nothing.

LORD BRADLEY: I wouldn't say nothing, Sammy. It was a surprise to me that you got along with Blake so well. I thought the conflicting backgrounds would lead to interesting scenarios. (*runs finger along edge of knife*) But an ex-convict befriending an ace detective? I wasn't expecting that. You were supposed to be my red herring.

SAMUEL: That was years ago. I-I've changed.

LORD BRADLEY: Apparently you didn't change enough to be comfortable telling Blake or Sheila.

SAMUEL: They deserve better than me...

LORD BRADLEY: Oh, cheer up, old chap. You redeemed yourself in a small way. You had "friends" that genuinely cared about you. (*laughs maniacally*) And look at all the good they did you.

Scene 5

A room in LORD BRADLEY'S *mansion, right after the banquet. The room itself seems to be a miniature library of sorts. The back wall is lined with books. There is a fireplace in the middle, currently out. A large, cushioned chair and a small table are by the fireplace. The room is devoid of people. Running can be heard to the left.*

(BLAKE & SHEILA *enter left, running. Stop and catch their breath*)

BLAKE: We should be safe here. Let's figure out a plan. (*locks doors*)

SHEILA: Blake...

BLAKE (*ignoring* SHEILA): We can make a run for it after. If I remember correctly, the exit shouldn't be far.

SHEILA: Blake.

BLAKE: If they find us, at least we have an advantage. We can ambush them.

SHEILA: Blake! Listen to me.

BLAKE: What?

SHEILA: What are you doing?

BLAKE: Trying to get us out of here alive. What else?

SHEILA: You and I both know that's unlikely.

BLAKE: What? Sheila, don't say that. We have to try.

SHEILA: He can open and close doors with a push of a button. What use is locking them. He's probably watching us with hidden cameras too.

BLAKE: We don't know that for sure. As crazy as he is, Bradley is incompetent in many things. I'd wager that he'd slipped up somewhere.

SHEILA: Blake. I know you mean well, but... it's just... I...

BLAKE (*goes up to* SHEILA *and grabs her arm*): Hey, it's okay. It's going to be okay. We can't let him win.

SHEILA: He's already won. (*tears away from* BLAKE) I don't want to accept it, but he *is* in control.

BLAKE: Sheila...

SHEILA: This is his mansion. We were doomed from the start. We let Jamie drive us miles away from civilization. We were too drunk to even remember the way we got here! (starts breaking down) Even if we do manage to escape somehow, we'll walk for days without sense of direction. I can't take it! (*crying*) Just look at what he did to Cassandra! To Kevin! To Sam! And what will he did to you Blake? He ruined his plans! He's a monster! He'll kill or torture or-or... (SHEILA'S *sobs prevent her from continuing*)

BLAKE (*takes* SHEILA'S *hand*): Look at me. Sheila, please. Just look at me. (SHEILA *is unresponsive, so* BLAKE *cups her face*) Sheila. I know things are bad. I won't deny that. You're scared. But I'm scared too. Scared of losing you. You're everything to me Sheila. So I have to stay strong. I have to believe we can make it out of this. And if you can go on, I'll carry you. I'll be strong not just for me, but for us. I love you Sheila.

SHEILA: Blake, no. I-I don't-

BLAKE (*Interrupts with a kiss*): It's okay, Sheila. Don't be afraid. I'm here. (*presses* SHEILA'S *to his chest*) I'm here. And I'll never let anything happen to you. It's going to be okay.

SHEILA (*calms down*): Thank-Thank you, Blake. I'm sorry. It's just all too much.

BLAKE: We have each other. That's all that matters now.

SHEILA (*stifles remaining tears*): Blake, do you remember the first time we met?

BLAKE: Of course. How could I forget? Wait... (*chuckles*)

SHEILA (*giggles*): It was at a banquet, all those years ago.

BLAKE: How ironic. You *would* get a kick out of this.

SHEILA: You were celebrating your latest case.

BLAKE: It was Wesley's idea. I wasn't much of a partier.

SHEILA: But you went anyway, sulking in the corner.

BLAKE: And then you went up to me and told me I was a buzzkill.

SHEILA: I'm sure it was much more colorful than that.

BLAKE: Probably was. The first of many sly quips.

SHEILA: If only this was like then… If only I'd…

BLAKE: I wouldn't change anything for the world, Sheila, as long as I'm with you.

SHEILA: You're such a hopeless romantic you know? At least you're hopeless for me.

(BRIANNE *bursts in right and opens fire*)

SHEILA: Blake! (*takes bullet for* BLAKE *and collapses*)

BLAKE: No! (*shoots* BRIANNE *and kills her*) Sheila! No! (*kneels by* SHEILA'S *side*) It's going to be okay. Just don't move. There has to be a med kit somewhere. (*starts standing but* SHEILA *grabs* BLAKE'S *arm*)

SHEILA (*weakly between shallow breaths*): Blake. Don't.

BLAKE: No. I-I can't lose you. I can't let another person die!

SHEILA (*cups* BLAKE'S *face*): It's not your fault. There were nothing you could do.

BLAKE: The bullet was meant for me! I'm supposed to be protecting you! And I failed… (*starts breaking down*)

SHEILA: No, Blake. You didn't. You've protected me all these years. You put up with my snarky comments. You made me feel loved. So let me protect you, just this once. For all that you've given.

BLAKE: I don't want that! I want you to live, Sheila! I love you!

SHEILA: We can't have everything, Blake. But… at least I had you… until the very end.

(*hand falls to the ground*)

BLAKE: Sheila! Sheila! No no no. You can't- (*chokes on words and sobs for a few moments*) You were my everything, you know…(*brushes* SHEILA'S *cheek*) You annoyed me to no end and I cherished every moment. (*kisses her forehead*) Sweet dreams, my love. (*clapping is heard offstage*)

LORD BRADLEY (*offstage*): Bravo, bravo! A splendid performance, Blake. (*enters right*) A little melodramatic and cheesy at the end, but wonderfully acted out. Solid 9/10 from me.

BLAKE: You think this is a game?! (*stands and aims gun*) You murdered all those innocent people!

LORD BRADLEY: Murder is such a nasty word. I prefer liquidated.

BLAKE: Damn you! Have you no conscience? Not a single sliver of morality?

LORD BRADLEY: I don't think so. But don't you dare act all high and mighty with me. You killed poor Brianne over there! Her 5 year anniversary of working for me was next week.

BLAKE: I didn't kill her in cold-blood! I didn't kill her for fun! I didn't carve her body up!

LORD BRADLEY: Does that really make a difference? At the end of the day, we're both murderers. Kindred spirits in a way.

BLAKE: I am nothing like you…

LORD BRADLEY: Oh, you with your hyperboles. We're both relatively hand-some, young bachelors looking for love. And it looks like your search is going to begin all over again.

(BLAKE *shoots* LORD BRADLEY *in the leg*)

LORD BRADLEY(*grunts in pains before regaining composure*): Touchy subject for you. Don't worry, you'll find someone soon.

(BLAKE *shoots other leg*)

LORD BRADLEY: Okay! Let's move on to a different subject. Nice weather we're having right?

BLAKE: Why?

LORD BRADLEY: Hmmm, you're right. It is late at night, so I wouldn't call it nice per say.

BLAKE: Why did you do this?! We bring us all here to kill us?!

LORD BRADLEY: Sadly, it's not because you arrested my brother and I was out for vengeance. Nothing that exciting. quite simply, I was bored.

BLAKE (*voice shaking with anger*): You-you were bored?! You kill my friend for en-tertainment?!

LORD BRADLEY (*laughs*): I was always a fan of the whodunit mysteries. I thought it might be fun. But, you ruined it by figuring it out right away! I can't com-plain though. You ultimately provided me a good story. A story story. That was all I wanted.

(BLAKE *presses gun to* LORD BRADLEY'S *head*)

LORD BRADLEY: Another plot twist! You're full of surprises, Blake.

BLAKE: Give me one good reason I shouldn't blow your brains out.

LORD BRADLEY (*laughs*): I've got nothing. I'm a pathetic excuse for a human being. Go right ahead, Blake. Kill me.

(BLAKE *gun hand is shaking uncontrollably*)

LORD BRADLEY: Go on. Do it. (*grabs gun with both hands*) Do it! Kill me! I deserve it! Paint my mansion red!

BLAKE (*pistol whips* LORD BRADLEY): No. You don't deserve a clean death.

LORD BRADLEY (*sighs*): That was expected. You already made up your mind, otherwise you wouldn't have asked. Now what?

BLAKE: Now I go back home and file a warrant for your arrest.

LORD BRADLEY: We both know that's not happen. Even if you did manage to get back, and even if you did manage to convince your department of the murders, I have money. I'll just hired the best lawyers, bribe some officials, and I'm a free man.

BLAKE: Then I'll just go home. There's nothing worth a damn here. (*tosses gun on the ground and starts walking to the left*)

LORD BRADLEY: You're leaving a lethal weapon unguarded with a madman? What if he decides to take your life?

BLAKE: Go ahead. You've already taken everything else.

LORD BRADLEY: Fine. (*crawls to gun and picks it up*) If you won't do it, I will. (*points gun to his head and pulls trigger*)

BLAKE: No! (*runs over to* LORD BRADLEY'S *body*) And you would take away my dignity too. My one act of good, squandered. (*falls to knees*) You killed Cassandra. You killed Kevin. You killed Sam. You killed Sheila. And now, you're dead too. You won't have to live with what you've done. But I do… (*starts sobbing again, which eventually becomes hysterical laughter*)

JAMIE: (*enters left*) Enough, Blake. There is much to be done now that Lord Bradley is dead.

(BLAKE *continues laughing*)

JAMIE (*sighs*): The fools I'm forced to serve.

Epilogue

Inside of the library of the Bradley Mansion. Noon. BLAKE *is sitting in the cushioned chair, reading a book.* JAMIE *enters with a bottle.*

JAMIE: Here you are, Master Blake. Cheap, store-bought liquor. (*places bottle on the table*)

BLAKE: Thank you, Jamie.

JAMIE: Would you like a glass with that, Master Blake?

BLAKE: No, that will be all. You are dismissed.

JAMIE (*bows and turns to leave*): Oh, I almost forgot. (*turns back to face* BLAKE) The guest will be arriving by tonight.

BLAKE (*puts book down*): Is that so? Are all preparations done.

JAMIE: Yes, sir. Everything is in place.

BLAKE: Good. (*laughs creepily*) Let's give our guest a banquet they won't soon forget.

I'M OKAY WITH THAT
Noah Sabatini

CHARACTERS:

DREW, *Republican candidate, about 40, wears a suit throughout the play.*
ROBIN, *Democrat candidate, about 35 years old, who wears a suit and tie throughout the play.*
JOHNSON, *a friend of Drew's, about 35, wears a suit throughout the play.*
OTHERS, *Reporters, audience of the debate, etc. Can be various ages and genders, wearing mostly formal attire.*

Scene 1
Campaign office.

(Candidates Drew and Robin are sharing ideas. Campaign managers signal for debate in two minutes.)

DREW: I can't wait to beat you tonight.
ROBIN: That's not going to happen, Drew. Believe it or not, the audience leans toward more handsome candidates. *Not* old men.
DREW: While you may be handsome and attractive--
ROBIN: Wait, what?
DREW: What?
ROBIN: *You* think *I'm* attractive?
DREW: Please. Quit interrupting me. While you may be handsome, you're too young to be wise.
ROBIN: I'm only five years younger than you, Drew.
DREW: Exactly. Now let's get on with this debate.
(Twenty minutes into the debate, the press asks questions)
PERSON 1: Robin, what's your opinion on the LGBTQ+ community?
DREW *(to himself)*: Here we go again.
ROBIN: I think they are a great group of people. I have nothing against them. In fact, when I was younger -- this might come as a shocker -- I experimented with a roommate.

(Audience gasps)

ROBIN: We were hormonal teenage boys, what can I say?

(Drew stares down Robin.)

ROBIN *(aside to Drew, gesturing towards the audience)*: You can't win 'em over any more than with a heart-to-heart.
PERSON 2: Drew, as a Republican, what's your opinion on this?
DREW: I have to say that I am outraged and disgusted. God created us to be men and women, no more, no less. This man has betrayed God's words, and he's trying to run for the Senate? Outrageous. I am against the LGBTQ+ community. They are all simply confused adolescents.
ROBIN: Some of them aren't teenagers. Many of them are adults just trying to be comfortable--
DREW: A lot of confused adults.
ROBIN: First of all, that is completely uncalled for. Second of all, show me exactly where in the Bible it says that men cannot lay with men and vice versa.
DREW: I-it's implied.
ROBIN: So it doesn't state it anywhere? You are making assumptions, and you know what they say about assumptions.
DREW: Was that necessary?
ROBIN: I don't know, was it necessary to insult a community of people?
DREW: You are not being very professional, Robin. Ever hear of freedom of speech?
ROBIN: Being professional means respecting others. You're the one that sounds confused.
DREW: You don't need to keep insulting me.
ROBIN: You don't need to keep being an idiot.
DREW: Well, that was uncalled for.
ROBIN: You seem to know a lot about being uncalled for, Drew.
DREW: What has gotten into you, Robin?
ROBIN: I could ask you the same thing.
ANNOUNCER: Okay, gentlemen. That's enough for today's debate. Thank you all so much for coming out. You may exit through the back door.

Scene 2
Backstage

(Drew and Robin are standing, chatting.)

DREW: Thanks to your little outburst, I actually might lose. Thanks.
ROBIN: Does it look like I care? You're so inconsiderate to people of different ideologies. The Bible says God loves all, what makes them any different?
DREW: Why are you so worked up over this? You didn't care when the other candidates had similar opinions.

ROBIN: Well, it's a big deal because…
DREW: Because…?
ROBIN: Because it's you.
DREW: I don't understand.
ROBIN: Never mind. I'd rather not say.
DREW: Damn it, Robin. Just say it.
ROBIN: Please, stop.
DREW: No, tell me what your problem is.
ROBIN: Leave me alone, Drew.
DREW *(grabbing his suit)*: Out with it already!
ROBIN: Drew, stop.
DREW: What are you, Robin, six? Quit crying and tell me the problem.

(ROBIN kisses Drew on the lips before being pushed away. Drew wipes his mouth on his sleeve.)

DREW: Robin, get off me now. That's… disgusting.
ROBIN: I know.
DREW: I have to go wash my mouth.

Scene 3
Washroom

(DREW is in the washroom with JOHNSON.)

DREW: What in God's name was that? He was acting so weird.
JOHNSON: I don't know, sir.
DREW: I mean, I've known the guy for years, but he's never acted so strangely.

(rinses out his mouth over the sink)

I can still taste his lips.
JOHNSON: Keep washing. It'll get out eventually, sir.
DREW: I'm trying.
JOHNSON: Sir, didn't he say he experimented with some roommates? Could this be another exper--?
DREW: God, I hope not. I don't want to get involved in this. I'm too old.
JOHNSON: Age means nothing in relationships, sir.
DREW: What are you getting at, Johnson? I'm not interested.
JOHNSON: You don't need to get defensive, sir. I would believe you more if you didn't get so flustered when I said it.
DREW: It's just impossible. I've hated him since the day we met. Something about him always put me off. Maybe it was this.

JOHNSON: Maybe it was jealousy.

DREW: Jealousy of what? What are you trying to insinuate, Johnson?

JOHNSON: Hear me out on this, sir. Maybe you didn't like him because you wished you were as confident about your sexuality as he was.

DREW: What?

JOHNSON: Don't interrupt me. You're not fooling anyone, Drew. All you do is talk about him, do you really think I don't notice?

DREW: I talk about how much I hate him.

JOHNSON: Be quiet. I see the way you eye him. I know what you're hiding. You have to be honest with yourself or live in constant self-loathing and envy of Robin. Stop lying, Drew. It's best for everyone. You must come to terms with who you really are.

DREW: Since when did you become an expert on life advice? You couldn't even keep a straight A in any of your classes.

JOHNSON: Doesn't mean I don't know what's going on, sir.

(Washroom door opens, with Robin behind it.)

JOHNSON: I'll leave you to it then.

DREW: Johnson, don't you dare leave me.

(Johnson closes the door behind him.)

ROBIN: Hey, I wa-

DREW: Not now, Robin. I don't want to talk to you.

ROBIN: I just want to apologize. Why won't you let me do that?

DREW: I'd rather you not.

ROBIN: W-what?

DREW: I want to apologize. I didn't mean any of what I said, and the truth is, I envy you for being so confident in your sexuality. I wish I were that confident.

ROBIN: What are you getting at...? Drew, you're making me anxious.

DREW: Here, just... let me try something.

(Drew kisses Robin for a solid minute)

ROBIN: Drew…. That was super gay.

DREW: I know. And I think I'm okay with that.

NO NAME TANK
BRENNA RAMIREZ

CHARACTERS:

CONRAD, *one of the home's oldest residents, he has gotten used to doing what he wants without much interference from the staff. He no longer has family to come visit him, but he doesn't seem to mind. Though he is very kind, he has no real ties to anyone and doesn't seem to want any.*

ALEX, *she is relatively new to the Home and has yet to settle in completely. Anywhere from her late twenties to early thirties, the most defining factor in her is the love she holds for each patient. Her new position at the Home is only threatened by her relationship with* DR. TRACK.

DR. (JAMES) TRACK, *Head doctor at the Home, he is a relaxed kind of doctor. Mid-thirties. Wants to be open with his and* ALEX's *relationship but understands that she isn't ready for it.*

Scene 1

(*The* CONRAD *is sitting on a bench in the open air gardens of the nursing home. His oxygen tank is sitting next to him and he feeds his bread to the pigeons.* ALEX *enters.*)

ALEX: Excuse me, Sir?
CONRAD: Yes?
ALEX: You do know that you aren't supposed to feed the birds here, right?
CONRAD (*laughs and continues to feed the birds*): There are a great many things we aren't supposed to do, dear.
ALEX: Yes, but feeding the birds is one of the House Rules you agreed to.
CONRAD: Yes, and having a relationship with the head doctor is also against House Rules, but you seem rather fond of breaking that one.
ALEX (*taken back, sputtering for words*): Sir, I am by no means in a relationship with Dr. Track.
CONRAD (*still feeding the birds*): Then you want to be, with all of the attention you give him.
ALEX: How did you know? Is it obvious? (*she now takes a seat on the bench with him*)
CONRAD: Only to someone who has been around as long as I have, my dear. You have nothing to worry about; I won't tell a soul.
ALEX (*sighs in relief*): We've tried very hard to keep it quiet here at work. Neither of

us need that kind of scandal on our résumés.

CONRAD: Love will be a scandal no matter where it happens.

ALEX: Well, I wouldn't exactly call it love just yet. We've only been seeing each other for a few weeks now.

CONRAD: Do you want it to be love?

ALEX: Doesn't everyone?

CONRAD: Not everyone. Some are content to be alone.

ALEX: But doesn't that get lonely?

CONRAD: Alone does not always equate to lonely.

ALEX *(sits quietly, watching the birds eat the last of the crumbs)*: Are you lonely?

CONRAD *(Smiles)*: No, just alone.

(He stands and takes his oxygen tank by the handle, leaving ALEX alone.)

Scene 2

(DR. TRACK and ALEX are sitting in the break room late at night discussing patients.)

DR. TRACK: I saw you talking to Conrad today.

ALEX: Conrad?

DR. TRACK: The man feeding the pigeons in the garden today.

ALEX: Oh, him. I didn't know his name.

DR. TRACK *(Chuckling)*: He's a character isn't he?

ALEX: *(Smiles)* He guessed our relationship before I said more than a few words.

DR. TRACK: Did he now?

ALEX: Yes, he did. He was pretty sure about it too. You aren't telling anyone, are you?

DR. TRACK: No, of course not. You said you wanted to keep our relationship separate from our workplace.

(Both are silent for a moment before going back to paperwork. Glancing at each other, trying to be discreet.)

DR. TRACK *(Throws down pen in frustration)*: This is dumb. No one else is here, Alex.

ALEX: We're still at work, James. I don't want to risk it.

DR. TRACK: Risk what? We're the only ones on duty right now. Everyone else went home almost an hour ago.

ALEX: We talked about this. You said you were fine with waiting.

DR. TRACK: But you never gave me a time frame.

ALEX: You don't think I'm just as frustrated by this?

DR. TRACK: Honestly, I don't know how you feel about this. You just keep saying "Wait."

ALEX: I'm still new here, James. It wouldn't be professional if word came out that we're seeing each other.

DR. TRACK: No one would care, Alex! No one cares now!

ALEX: What is that supposed to mean?

DR. TRACK: *(Takes off glasses, rubbing his eyes)*: It means that there have, and still are, relationships going on between the staff here. No one cares about that stupid rule but you.

(Again, they fall into silence, staring at each other.)

ALEX *(Lets out a breath, closing her eyes)*: I'm not used to this.

DR. TRACK: Used to what? Being in a relationship with someone you work with?

ALEX: Yes, every other place I've worked at has frowned down on this kind of thing. It's what gets people fired.

DR. TRACK *(Takes her hands in his)*: It's different here, okay? No one will fire you because of this.

ALEX: Alright. I'm just nervous is all.

DR. TRACK: I know, but we have nothing to worry about.

ALEX: I know; our relationship is just so new still. We've been on a couple dates.

DR. TRACK: I think twelve dates is a bit more than a couple.

ALEX: I just don't want to screw this up. We have to work together.

DR. TRACK: Yes, but I think it's safe to say that we can still be professional at work *and* have a romantic relationship at the same time.

ALEX: Aren't you worried about it though? What if we don't work out and things get complicated? Or mean? Or-

DR. TRACK: Hey, hey, that won't happen. Even if we don't work there is absolutely no way things will get mean. I respect you and your work way too much to get mean.

ALEX *(Smiles)*: How did you become some such a sweet man?

DR. TRACK: My mama didn't raise me to be anything but cordial to ladies. Anything less, and I got smacked upside the head.

ALEX *(Laughing)*: She sounds like a wonderful woman.

DR. TRACK *(Grinning)*: She is a very wonderful woman. Very caring, you remind me of her quite a bit.

ALEX *(Embarrassed)*: Why, James, are you flirting with me?

DR. TRACK: I do believe that I am, Alex. Tell me, am I doing a good job with it?

ALEX *(Leaning in)*: I'd say you're doing a pretty fine job.

DR. TRACK *(Leaning in more)*: Yeah? Do I get anything for my efforts?

ALEX: Depends.

DR. TRACK: On?

ALEX *(Almost, but not quite touching lips, whispering)*: Will you do my paperwork tonight?

(Both burst out laughing, rocking back in their chairs.)

DR. TRACK: Heck, no! I've got paperwork of my own to do!
ALEX *(Laughing)*: I figured as much. Oh well, you're still eye candy for the night.
DR. TRACK: I'm so glad that I can be of some assistance to you.

(Both smile.)

Scene 3

(ALEX is looking for CONRAD in the dining room at breakfast. She finds him sitting alone at a table, his oxygen tank in the chair next to him.)

ALEX *(She takes the seat next to him)*: Good morning, Conrad.
CONRAD *(Without looking away from his newspaper)*: Good morning.
ALEX: Why are you sitting alone?
CONRAD: I am not alone. I have my tank. *(He pays in affectionately like you would a dog)*
ALEX: But that's not a person. There are so many people here to talk and interact with.
CONRAD: I have no interest in the people surrounding me, nor do I care to get to know them.
ALEX: Why not?

(CONRAD closes his newspaper, folding it carefully before looking at ALEX. He does not speak for a while; he just looks at her. She fidgets a little in her seat, glancing away from him. He gets up, moving his tank from the chair to the ground.)

CONRAD: I believe it is time for my walk.
ALEX: Oh, of course. I apologize if I overstepped any boundaries.
CONRAD: Of course not. Would you care to join us? *(He pockets a biscuit)*
ALEX: Who's "us"?
CONRAD: My tank and me, of course. See? He has a name tag and everything.
ALEX: It's blank.
CONRAD: Yes, well, I've yet to name him. Or her. I'm not quite sure which one will win out.
ALEX: Ah, okay. Then yes, I'd love to take a walk with you.

(Both rise, ALEX taking a biscuit of her own, and head for the exit to the garden. They pass DR. TRACK on their way out.)

DR. TRACK: Good morning, Conrad, Alex.
ALEX: Good morning, Dr. Track.
CONRAD: Oh good, you talked about things.

(*Both stare at him.*)

DR. TRACK: I shouldn't even be surprised anymore. You know what goes on here before even I do.
CONRAD: I have been here longer than you have.
DR. TRACK: This is true.
ALEX: How long have you been here, exactly?
CONRAD: Longer than anyone else.
ALEX: That's not a straight answer, Conrad.
CONRAD: No, but it is an answer. Now, to our walk.

(*He walks ahead, leaving* ALEX *and* DR. TRACK *to themselves.*)

DR. TRACK: He seems to have taken a liking to you.
ALEX: Yeah? He must have other friends here. It's not possible that he's been on his own for so many years.
DR. TRACK (*Shaking head*): Nope, not one person. He likes to be on his own. You are the first person I've seen him with while on his free time.
ALEX: Well, I won't mess this up then.

(*Both smile before* DR. TRACK *looks around and pecks* ALEX *quickly on the lips.*)

ALEX (*Blushing*): I'll see you later?
DR. TRACK: I'll be here.

(ALEX *leaves, catching up to* CONRAD *who had been waiting just outside the door for her. Birds have already started to gather around him.*)

CONRAD: How was your little chat?
ALEX: Very nice, thank you very much.
CONRAD: Good.

(*They walk in silence for a while watching the birds. When they come to the bench from the day before,* CONRAD *sits, motioning for* ALEX *to sit next to him. They begin to feed the birds.*)

ALEX: Do you always come here?
CONRAD: This is my bench.
ALEX: So everyone knows that you come here?
CONRAD: Every day I come here and feed these birds. Before them, I fed their parents, and the parents before them. I have done this for as long as I have been here. When I got too old to stand, I put a bench here.
ALEX: What do you mean you put the bench here?
CONRAD: Lovely day isn't it? Are you going to feed them the rest of your bread?

No? May I then? Wonderful, thank you my dear.

ALEX: Conrad, you can't just do that. You can't just ignore questions like that straight out.

CONRAD: Why not?

ALEX: Because, people are going to think you're going senile.

CONRAD: Oh, who cares, they'll think that no matter what. No one pays any attention to an old man like me. Not anymore.

ALEX: I'm listening to you.

CONRAD: Yes, well, you are the special case.

ALEX: Why is that?

CONRAD: Thirty-nine years I have broken the rules of feeding the birds. Not one nurse, doctor, or grounds man has said anything to me. And do you know why?

ALEX: Why?

CONRAD: Because I am old. And no one pays attention to the old. We're all stuck into these homes and forgotten about like yesterday's paper.

ALEX: I'm sorry, Conrad

CONRAD: Why are you sorry? You haven't done it. You are one of the kind souls that has found a voice for us. You have taken the time to listen.

ALEX: With all due respect, you don't really know me, Conrad. You barely met me yesterday.

CONRAD: Wrong.

ALEX: Wrong?

CONRAD: Wrong. I have watched you since you started this job almost a month ago. I have yet to see a nurse exercise the same level of kindness and empathy with each house mate. You sing quietly while you work and play checkers with Martha, who is ninety-six and tries to unwrap the game pieces because she thinks they are candy. Each morning you come in with a smile on your face even though you had the late shift the night before. You *(points to her chest)* have the soul of a caretaker.

(ALEX *is silent, stunned by the sudden compliments.*)

CONRAD: You remind me quite a bit of my sister. She was kind and gentle and stubborn as a bull. Never let anyone tell her what was possible. And she worked hard, harder than anyone I have ever known. She would have liked you very much, Alex.

ALEX: These are all very kind things to say, but I'm not sure where they're coming from.

CONRAD *(Pats her hand and stands up)*: That's quite alright, my dear.

(He *leaves her, his tank trailing behind him.*)

Scene 4

ALEX: I still don't get it. He hasn't said more than five words at a time to me. Did

I do something?

DR. TRACK: Don't take it personally, sweetheart. He's like this with everyone.

ALEX: But he wasn't like this with me at first.

DR. TRACK *(He takes her hands)*: It'll be okay. He's just a finicky old man. Don't worry about it too much, Alex.

ALEX: I know, you're right, I just can't help but worry. What if something's wrong? I didn't even see him at breakfast this morning, or dinner last night.

DR. TRACK: What could be wrong? He's just moody is all.

ALEX: Yeah, you're right. Alright, I have work to do. I'll see you later?

DR. TRACK: I'll be here.

(They kiss, and ALEX leaves. Instead of making her rounds, though, she goes to the computer with the patient information.)

ALEX: I just need to know more about you. This is for your own good. Not an invasion of privacy.

(She searches his name, but finds nothing.)

ALEX: What do you mean there's no one here enrolled by that name? He's here every day, I've seen him leave his room.

(She gets up and goes for the door. Walking with purpose, she goes to CONRAD's room and knocks. When there is no reply, she reaches for the handle, but finds it locked.)

ALEX: Conrad? Can you hear me? Can you please open the door?

(Silence)

ALEX: Conrad? Conrad, open the door.

(She pounds once more on the door before pulling out her master key and opening it herself. Stepping inside to see CONRAD laying on the bed.)

ALEX *(In a gentle, almost whisper)*: Conrad?

CONRAD *(Raspy voice)*: Bethany?

ALEX *(Approaches the bed slowly, taking CONRAD's hand)*: Who's Bethany?

CONRAD *(Laughing)*: Oh, don't joke with me now, sister. It has been so long since I've seen you.

ALEX: Conrad, it's me, Alex. Are you okay?

CONRAD: Bethany, please do stop pretending. Tell me, how was Rome? You never got the chance to show me your pictures before you got back. So busy trying to catch up at the Home.

ALEX *(To herself)*: Oh, you've finally lost yourself, haven't you? *(To CONRAD)*

Conrad, I am going to go get help, I'll be right back, okay?

CONRAD: No! Don't leave again. Please, Bethany, don't leave again. Not when I'm so close to finally seeing you again.

ALEX *(Starting to cry)*: You're seeing me right now, Conrad. What are you talking about?

CONRAD *(Smiling)*: Yes, I am, but not really. I'll see you more clearly once we're on the same plane again, sister. But I need to do something first.

ALEX *(Holding back tears)*: Of course, what is it?

CONRAD: Why are you crying Bethany? It's only one thing. Then, I'll be with you, I promise. Here, *(he reaches for the side table, struggling, and picks up an envelope)* this must go to Alex, *(pause)* as well as the lawyers, I suppose, but mostly Alex.

ALEX: What is it?

CONRAD: The deed to the Home of course. She's the best hands I can think to put all of your work into, sister. Oh, how I wish you could have met her. I do believe that you would have gotten along swimmingly. I hope you...you don't...don't mind... *(he drifts off)*

ALEX *(Crying)*: CONRAD! Conrad, wake up right now. I swear, you'd better finish that sentence.

CONRAD *(Takes a shaky breath)*: What was that Bethany? I... I believe I'm getting very tired now.

ALEX: You, you said you hoped I didn't mind. *(She forces a smile through her tears)*

CONRAD: Ah, yes, I... I hope you don't mind that.... that she sat on...on our bench. In your...seat. She just reminded me so much of...of you. I just...wanted you back...for just a little.

ALEX *(Grips his hand tightly, kissing his forehead, still crying.)*: You have me right now. And you'll be with me soon. I'll make sure that I- that Alex, gets the letter.

CONRAD: How will you do that?

ALEX: Don't you worry about that; you just sleep now. And when you wake up I'll be there.

CONRAD: Promise?

ALEX *(Nodding)*: I promise.

(CONRAD smiles one last time at ALEX before closing his eyes.)

Scene 5

DR. TRACK: Are you alright?

ALEX: Not really.

DR. TRACK: I'm sorry, Alex. *(He pulls her into a hug)*

(She clings to him, but does not cry.)

ALEX: *(Muffled speech)*

DR. TRACK *(Pulling back a little)*: What was that?
ALEX: I said he left me the Home, and everything else he owned.
DR. TRACK: What? Why would he do that?

(She hands him the letter CONRAD *had written to her right before he died.* DR. TRACK *reads it aloud.)*

Dr. TRACK: My dearest Alex, you have only just begun to work at this Home, but I assure you that I am making the right choice. I see a kindred spirit in you. I see my sister, Bethany, who was the one to first open the Home. I now leave that in your hands. I have the utmost trust that you will do great things with it. I only ask you one thing; feed the birds so that they do not go hungry.

- Conrad M.G

(ALEX *and* DR. TRACK *leave, hand in hand, trailing* CONRAD*'s nameless oxygen tank behind them.)*

ABOUT THE AUTHORS

SADIE ADAMS
Born and raised in Southern California, Sadie Adams developed a love of writing and a particular fascination for poetry. Her favorite poem is "Ardella" by Langston Hughes. She will pursue writing in the future and hopes to eventually publish her own books.

EMILY CHAU
A voracious reader, Emily Chau was raised in Westminster, where her love for fiction and Broadway theater developed her respect for all art forms. Although she argues that reading books all day can be a real career, she's open to life guiding her to unexplored destinations.

JENNIFER CHAU
A lover of writing and music, Jennifer Chau explores her creativity by playing the violin in orchestra and writing poems and short stories. When she is not scribbling words on paper, she enjoys watching movies and making DIYs.

TUYET DUONG
Born in Vietnam, Tuyet moved to California when she was two. Growing up, her small size earned her the nick-name Twiggy. Her love for books and writing stemmed from the Harry Potter series. She wishes to one day be a pediatrician.

HANNAH GROVE
Product of a city where white people are the minority, Hannah enjoys taking complicated plots and figuring out how they make a story. A fantasy book makes her excited, and the only thing better than reading it is writing it. Something to live for? You guessed it. Writing fantasy.

KEVIN HO

Born and raised on the West Coast, Kevin grew up influenced by animations of every genre. Whether it be cartoons or Japanese anime, Kevin strives to create a writing style base on his influences, and "The Future is Brighter with You" is his first published story.

TRACEY HOANG

Tracey Hoang is a quirky person who enjoys writing when inspiration hits. She has written a lot of short stories, but "The Coffee Shop" is one of the few works she's completed. When not writing, she enjoys listening to music, being with her friends and family, and volunteering.

ZACHARY KING

Zach King has lived in California and has spent most of his life in his living room or his room playing video games (and sometimes going to school). "A Night at the Pizzeria" is a perfect example of how he incorporates this love for games into his writing.

NANCY LE

Born and raised in Fountain Valley, California, Nancy grew up like any other average child. It wasn't until high school that she discovered her desire to express herself through writing stories which allows her mind to wander into unique places. Her first published story is "Lily's Legacy."

NICOLE LE

Nicole Le is an average student with average grades whose only social life is school and the three friends she has online. She doesn't know what to do with her life or her biography. She is a small meme, trying her best.

CHRISTINA NGUYEN

Born in California, Christina grew up in Santa Ana with her family, where she fell in love with fast food and fiction. Although dabbling with writing stories online, "Picking Up the Pieces" is her first published story.

GINA NGUYEN
Gina Nguyen joined a writing class purely because she likes to express her mind and opinions about everything. In the future, she wishes to be a psychology or a high school English teacher, a therapist, a foster mother, an entrepreneur, an author, and a philosophy college professor. She just prays she has enough time and energy to fulfill her life plans.

KARI NGUYEN
Kari Nguyen is a student who loves experimenting with different forms of art. Although she has always had a passion for writing, she was able to discover her true potential during senior year, when she took a creative writing class. Now, when not writing, she spends time creating artworks and watching YouTube videos.

DAWN PHAM
Born and raised in California, Dawn Pham never expected to become a published author. She enjoys writing poems and short stories as well as acting in theater. Her life goal, however, is to become an accomplished nurse and help everyone that needs it, especially her beloved friends and family.

THONG PHAM
Thong Thien Pham experienced childhood and adolescence in Southern California, with origins in Vietnam. Ironically, he was quite adamant against writing in elementary school. However, with the aid of great books and greater teachers, he grew to love the art. Although a fantasy fanatic at heart, he has a place for mysteries as well.

EMILY PLASENCIA
Born in the big bear state, Emily developed a strong passion for art. (She won several art awards, and some of her artwork have been used for display). Although determined to become a fine artist, her first published story, "Remembering" helped her to discover the art in writing.

MAGALY PLASENCIA
A girl born with a determined heart in the state of California, Magaly developed her own style in drawing as well as in writing works of fiction. Her first published work, "Back Home," is the first step for her taking on risks and spreading her ideas with others.

DANNY QUACH

Danny Quach grew up in Garden Grove where he developed a love for drama, making music, and playing games. Danny took the creative writing class in hopes that he could improve his writing. With hard work, he was able to publish his story, "The Toilet Paper."

ALEXANDRA QUANG

Constantly craving fro-yo, Alexandra Quang is a student from the city of Westminster, California. She self-indulges in salt-n-pepper kettle chips, cat videos on YouTube, and writing her ideas on everything but paper.

BRENNA RAMIREZ

Born and raised in Southern California, Brenna Ramirez was exposed to many things early in life. While writing was not one of them, she eventually found a joy in that as well. "No Name Tank" and "Tour Guide," which she proudly presents, are her first completed and published works.

EMANUEL RAMIREZ

Made in Westminster, Emanuel grew up in Santa Ana, California and at a young age grew interested in poetry. He loves the way poets express emotions and ideas through their words. He tries to do the exact same thing in each of his poems, hopefully allowing the reader to take something they like out of each one.

ASHLEY RIVERA

Ashley Marilyn Rivera grew up in Garden Grove, where she developed a love for art, painting and drawing, all of which she enjoys during her spare time. Although art was her original love, she has found interest in expressing herself through writing. "Jordan & Johnathan" is her newest story.

NOAH SABATINI

Noah Sabatini, the boy with a passion for anthropomorphic art, decided to broaden his creative expression by working on his writing skills in the Creative Writing class at LQ. Through lots of determination and frustration, he manages to pour out emotional pieces of art representing himself.

THANA SITHISOMBATH

Growing up in Southern California, Thana Sithisombath realized his interest in drawing and writing, activities that involved his creativity and the paper in front of him. One day, he hopes to use his creative talents in a career that requires it.

AISLINN STOLZE

Aislinn Stolze grew up in the city of Westminster, California, the place where she discovered writing, art and music. On most days, she can be found writing stories or drawing. Her first published story, "Once Upon a Mermaid's Dream," was inspired by her love for the ocean.

AMY TRAN

Originally from Southern California, Amy Tran is an aspiring writer and hopes to major in psychology in the near future. She is a full-time Libra with the personality of a Pisces, who spends her spare time watching anime, listening to K-pop, and freestyle dancing to EDM when time permits.

DAN TRAN

Born and raised in sunny Southern California, Dan Tran read stories like the Harry Potter and Percy Jackson series which fostered his love of storytelling. This love grew to encompass sketching, music, and writing. Though "Ascent" is his first published work, he hopes to continue writing and become a teacher.

YEN TRAN

Born and raised in California, Yen Tran is the oldest of eight children. She enjoys dabbling in the arts and indulging in anime and manga. Her interests cover a wide range, from reading books to playing indie horror games, which may make her seem eccentric to others.

RICHARD TREJO

Richard Kyle Trejo got back into writing during the summer after his sophomore year. He writes dark stories but has moved towards romance even though he is not, ironically, a fan of romance. His YouTube channel is Wolf and Friends Gaming.

MONICA VAN

Monica Van grew up in California, where she discovered her creative side. During her almost nonexistent free time, she sings in her band, Lost Avenues, draws, and writes stories and poetry.

KIMBERLY VIRAMONTES

Born and raised in California, Kimberly Viramontes grew up in Santa Ana, where she developed an appreciation for writing, her Mexican culture, and the weather. Although she's written stories before, "Zombie Surprise" is her first published story. Kimberly aspires to graduate from college with a degree in Psychology.

STEPHANY VIVAR

Stephany Vivar grew up in Santa Ana where she met the love of her life, tacos. Tacos changed her life, and she began to write about how she loved tacos then ended up writing about more than just tacos. Next came short stories, long stories, and poetry. "Case 66," which is not about tacos, is her first published story.